ROBERT B. PARKER'S

# Fool's Paradise

## The Spenser Novels

*Robert B. Parker's Angel Eyes*
  (by Ace Atkins)

*Robert B. Parker's Old Black Magic*
  (by Ace Atkins)

*Robert B. Parker's Little White Lies*
  (by Ace Atkins)

*Robert B. Parker's Slow Burn*
  (by Ace Atkins)

*Robert B. Parker's Kickback*
  (by Ace Atkins)

*Robert B. Parker's Cheap Shot*
  (by Ace Atkins)

*Silent Night*
  (with Helen Brann)

*Robert B. Parker's Wonderland*
  (by Ace Atkins)

*Robert B. Parker's Lullaby*
  (by Ace Atkins)

*Sixkill*

*Painted Ladies*

*The Professional*

*Rough Weather*

*Now & Then*

*Hundred-Dollar Baby*

*School Days*

*Cold Service*

*Bad Business*

*Back Story*

*Widow's Walk*

*Potshot*

*Hugger Mugger*

*Hush Money*

*Sudden Mischief*

*Small Vices*

*Chance*

*Thin Air*

*Walking Shadow*

*Paper Doll*

*Double Deuce*

*Pastime*

*Stardust*

*Playmates*

*Crimson Joy*

*Pale Kings and Princes*

*Taming a Sea-Horse*

*A Catskill Eagle*

*Valediction*

*The Widening Gyre*

*Ceremony*

*A Savage Place*

*Early Autumn*

*Looking for Rachel Wallace*

*The Judas Goat*

*Promised Land*

*Mortal Stakes*

*God Save the Child*

*The Godwulf Manuscript*

## The Jesse Stone Novels

*Robert B. Parker's Fool's Paradise*
  (by Mike Lupica)

*Robert B. Parker's The Bitterest Pill*
  (by Reed Farrel Coleman)

*Robert B. Parker's Colorblind*
  (by Reed Farrel Coleman)

*Robert B. Parker's The Hangman's Sonnet*
  (by Reed Farrel Coleman)

*Robert B. Parker's Debt to Pay*
  (by Reed Farrel Coleman)

*Robert B. Parker's The Devil Wins*
  (by Reed Farrel Coleman)

*Robert B. Parker's Blind Spot*
  (by Reed Farrel Coleman)

*Robert B. Parker's Damned If You Do*
  (by Michael Brandman)

*Robert B. Parker's Fool Me Twice*
  (by Michael Brandman)

*Robert B. Parker's Killing the Blues*
  (by Michael Brandman)

*Split Image*

*Night and Day*

*Stranger in Paradise*

*High Profile*

*Sea Change*

*Stone Cold*

*Death in Paradise*

*Trouble in Paradise*

*Night Passage*

## The Sunny Randall Novels

*Robert B. Parker's Grudge Match*
  (by Mike Lupica)

*Robert B. Parker's Blood Feud*
  (by Mike Lupica)

*Spare Change*

*Blue Screen*

*Melancholy Baby*

*Shrink Rap*

*Perish Twice*

*Family Honor*

## The Cole/Hitch Westerns

*Robert B. Parker's Buckskin*
  (by Robert Knott)

*Robert B. Parker's Revelation*
  (by Robert Knott)

*Robert B. Parker's Blackjack*
  (by Robert Knott)

*Robert B. Parker's The Bridge*
  (by Robert Knott)

*Robert B. Parker's Bull River*
  (by Robert Knott)

*Robert B. Parker's Ironhorse*
  (by Robert Knott)

*Blue-Eyed Devil*

*Brimstone*

*Resolution*

*Appaloosa*

## Also by Robert B. Parker

*Double Play*

*Gunman's Rhapsody*

*All Our Yesterdays*

*A Year at the Races*
  (with Joan H. Parker)

*Perchance to Dream*

*Poodle Springs*
  (with Raymond Chandler)

*Love and Glory*

*Wilderness*

*Three Weeks in Spring*
  (with Joan H. Parker)

*Training with Weights*
  (with John R. Marsh)

ROBERT B. PARKER'S

# Fool's Paradise

A Jesse Stone Novel

## Mike Lupica

G. P. Putnam's Sons
New York

**PUTNAM**
— EST. 1838 —

G. P. PUTNAM'S SONS
*Publishers Since 1838*
An imprint of Penguin Random House LLC
penguinrandomhouse.com

LIBRARY OF CONGRESS CATALOGING-IN-PUBLICATION DATA

Names: Lupica, Mike, author. | Parker, Robert B., 1932–2010, creator.
Title: Fool's paradise / Mike Lupica.
Other titles: At head of title: Robert B. Parker's
Description: New York : G. P. Putnam's Sons, 2020. | Series: A Jesse Stone novel
Identifiers: LCCN 2020018116 (print) | LCCN 2020018117 (ebook) |
ISBN 9780525542087 (hardcover) | ISBN 9780525542094 (ebook)
Subjects: LCSH: Stone, Jesse (Fictitious character)—Fiction. |
Police chiefs—Fiction. | GSAFD: Suspense fiction. | Mystery fiction.
Classification: LCC PS3562.U59 F66 2020 (print) | LCC PS3562.U59 (ebook) |
DDC 813/.54—dc23
LC record available at https://lccn.loc.gov/2020018116
LC ebook record available at https://lccn.loc.gov/2020018117

Printed in the United States of America
10 9 8 7 6 5 4 3 2 1

Book design by Nancy Resnick

For John Fisher, Chief of Police, Carlisle, Mass.

ROBERT B. PARKER'S

# Fool's Paradise

# One

Jesse Stone opened his eyes even before the alarm on his phone started to chirp, 5:58 a.m. Sunday, Fourth of July weekend, cold sober. Stone cold. Private joke. His drinking never was. Jesse had never been a happy drunk, or a funny one. Just a drunk.

Once he would still have been drunk at this time of the morning, trying to decide whether he was waking up or coming to, and likely scared shitless about what he might have done the night before.

Good times.

Now he set the alarm for six, seven days a week.

Last night had been another early one for him, after the relighting of the marquee above the entrance to the Paradise Cinema. The theater had burned to the ground the year before. But somehow that day the volunteers from the Paradise Fire Department had managed to save the marquee. In the immediate aftermath of the fire, a not-for-profit committee had been formed by Lily Cain, part of the town's royal and ruling class. It was called Friends of Paradise. No better friend than Lily, who, being Lily, had quickly raised enough money to invade New Hampshire. The Paradise Cinema had been rebuilt in less than a year and had officially reopened last night.

Jesse had looked around the crowd during the ceremony and seen all these happy faces lining Main Street. So many more faces of color than there had been in Paradise when he'd first arrived here. The town wasn't just more diverse than it had been twenty years ago. He knew it was *better* because of the diversity, livelier and more welcoming. Even though he knew people of color still scared the money in town, and there was still a boatload of that.

But for this one night, they all stood shoulder to shoulder on Main Street, cheering the reopening of a theater that always looked to Jesse as if it had been a fixture in Paradise almost as long as the ocean. It always amazed Jesse how little it took to make other people happy.

Molly Crane, his deputy and friend, had seen him staring into the crowd before Lily Cain threw the switch to light the marquee.

"Looking for potential perps?" she said.

"Nope," he said. "Just trying to figure out why something like this could make this many people feel this good."

"Maybe because these people don't think feeling good is against the law in Paradise, Massachusetts," she said.

"I'm the chief," Jesse said. "I should know shit like that."

"Not about being happy," Molly said.

"I think of myself as a work in progress," he said.

She'd sighed and said, "So much work."

Fireworks had lit the sky as soon as the ceremony ended. Most of Paradise had gone out to party after that, in bars, all the way to the beach. Jesse had gone home to bed. Alone. But sober.

Sober, he knew, was why he was still the chief of police. Alone was because he'd arrived at the decision, at least for the time being, that he was about as good at romantic relationships as he had been with scotch.

Molly Crane had always said he was the alonest man she'd ever known.

His phone started chirping again. Incoming call this time. The display said *Suit*.

"Got a body at the lake," Suitcase Simpson said.

Jesse had made Suit a detective at the same time he'd officially made Molly his deputy, and had gotten both of them raises, despite the objections of the cheapskates on the Board of Selectmen. When Jesse had first met Luther Simpson, nicknamed Suitcase after an old-time ballplayer, he'd been a former high school football player, a local who'd just drifted into police work, after he'd taken the test, passed it. Molly had been working the desk and acting as a dispatcher. Now Suit had grown into being a terrific cop, even if Jesse still looked at him and saw the big, open-faced kid he'd met originally. Molly had grown into being a first-rate cop herself, in addition to being completely indispensable.

"Man or woman?"

Jesse sat up.

"Man."

"How?" Jesse said.

"Looks like a bullet to the back of the head," Suit said. "Or two. Lot of blood."

"ID?"

"Not yet. But we just got here. I wanted to call you first thing."

"You're a detective," Jesse said. "It means you're authorized to start detecting without me."

"Just going by the book," Suit said. "Yours."

"Floater?"

"No, praise Jesus and all of His apostles."

Suit now knew more about floaters than he'd ever wanted to, things that Jesse had learned a long time ago in Los Angeles, about how bodies in the water first sank and then eventually came back to the surface as the air in them was replaced with gas that inflated them like toy dolls. The longer they had been in the water, especially seawater, the better the chance that fish and crabs and sea lice had been feeding on them, turning them into something you never forgot.

Suit told Jesse exactly where he was at the lake, a part of the closest thing Paradise had to a Central Park, close to town, full of wooded areas, but somehow feeling remote at the same time. It was on the west side of Paradise, next to the field where Jesse still played in the Paradise Men's Softball League. What he called the Men of Summer. It's where they'd once found a teenage girl named Elinor Bishop. Jesse had seen more than his share of floaters when he'd worked Robbery Homicide. Suit had never seen one before Elinor Bishop. He still said he'd rather be caught wearing women's clothing than catch another floater.

He'd admitted later to Jesse that the first chance he got

that night, and hoping that nobody else noticed, he went into the woods and nearly puked up a lung.

Jesse told Suit he was on his way, and ended the call. Then he was out of bed, having already decided not to shower, getting into the jeans he'd left hanging over the chair next to his bed, grateful there was no hangover for him to manage. Before the lighting of the marquee, he had been at an AA meeting in Marshport, the next town over from Paradise. At one point the speaker had said having a hangover was like having a second job.

Jesse was still making it. Day at a goddamn time. Still on the job as chief. Maybe that was all the proof he needed that the Higher Power they talked about in AA really was looking out for him. Serving and protecting *him*.

Jesse felt a different kind of buzz now. One that had never had anything to do with booze. Just cop adrenaline and a dead body making him feel more alive than he had in a while.

He went into the kitchen, poured some coffee into a travel mug, mixed in cream and sugar, and headed out the door. Before he did, he stopped, having caught his reflection in the mirror in his living room.

Toasted himself with the mug as he did.

*First of the day,* Jesse Stone thought.

# Two

Jesse drove his new black Ford Explorer through the empty streets of Paradise, the theater marquee looking like some kind of ghost light sitting on top of morning fog. Suit had told him it was time to upgrade, that this year's Explorer got a better "pursuit rating" than Jesse's model, that they had beefed-up suspensions and performed better, and that you could get them even more easily prewired than before for police radios and what Suit called "all the other fun cop shit."

Jesse had told him to stop, he was sold, had gone to the Board, and had been issued the Explorer he was driving now. He got them to issue Suit one, too. Molly said she was sticking with her old Cherokee.

She'd just shook her head at the time and said, "Boys with their souped-up toys."

As Jesse got to the lake he saw the flashing blue lights, like a different kind of light show now in the first hour after sunrise. He parked the car, got out, and ducked underneath the yellow crime tape, noticing Suit's Explorer parked next to the medical examiner's van and two other patrol cars. No onlookers here yet, no cell phone pictures being taken. Soon, though. Word would get out. It always did. In the old days, before the advent of digital portable radios, there had briefly been an app people in Paradise could download onto their phones that live-streamed the PPD's police scanners. All in the name of transparency. Jesse had shut it down first chance he got.

*Yeah,* Jesse always thought, *what the world needs.*

*More fucking transparency.*

He walked toward the water. The new state medical examiner, Dev Chadha, and Suit were standing over the body. Peter Perkins was there, too. He'd been with Jesse on the PPD as long as Molly and Suit had, and hadn't even changed after his morning run. He was in a faded Patriots Super Bowl T-shirt and gray sweatpants and New Balance sneakers the color of tangerines, already walking the immediate area. Gabe Weathers was doing the same. Jesse just assumed both Peter and Gabe had heard on the new portable radios that had been issued to everybody in the department. Now they were both taking photographs and video with their phones, trying to get as complete a picture of the scene as possible.

There were twelve men and women in the Paradise Police Department. A third of them were here now, before seven on a Sunday morning. They all understood why. It never mattered whether it was a big city or a small town. Murder was still the main event.

The body was still facedown about twenty yards from the

water's edge, the back of his head matted with blood that did not yet appear completely dry. Jesse didn't know how many bodies there had been for him in his cop life, in L.A. and here. Had never tried to process his personal body count. Just knew there had been too many. The first one had been a shooting victim on a side street near Dodger Stadium. Slumped over the wheel of a car, two bullets to the back of the head. Hector Rodriguez. The shit you remembered. He'd wanted to throw up, too, but knew if he did he would never hear the end of it. Death before dishonor.

"You call I-and-I yet?" Jesse said to Suit.

The Identification and Information unit from the State Police, with an office in Marshport now, was attached to the new police lab there.

Suit grinned.

"I might have waited until I saw the chief's vehicle arriving at the crime scene," Suit said.

"But they're on their way?" Jesse said.

Suit was still grinning. "Well, yeah, *now* they are."

Jesse turned to Dev.

"How'd you get here so fast?"

"Don't sleep," he said. "Got no life other than this job right now." Now he grinned. "And this is the first homicide I've caught since I *got* this job."

"No ID?" Jesse said to Suit.

Suit shook his head. He was wearing jeans but had put on a blue PPD windbreaker over a polo shirt. Jesse had never met a cop happier to no longer be in uniform than Luther "Suit-case" Simpson.

"Nothing in the back pockets of his jeans, or in the general vicinity," Suit said. "Dev and I were waiting for you to roll him over."

"You didn't have to wait."

"You suddenly stop being a control freak overnight?" he said. "I need to tell Gabe and Peter."

It was part of the ongoing dynamic between the two of them. Even before the son Jesse didn't know he had, Cole, had shown up from Los Angeles, he'd treated Suit like a son. But Suit constantly reminded him that he was about to turn forty and didn't need Jesse to still hold his hand on the job.

Suit had still waited for Jesse to show up and take full control of the scene. Usually the Staties would take charge of the investigation as soon as they showed up. But both Jesse and Suit knew the rules of engagement were different in Paradise. Jesse had the same standing with Brian Lundquist, the chief homicide investigator with the Massachusetts State Police, that he'd had with Healy, Lundquist's predecessor, now retired. Neither one of them had ever treated Jesse Stone like just another small-town cop. Mostly because they knew better.

"The control thing is just one more habit I'm trying to quit," Jesse said.

"I'm gonna have to see some evidence of that before I believe it," Suit said.

"And don't do it all at once," Dev said. "You risk decompression syndrome."

"Decompression syndrome?" Jesse said.

"The bends," Dev said.

Jesse knew the drill by now. They all did. They weren't showing disrespect to the dead by standing over the body and talking some cop smack with one another. Somehow it just made standing over the body easier for them all to handle. Just more rituals of the job. Ones you'd never find in any book.

"Who found him?" Jesse asked Suit.

"Woman who lives between the lake and the park," Suit said. "Christina Sample. I played football with her brother Tommy in high school."

Sometimes Jesse thought Suit had played football with every male in Paradise who was around his age.

"Christina was out early walking her dog," Suit continued. "She's pretty upset. She thought it was somebody who might have been sleeping it off after partying too hard last night."

Jesse turned to Dev.

"Lot of blood," Jesse said.

"Whoa," Dev said. "You don't miss anything."

"Fuck off," Jesse said.

Dev grinned and saluted. "Yes, *sir*," he said.

Molly said one time that Dev was a dead ringer for the actor who starred in *Slumdog Millionaire*. Jesse had asked her which Clint Eastwood Western that was. But when he'd looked up the actor on the Internet, he'd seen Molly was right. Molly just knew a lot of things, about a lot of topics that didn't interest Jesse in the slightest.

"When there's this much it can take hours to dry completely," Dev said. "The guys say they can't see any sign that the body has been moved. So it must have happened here."

"How do you shoot somebody here and nobody hears the shot?" Jesse said.

"My guess?" Dev said. "Happened during the fireworks."

Jesse said. "Shell casing?"

Suit shook his head. "Guy must have grabbed it."

"What about the round?" Jesse said.

"It'll depend on the caliber," Dev said. "But from the looks of the entrance wound, it's probably still inside him."

"You said nothing in the back pockets?" Jesse said to Suit.

"No phone," Suit said. "No wallet. Weird, unless it was a robbery."

"Okay," Jesse said. "Let's turn him over."

"You don't think we'll catch some shit from the CPACs?" Suit said.

State Police detectives, from Crime Prevention and Control. They were the ones who investigated untimely deaths. Jesse had always wondered about that with homicides. If they weren't untimely, what the hell were they?

"It would be me catching the shit," Jesse said. "But I won't."

With Suit's help they gently rolled the body over. There was no exit wound to the forehead. So the bullet *was still* inside him. As Jesse reached down to close the man's eyes, Suit said, "I don't know the guy."

"I do," Jesse said.

# Three

**M**an, I still can't believe you met this guy at your AA meeting," Suit said.

"Well," Jesse said. "It wasn't just mine."

"But you'd never met him before?" Suit said.

"I'd never been to this meeting before," Jesse said. "I just felt like I needed one last night. There wasn't one here, so I went on the website and found one in Marshport."

Suit looked at him, frowning.

"So you needed a meeting like you used to need a drink?"

Jesse grinned. "You're probably noticing the connection, Detective."

"You're making fun of me," Suit said.

"Am not," Jesse said.

"You sure?"

"I am," Jesse said.

They were in Jesse's office back at the station. Dev was with the body at the lab in Marshport. The two CPACs who'd shown up, Crandall and Scoppetta, were still with Peter Perkins and Gabe at the scene.

Jesse and Suit had stopped to pick up donuts, even though Suit swore he didn't eat them anymore. Since he'd married Elena he not only was in the best shape of his life, he bragged constantly about his low cholesterol numbers the way ballplayers bragged about high batting averages.

Or getting laid.

"You meet this guy last night in the next town over and the next morning he shows up dead in ours," Suit said. "What are the odds?"

"I really didn't do much more than say hello," Jesse said. "He wasn't the main speaker. But at the end they ask if anybody else wants to say something and this guy said his name was Paul, and that he was grateful to be in the room, because he felt as if he needed a meeting as much as he ever had."

"That was it?" Suit said.

"Then he said that he knew part of the process in AA was making amends, but wondered if amends worked both ways. And everybody kicked that around for a few minutes."

Suit said, "He explain what he meant by that?"

Jesse shook his head.

"And you only got his first name," Suit said.

"The way it works, Suit," Jesse said. "'Hi, I'm Jesse and I'm an alcoholic.' Then it's all the slogans. They're a bear for slogans. 'One day at a time.' 'Easy does it.' 'Friend of Bill.'"

"Who's Bill?"

"One of the guys who started AA."

"Didn't you have a sponsor named Bill?"

"Coincidence," Jesse said.

"I'm not gonna lie, Jesse, it still sounds weird to me," Suit said. "Hearing you call yourself an alcoholic. It still makes me think of skid-row bums a little bit."

"It's no different than me saying I used to play shortstop, or used to be married to Jenn," Jesse said.

"You still miss it?" Suit said. "The drinking?"

"Other than every day," Jesse said, "not so much."

They each sipped coffee. There was a Cuisinart coffee-maker in the corner, one Jesse hadn't fired up yet. The machine had been a gift to the PPD from Sunny Randall, back in Jesse's life now if not his bed. They each had their reasons. But then sometimes Jesse thought sex was more complicated than the tax code.

"Did the guy know that you were a cop?" Suit said. "At the meeting?"

Jesse shook his head. "He was Paul, I was Jesse. I didn't ask for his last name and he didn't ask for mine. Now I wish I had."

"Did he say he was on his way over here?"

"Nope," Jesse said. "Sometimes you hang around after a particularly good meeting, but I didn't want to be late for Lily's big night. I shook his hand and left."

"You think he lives in Paradise?" Suit said.

"Don't know that he doesn't."

"But would it make sense for him to go to an AA meeting in Marshport?"

"Not that far away, and people are always looking for meetings that meet their schedule or their needs." Jesse shrugged and drank coffee. "I was there."

"So either he had his own car," Suit said. "Or took a car service."

"Or hitched a ride with somebody else from the meeting if he didn't have a car," Jesse said.

"Who doesn't have a car?"

"Maybe a drunk who lost his license for being a drunk."

"You really think he might be from here?" Suit said.

"This is a small town, Suit," Jesse said. "You grew up here. I've been here a long time. But we don't know everybody."

"Maybe his prints will be in the system."

Jesse grinned. "Wish to build a dream on," he said.

The phones were quiet. By some minor miracle the four cells near the squad room were empty, even after all the drinking that Jesse knew had to have gone on late into the night. Jesse wasn't spiking the ball yet, but maybe this was going to be a holiday weekend when the town didn't turn into Stupidville.

"You going back to Marshport?" Suit said to Jesse.

"There's a six o'clock meeting at the same church every night," Jesse said. "Maybe Paul talked to more people after I left."

"And some of them might be back there tonight?"

"You get a good meeting, you generally stay with it," Jesse said.

"Every day?"

"Some people go to two a day," Jesse said.

"You're shitting."

"Whatever it takes."

Suit stood. He said he was going back to the lake to relieve Peter and Gabe, see if there was anything he'd missed, or they had. Said he might go back and interview Christina Sample again. When he got back, he said he'd start checking

Uber and Lyft, in addition to taxi companies and other local car services who hadn't been put out of business by Uber and Lyft, at least not yet.

"I'm sorry the guy died," Suit said. "But I still got this feeling, you know? Like it's game on, or something. You know what I mean?"

"I do," Jesse said.

"That feeling ever get old?"

"Not until we're the ones dead," Jesse said.

Jesse was alone in his office after Suit left. Molly had just texted him to let him know she was on her way in, she'd been dealing with something at home. A kid named Jeff Alonso, who'd started out on the cops in Rhode Island, was working the front desk. Jesse reached into one of the bottom drawers of his desk for the old ball he kept there, and the Rawlings glove that was an exact replica of the one he'd worn in the minors. Cole had somehow found it, and had given it to Jesse as a gift. He put the glove on his left hand now, began to pound the ball into the pocket.

*Damn damn damn*, he thought. *It still feels sweet.*

He still loved the feel of it all, ball and glove, the seams underneath his fingers. Loved the sound of the ball hitting the pocket. Jesse had always been able to get the ball in the hole or behind second, and throw it hard across the diamond, and accurately. Even when he and Suit played catch with a softball, Suit would talk about the hissing sound he swore the ball made when Jesse threw it. Jesse was always a better fielder than hitter but had always believed he was a good enough hitter to make it to the bigs, until he got hurt.

He returned the glove to his drawer and then leaned back

in his chair, fingers laced behind his head, and thought of Paul, sitting in the church basement, full of his own sobriety less than twenty-four hours ago. Now he was on Dev's table at the new lab in Marshport and it was Jesse's job to find out how he got there.

He spent so much time thinking about what he couldn't do, thinking about who he used to be and who he was now. Or what he was. Wondering what he missed more, baseball or drinking. Or all the women in his life that he'd lost. Some had quit him, the way baseball had. He'd quit more. Maybe that was the real question in the end: Had he lost more in his life than he had gained?

Amazing how much goddamn time he spent organizing his life around drinking. Every goddamn day.

*Fuck it,* he thought, and told himself all over again that he needed this job more than he needed a drink.

Think about *that.*

Jesse knew he'd never be a bear himself on all the AA slogans, or the Twelve Steps. But he knew what the steps were.

Number eight was the one about making amends.

Paul had talked about amends.

# Four

Jesse was still at his desk when Molly Crane burst into his office as if sparks should have been shooting off her, like a car riding on rims.

"My friends are dumber than housewives shows," she said, plopping herself down in one of the chairs across from him.

"You watch those shows?" Jesse said.

"Just enough to know that my friends are wicked dumber than them," Molly said.

"All of them," Jesse said, "or one in particular?"

"One," she said. "Annie. Who was nearly raped last night after I left her at the Scupper."

"Tell me," Jesse said.

The Scupper was in a section of Paradise known as the Swap, and was as close to a dive as any bar in town. Jesse had never had anything against dive bars, he'd always thought they were more real than modern places where the beer list was longer than a police manual. Jesse had just never understood the appeal of this one, even for kids just looking to get a load on. He thought you went to the Scupper only if the Gray Gull was too crowded. Or if you were just too overserved to give a shit.

"You, Deputy Chief Molly Crane, went to the Scupper?" Jesse said. "And not at gunpoint?"

"You want to hear about this or not?" Molly said.

"You know I do," Jesse said. "Did the attempted rape happen in the Swap?"

"In the park," she said. "You know that little wooded area?" Jesse told her he did.

"Guess there were a lot of fireworks last night," Jesse said.

"You mean the body at the lake," Molly said.

Jesse nodded.

Molly said, "Let me finish telling you mine, then you tell me yours. Okay?"

Molly and Annie had walked down to the Scupper after the fireworks. But it had gotten too loud and too crowded. Molly finally left, and ran into Suit and Elena on the street. They gave her a ride home. Annie wanted to stay. Her husband was out of town, their kids were at camp.

"Told me she wanted to kick up her heels a little," Molly said.

"She actually said that?" Jesse said.

"She's a tiny bit older than she looks," Molly said.

"She looks like your older sister to me."

Molly finally managed a smile. "How *much* older?" she said.

"When did you find out what happened?"

"She woke me up a little while ago," Molly said. "She still sounded half drunk."

"Know the feeling," Jesse said. "She fool around, by the way? When her husband isn't around and the kids are at camp?"

"That's the thing," Molly said. "Not that I've ever known, though that doesn't mean she doesn't."

Annie told Molly that she kept drinking like the world was about to end after Molly left her, had some laughs chatting up some young guy who showed her the motorcycle he had parked out front, declined a ride home on it after watching him come back inside and match her drink for drink. She staggered out of there finally. Alone. Can't remember what time. Streets were still filled with people. A guy started walking with her on the street. Big beard, she remembers that. Told her it was too early to go home, they needed to get to this party. What party? Annie wanted to know. The guy said the one in the park for just the two of them.

"She still wanted to kick up her heels," Jesse said.

"Or get them all the way up in the air," Molly said.

"Hey, we both know that can happen to the best of them," Jesse said, grinning at her.

They both knew what he meant, the one time in her marriage she had been unfaithful to *her* husband.

"We're talking about Annie here," Molly said. "Focus."

"Been meaning to ask," Jesse said. "You ever hear from your old friend Crow?"

She gave him a look as if she might go outside and key his car.

"Are you gonna let me tell this or not?"

"Sorry."

"So they end up at the park, just the two of them. On the swings first. Turns out he's got a flask with him. She drinks.

He drinks. They start making out. And then bullshit bullshit bullshit, as you like to say, and he's pulling her into the trees on the lake side and he's on top of her. As drunk as she was, and whatever she thought she wanted, she didn't want *that*. She tried to scream, but he put a hand over her mouth. At that point, she just thought she'd have to let it happen. He was too big and she was too drunk."

"Bullshit bullshit bullshit," Jesse said.

"Exactly."

"But you say it didn't happen."

"All of a sudden, they hear a gunshot, she says, and it sounds pretty close," Molly said.

"Not fireworks?"

Molly shook her head. "I asked her. She said even she could tell the difference."

"So unless somebody else fired a gun last night, it was the gunshot from the lake."

"Anyway," Molly said, "the guy just says, 'Fuck it, bitch, I didn't really want you anyway,' and just leaves her there."

"Virtue intact."

"Barely," Molly said.

"Would she remember the guy if she saw him again?"

"She says no. Said he was wearing some kind of trucker hat pulled down low over his eyes."

"You should tell her to come in," Jesse said.

"That's the thing, she won't," Molly said. "I already asked her that, too. She's embarrassed that she was even in that situation. She doesn't want Mitch to find out. Said she was telling me as her friend, not a cop."

"She still ought to come in," Jesse said. "I don't want

somebody like the trucker-hat asshole running loose in our town."

"I told her I wouldn't tell," Molly said. "But I never count you when I say I won't tell anybody. You, I tell you everything. Even when I wish I wouldn't. Starting with my night with Crow." She shook her head, disgusted. "To my everlasting regret."

"At least you made your own choices with Crow," Jesse said.

"I'm not blaming the victim here, I'm really not," Molly said. "But she ought to want the guy caught same as us."

"Give her some time," Jesse said. "Then make another run at her."

He noticed his coffee cup was empty. He'd forgotten to make more.

"Want coffee?" he said.

"Not if I have to make it."

"I forget sometimes you're deputy chief," he said.

Molly grinned. "Fuckin' ay," she said.

He walked across the room and filled a paper filter with Dunkin' coffee and filled the machine with water. While they both waited for the coffee to brew, Molly took a donut out of the box in front of Jesse. She complained constantly about her weight but never put on an extra pound as far as Jesse could tell. It was a Molly thing. By now he thought that her talking about her hips should be the start of a drinking game.

Just not for him.

"A guy who acts out like that," Jesse said. "He'll do it again. Just a matter of time and opportunity. Hate to think we've got an ape like that wandering around town."

"Along with a murderer," Molly said. "You know who the vic is yet?"

"Sort of," Jesse said. And told her.

"Where's Suit?" she asked.

"Back at the lake," Jesse said. "Probably making calls about car services from there. Peter and Gabe are canvassing the lake houses, all the way around to the other side."

They talked about Paul not having a phone or wallet on him, and why the killer would have lifted them both.

"You think it was a robbery gone bad?" Molly said.

"I'll make that one of the first things I ask him when I catch his ass," Jesse said.

"At least Annie made it home from the park," Molly said.

"I'm going to find out what happened to this guy," Jesse said.

"You only talked to him for a couple minutes," she said. "That doesn't mean this has to be personal."

"Feels that way."

"It always does when it happens in your town," Molly said.

"Yours, too," Jesse said.

His cell phone was on the desk in front of him. He heard it buzzing now. Picked it up and saw it was Suit again. The way his day had begun.

"Got lucky," Suit said. "Got nothing from Uber or Lyft. But the second cab company I called in Marshport told me one of their drivers picked your guy up a block from the church and drove him over here."

"Good work," Jesse said.

"Aw, shucks," Suit said.

"How'd the guy pay?"

"Cash."

"Where'd he get dropped?" Jesse said.

There was a pause at Suit's end of the phone and then he said, "That's the interesting part."

Jesse waited.

"Lily Cain's house," Suit said.

# Five

Jesse ordered sandwiches from Daisy's, which Daisy Dyke herself delivered. When she did, Jesse asked her why she continued to be so good to him.

"Because you continue to give me hope," she said, "that not all men should have a bounty on them."

Everybody in town called her Daisy Dyke. *She* called herself Daisy Dyke. In the world of political correctness, it made Jesse love her even more. But there were other reasons. She had a heart as big as the ocean, and was tough enough to clean up Afghanistan all by herself. Her short hair was a purple color these days. Jesse told her he liked it. Daisy told him she'd gone with it because one of the women on the U.S. World Cup team had the same color. Jesse told Daisy he didn't know she liked soccer. She said she didn't, she just had a thing for the soccer woman with the purple hair and tattoos.

"You sure you don't want to go steady?" Jesse said before she left.

"Don't be vulgar," she said.

Jesse couldn't remember the last time that he and Suit and Molly had been in the conference room on a Sunday morning. They were now. Gabe was looking at security footage from the new camera that had been mounted on a front corner of the Paradise Cinema, wanting to see if Paul might have been in the crowd the previous night, before somehow making his way to the lake. Peter Perkins was still knocking on doors at the lake houses closest to where the body had been found.

"You going to eat your fries?" Suit said to Molly.

"I thought fried food was the enemy now," Molly said.

"A man still has needs," Suit said.

"Well, try to keep them under control," Molly said. "*All* of them."

Jesse took a bite of his pastrami sandwich, washed it down with coffee. It was the second fresh pot he'd made. Maybe he did have to quit caffeine next.

"We've got the guy at the meeting in Marshport," Jesse said. "We've got Lily's address. But until we got an ID, we've got shit."

"It's still kind of early," Molly said.

"It's a murder investigation," Jesse said. "There was an old ballplayer one time who said it gets late early around here. First twenty-four hours are the most important sometimes."

"If this guy's prints aren't in the system, how do we find out who the hell he is and where he comes from?" Suit said.

"There's different agencies," Jesse said, "for prints and dental records. One is the National Missing and Unidentified Persons System. They started up that Armed Forces DNA

Identification thing for soldiers back in the nineties. There's a few others."

"You just know this stuff off the top of your head?" Suit said.

"How many times do we have to go over this?" Jesse said. He ate some pickle. "I'm the chief."

Molly slapped away Suit's hand as he reached for one of the fries still in her container.

Jesse said, "We need to wait a couple days to put his picture out. Always gotta be careful with next-of-kin issues. If there are people looking for Paul and they see it on the *Crier* website or wherever, they'll want to shoot me out of a cannon."

The Paradise *Town Crier* was somehow still in business even with bigger papers in bigger cities going under all the time. The owner, Sam Brill, was always complaining about the cost of everything as he got ready to cut his staff again. Jesse thought of him as the real town crier.

Most of the bylines in the paper belonged to a kid named Nellie Shofner, who'd almost always gotten things right when it came to covering the PPD. Jesse liked her.

"I can't believe our friend Nellie hasn't called already," Molly said.

"She will soon. And when she does . . ."

"Yeah, yeah, yeah," Molly said. "I'll give her one and tell her you're unavailable for comment." She grinned. "Though I always get the feeling that Nellie wishes you were a lot more available to her."

"How many times do we have to go over this," Jesse said. "She's my son's age."

"Looks at you like she's all grown up," Molly said.

"Not all available women in Paradise want to jump my bones," Jesse said.

"Those are just the ones who don't want to wait in line," Molly said. "They must not know that the line moves."

Jesse told Molly he was on his way to see Lily Cain.

"You going to call first?" Molly said.

"You're the one who thinks every woman in town loves me," Jesse said. "I'll just give Lily a thrill and surprise her."

He saw Molly smiling at him.

"What?" he said.

"You've got that look," she said.

"What look?"

"The one that says you might nearly be happy right now." She was still smiling. "Maybe you don't need another woman in your life," she said. "Just a stiff."

"Works better with both sometimes," Jesse said.

"Don't be gross," she said, and Jesse told her that Daisy Dyke, even playing in a different league than Molly, had basically told him the same thing today.

# Six

Lily once joked to Jesse that she'd gotten to the big house on the water the old-fashioned way.

She'd married her way to it.

Jesse thought it had to be more about the money than love, because nothing else made sense. Whit Cain, before his stroke, had looked and acted like every rich asshole the country had produced over the last hundred years, as guys like him kept getting richer, as if somehow assholes like him had become our most predominant natural resource. Jesse had always heard he cheated on Lily, and copiously, at least when he could still get around. Jesse had never spent enough time in their social orbit to know for sure. What he did know was that Whit Cain, before the stroke, had been spending most of his time at his home in Palm Beach, as if he and Lily were leading separate lives. Lily told Jesse once she'd rather spend more time with her gynecologist than more in Palm Beach.

The Cain compound was at the end of Paradise Neck, the

harbor to the left and Stiles Island in the distance to the right. The Atlantic Ocean stretched out in front of them, like it was just one more thing in Paradise, Mass., that belonged to the Cains.

A carriage house built in the 1930s, the place had grown and grown. Like the family fortune. Sometimes Jesse thought that whomever said money didn't grow on trees was full of shit.

The legend around Paradise was that Whit Cain's father had started out in the bootlegging business with Joseph Kennedy, even though the Kennedys denied to this day that their old man had ever been involved in anything illegal, same as the Cains did.

Old Man Cain had moved north from Boston as the Kennedys had gone south to Hyannis Port, apparently on a mission to buy up every inch of oceanfront property from Gloucester to Salisbury, and more than a little real estate in downtown Boston, and everybody knew better than to get in his way. By the time World War II ended, Cain Enterprises owned the First National Bank of Paradise, the biggest construction business in town, and a real estate company that built houses that cost a vulgar amount of money on property that cost even more. They had even started a boatbuilding company, for which Michael Crane, Molly's husband, had once worked. And didn't miss a beat when the old man died. In fact, the rumor about his son Whit was that he was more of a ruthless ballbuster than his father had ever been. What Whit Cain couldn't buy, he found a way to steal. There were still local legends about rivals whom he eventually rolled. Or who simply left the area and never came back.

Now Whit was the old man, in an upstairs bedroom facing

the water, the family fortune of little use to him. Whit and Lily's only child, son Bryce, was overseeing the family's business interests, even though the feeling around town was that once Whit Cain had passed Bryce wanted to cash out and move to Palm Beach himself, and for good.

Jesse had gone home and changed before driving over the causeway to Paradise Neck. He wore a blazer and pressed gray pants and loafers that were as close as he had to dress shoes. There was something about Lily Cain that always made him want to look his best.

In another time, you would have been allowed to call Lily Cain a great broad. In private, Jesse knew she could swear like a champion. He'd told her once that she was where sailors went to learn all the ways to use the word *fuck*. He'd never had the nerve to ask if the pale area on her left forearm had once been a tattoo.

Lily answered the front door herself, even though Jesse knew how much help there was on the premises, at all times.

"Chief Stone," she said, leaning forward and presenting a cheek for a kiss. "Business or pleasure?"

"Business, Lily," he said. "But always a pleasure seeing you."

She was almost as tall as Jesse was. Her hair was some sort of beauty-parlor mix of blond and silver, worn long. Her eyes were as blue as the sky above the water. Jesse just assumed that for her skin to look as flawless as it did Lily'd had work done. But if she had, it was damned fine work. She still had a good figure, too. She must have been something to look at when she was young, Jesse thought, simply because she was still something to look at now. There was always a hint of mischief in her eyes. Or trouble. Jesse guessed she was around seventy.

But despite the almost regal way she carried herself, Jesse had always thought she gave off a bad-girl vibe, as if she'd been hell on wheels once and could prove it. Molly Crane liked to say that she herself was a good girl until she turned.

"Don't be so formal, Lily," Jesse said, winking at her. "You can just call me Chief."

She laughed a full, throaty laugh and showed him in. He had been in the big front foyer a few times before, the room looking as if it wanted to open up all the way through the screened-in porch to the water's edge, and then perhaps to Portugal.

*F. Scott Fitzgerald had it right,* Jesse thought. *The very rich were different from you and me. It started with the views.*

"Bryce and I are just finishing lunch," Lily said, leading Jesse toward the terrace.

Bryce Cain was at the table, staring at his phone.

"Chief," he said, looking up finally.

"Bryce."

They didn't shake hands. Bryce was still staring at his phone, as if waiting for a text message that might slow down climate change.

Lily took her seat. Jesse sat next to her. Lily asked if he wanted something to eat. He said he was fine. She asked if he wanted coffee. He said if he had any more today, he'd want to run down to the water and swim to Stiles Island and back.

"Wasn't last night lovely?" Lily said.

She'd still not asked about the reason for Jesse's visit.

"It was," Jesse said. "Nothing Paradise likes more than celebrating itself."

"Jesse Stone," she said, admonishing him. "You know re-building that theater was a good thing for our town."

"Was and is," he said. "And doesn't happen without you."

"I had plenty of help," she said.

"Takes a village," he said.

"And a whole lot of fucking arm-twisting," she said.

"Think we could have gotten along without *fuck* in there, Mom," Bryce said, putting down his phone, almost as a last resort.

"But what would the fucking fun be in that?" she said.

Bryce Cain was almost as pretty as his mother, maybe an inch taller, same skinny pipe-cleaner frame. Same blue eyes. He wore his own blond hair, starting to go gray, way too long for somebody his age, as if he wanted to look like Brad Pitt. His face looked pretty damn smooth, too. Maybe he and Mom shared the same nip-tuck guy.

"You look official today, Chief," Bryce said.

"I think of the look as firm and resolute," Jesse said.

"Or just ruggedly handsome," Lily said.

Dev had taken a picture of Paul with his phone, and asked an old friend with the State Police to do an artist's rendering, which Dev had delivered to Jesse himself. They both agreed it was very good. Jesse took the drawing out of its manila folder and handed it to Lily.

"This man was found dead at the lake early this morning," Jesse said. "Lily, he took a cab over to Paradise from Marsh-port last night. The driver said he dropped him here."

Lily looked at the drawing, then back at Jesse.

"I'm sure he did," Lily said. "But just getting to the gate doesn't get you in. When Whit and Karina, his nurse, are alone in the house at night, she deactivates the phone down there when she goes to bed. To get in, you need her phone number or mine. Or you're out of luck."

"Did the nurse mention a visitor before she went to bed?"

"She did not," Lily said.

"But she would mention it?"

"She thinks of herself as more than Whit's nurse," Lily said. "She sees herself as a gatekeeper. If somebody wanted to get inside the gate last night, she would certainly have told me."

Lily's reading glasses were on the table in front of her. She put them back on and took another look at the drawing, before handing it to her son.

"Is this an accurate rendering?" she said.

"It is," he said. "I didn't want to bring a photograph from the morgue."

"Do you know who this poor man is?" she said.

"Only have a first name," Jesse said. "Paul. I met him at an AA meeting in Marshport last night."

No point in holding back on that. Jesse assumed by now that if there was life on Mars, even they knew about his drinking problem. And he knew that Lily had been one of the people fighting for him to keep his job when he was in rehab.

"And you think he came here?" Lily said.

"Don't think," Jesse said. "Cabdriver said he dropped him."

"Then how did he get to the lake?" Bryce said. "Pretty long walk."

"Maybe the killer drove him," Jesse said.

"You're saying the killer picked him up here after the taxi let him off?" Bryce said. "How does that make any sense?"

"You don't have a security camera at the front gate?"

Bryce Cain shook his head, as if the subject frustrated him.

"Mom says it's not Buckingham Palace," Bryce said. "And she's not the queen."

Jesse grinned at Lily. "Beg to differ."

"You say you met this guy but have no idea who he is," Bryce said.

Jesse said, "No identification on him. I was hoping he'd paid the driver with a credit card, but he paid with cash."

"Maybe the guy was drunk and ended up getting robbed and killed," Bryce said. "Who the hell knows?" Bryce lifted his shoulders and let them drop. "But a drunk getting killed is hardly the crime of the century."

"Ex," Jesse said.

"Excuse me?" Bryce said.

"Ex-drunk," Jesse said. "Or recovering, take your pick, unless the toxicology shows different. I just know he was still sober at around seven o'clock last night when I left him."

"Maybe the night was young and he couldn't stop himself from getting hammered," Bryce said. "But you'd know better than me." He smiled. "No offense, of course."

"Of course."

"How did he die, if you don't mind me asking?" Bryce said.

"Shot," Jesse said.

"In our town?" Lily said.

"Happens in the best neighborhoods," Jesse said.

"I wish I could help you more, Jesse," she said. "But I have no idea who this man is, or what business he could possibly have had with us."

"Had to ask," Jesse said.

"Well, just make sure you keep my mother out of the media," Bryce said. "You know how much the fake-news people would love to have the Cains in a story like this."

"Not to make too fine a point of it," Jesse said, "but what part of the story would be fake?"

Jesse and Bryce Cain had never spent much time together. But it had been more than enough for them to know they didn't like each other. It seemed to bother Bryce that his mom liked Jesse as much as she did, and that she had fought for Jesse while he was in rehab. Jesse's reasons for disliking her son were far simpler. He just thought Bryce was a raging entitled rich-boy assclown.

"Sometimes, Chief," Bryce said, stepping hard on the last word, "I think you occasionally forget that you work for us, and not the other way around."

"Bryce," Lily said. Some snap in her voice. "Please cut the shit."

Jesse felt himself smiling.

Lily Cain, ladies and gentlemen.

"Sorry," Bryce said. "Not looking to tangle with you, Jesse."

Just like that he was Jesse.

"Dad's upstairs dying," Bryce said. "We don't need any extra noise."

Jesse saw Lily Cain smile.

"At this point, Bryce," she said, "extra noise is likely the least of his concerns."

She turned back to Jesse.

"You have my number," she said. "Send the picture to my phone. I'll ask Karina if she saw or heard anything unusual before bed."

"He was dropped here a few minutes after nine," Jesse said. "So you weren't back yet?"

"There was a big reception at Town Hall," she said. "Which I noticed you managed to avoid."

"You bet."

"I probably left a little after that, took one last look at my marquee, and then went home to bed."

"Thank you," Jesse said.

She smiled again. "I know you, Jesse Stone," she said. "You're going to be like a dog with a bone with this."

"Everybody has to be good at something," he said.

"Well, just leave us out of it," Bryce said, reaching for his own phone, pushing his chair back, walking away from them toward the water.

Jesse and Lily watched him go. Neither spoke until Lily sighed and said, "The pull of heredity."

"Ain't it grand," Jesse said.

# Seven

At a few minutes before six that night Jesse parked the Explorer in front of the First Episcopal Church of Marshport.

He always wondered if they'd originally planned to have a Second or Third Episcopal, with the thought of franchising them in the area like Taco Bells.

Jesse had never been one for attending any kind of church regularly. But with old ones like this, he loved the architecture more than the idea of them, the red brick and the spires and the ornate windows. Loved the way they were so obviously built to last. Wondered all over again where the financing had come from at the time they were being built. This one was more than one hundred years old. Maybe there had been a Friends of Marshport to raise the money back in the last century. The Ukrainian Mob had taken over the running of the town well into the start of this century, before a famous shooting war that was compared at the time to Gunfight at the

O.K. Corral made Marshport essentially start all over again. At the time, Jesse had heard that a private detective he knew from Boston had been in the middle of all that, after his best friend had nearly been shot to death by one of the Ukrainians. Jesse never found out for sure. But it sounded like the detective. Spenser, his name was. A total badass himself, with whom Jesse had worked a couple times. Even Sunny said he was the best.

The message board out front gave the schedule of Sunday services. Nothing there about the Higher Power the people in the basement were about to discuss. Maybe it was implied. It was church, after all.

Jesse left his revolver and badge in the glove compartment. He didn't like being without a gun, even in a house of worship. He was carrying a Glock .40, semiautomatic, magazine, no clip, fifteen to seventeen rounds. But even though he was here on official business, he was still one of them in the room, part of the club, not the chief of police from the next town over.

Hi, I'm Jesse.

He sat in the back. He always sat in the back, except at rehab, when they made you sit in a circle with a much smaller group. But he looked at the room differently than he had last night. Looking at it with cop eyes tonight. Checking for faces he recognized.

The speaker gave her name as Laura. She was a pretty blond woman in her thirties, maybe forties, who'd been there the night before. Said she'd been an advertising executive in Boston. Happily married to a man she described as a "biggie on the go." She smiled when joking that she knew it was going to shock them, but that she'd never thought she had a problem with alcohol. Thought she had her drinking under control, even during her girls-gone-wild days in college.

But then she was into the drinking life, full throttle. It was just part of the skill set of her business life, or so she told herself. Like bullshitting people. Business lunches and dinners got longer and longer. She got caught in her first affair. The biggie-on-the-go left her. Then she didn't need the excuse of a business dinner, she just started going to bars. Before long she was leaving with strange men.

Jesse thought of Annie leaving the Scupper, and the strange man she'd met on the way home.

"That's the way I thought of them," she said. "Strange. Never imagining the strange one was *me*."

She was on a downhill run by then. Lost her job. Lost the house. Ended up in a motel in Quincy, having been beaten up. She used her phone to call the cops. One of them, a woman, took her to a meeting that night.

Laura said she was eleven months sober. She was working again in the advertising business, from home. She'd run the Boston Marathon in April. The people in the room applauded when she finished. It was time for cookies and coffee. By now Jesse knew that cookies and coffee were the thirteenth step of AA, after the one about carrying the message to other alcoholics.

"First time you spoke?" Jesse said to her.

"You could tell?"

"Sometimes I can," he said. "It didn't sound like a story you'd told before."

"Finally screwed up my courage," she said.

"Pretty sure courage was going to the first meeting," he said.

He put out his hand.

"Jesse," he said.

"You're the cop," she said.

Jesse grinned. "Well, not the only one."

He took out his phone and showed her the picture of Paul. He heard the sharp intake of breath.

"Oh my God," she said. "He's dead. We were all just here." She looked up at Jesse. "How? When?" She shook her head quickly, almost furiously, as if flies were buzzing around it. "I'm stammering," she said.

He told her how Paul had died, and when.

"I had to get out of here last night," Jesse said. "A thing over in my town. I talked to him for a minute. Wondered if you might have after I left."

She didn't look to Jesse as if she'd taken a lot of time on hair and makeup. But this close to her, he saw the age around her eyes, or perhaps the mileage. The old Indiana Jones line. Not the years, the mileage. There was a tiny scar, unhidden by the makeup, on her chin. Her eyes were very blue, almost violet. She reminded him a little of Sunny. An older, sadder version of Sunny. Just not as pretty. Few were.

"We did sit here and talk," she said. "He said what he'd said when he put his hand up. He just needed a meeting. Said he needed a shot of courage tonight, not bourbon."

"All I've got is his first name," Jesse said. "No way to ID him, at least not yet. Did he say anything that might help me figure out how he ended up here?"

She tilted her head, ran a hand through her long hair, frowning.

"He really didn't," she said. "He asked me if I wanted to grab a burger. I thanked him and told him no, I already had plans. I really did, but I don't come here looking to meet guys. He said no worries, he sort of had to be somewhere, too. Then he asked me to wish him luck."

"He say why?"

"He did not. And I didn't ask."

"You ask where he was going?"

"That I *did ask*," Laura said. "He said Paradise. Then he said that from what he knew, maybe they should call it Fool's Paradise."

# Eight

Crossing over from Marshport into Paradise, Jesse found himself wanting a drink.

The urge came over him sometimes just like that, no particular trigger, no real precipitating event. A sudden storm, appearing over the water as if out of nowhere. Then he just wanted a drink *right fucking now.*

He felt himself squeezing the steering wheel, as if lessening his grip even slightly would transform the Explorer into one of those self-driving cars, and he would be on his way to the Gull. Or a liquor store still open on a Sunday night.

He took in as much air as he could, let it out slowly, telling himself the feeling would pass, that since rehab it had always passed, that he didn't need to pull over and sit on the side of the road until the feeling *did* pass.

It still didn't take much, even after a meeting. Or maybe it was because of the meeting, who the hell really knew? Sunny always said that drinking never really made her feel better about things when she felt as if her own life were turning to shit. But that it sure as hell never made her feel any worse.

What had Sinatra said that time when Jesse and some buddies had gotten drunk and gone to see him in Las Vegas, when Frank was old and starting to forget the lyrics and acting impatient for his own show to be over, as if it were a ball game that had gone all too long? "We feel sorry for all you people who don't drink, because when you wake up in the morning that's as good as you're going to feel the rest of the day."

Do you still miss it? Suit had asked.

Every day.

He slowed the car, making his way down Main Street in the gathering darkness. Past the theater. Taking the turn and driving past his old condominium, a couple blocks from the Gull. Then past the Gull and down through the Swap until he was in front of the Scupper, outside which Annie Fallon's night had changed, and nearly her life. He slowed as he passed the Scupper and looked through the front window and saw people laughing and talking, all of them with drinks in their hands. The people he served and protected.

He hadn't done much of a job protecting Paul from getting one to the back of the head, from the .22 that had killed him. Dev had the bullet. One shot, he said, rattling around inside the brain, goodbye.

When Jesse got home, he was so tired it was as if he'd walked from Marshport. But somehow his thirst had made him hungry. So he decided to fry up a burger, truck-stop style, and watch *Sunday Night Baseball.*

Baseball was usually all he watched on television. Baseball or Westerns. That was it, all the company he got from TV.

Cole hadn't been around much lately. He'd completed his state cop training, been assigned to their office in Northampton. He had a steady girlfriend there, even though he constantly told Jesse that talking about "going steady" dated Jesse more than his taste in music did.

That was Cole's life right now. Learning to be a cop in western Massachusetts. And girls. Or girl, singular, in this case. Katie was her name. Jesse still hadn't met her. But the kid seemed happy enough, even talking occasionally about going back to Los Angeles someday and seeing if he had the chops for Robbery Homicide.

He said one time that he'd thought about taking Jesse's name instead of his mom's, but Cole Stone sounded too much like he ought to be a fucking ice-cream store. He stayed with Cole Slayton.

When the burger and fried potatoes Jesse had cooked up with onions were ready he set up a TV table in front of the set. Did they even still call them that? Jesus, he was getting old. He pointed the remote and switched on the game, Red Sox against the Yankees, and saw that it was only in the fourth inning. Some people wrung their hands over how long the games were. Not Jesse. They could play all night as far as he was concerned.

Long games made his nights feel shorter.

He reached for his iced tea, held up the same tall glass that used to hold Johnny Walker or Dewar's, saw the same amber color he used to see when it was scotch in the glass, with just the right amount of soda.

He'd always liked watching baseball when he'd had a few, no way of getting around that.

"Here's looking at you," he said, his voice sounding too loud in the empty room, even over the sound of the announcers.

When he'd finished eating and cleaned his plates, he called Sunny Randall.

She answered right away.

"Damn," she said. "It's never good when the police call."

Just the sound of her voice made him feel better. Less like the alonest man around. He'd told Sunny once that Molly had said that about him and Sunny had said, "Wait, somebody else besides me picked up on that?"

"Your father was a cop," Jesse said. "You say that when he calls?"

"Are you calling to chat," Sunny said, "or do you need crime-stopping tips?"

Jesse said, "What are you wearing?"

"Does asking a question like that make you feel out of step in the modern world?" Sunny said.

"And proud of it."

"What would you say if I told you I just got out of the shower and was wearing nothing except a towel?"

"I'd go downstairs and get in the car and drive down there with the siren on," he said.

"Actually," she said, "I've got goop on my face, and am wearing baggy gray sweats."

"Still coming," Jesse said. "Just no siren."

She laughed.

"If you're gooped and saggy, you must be alone."

"I said baggy, Chief Stone. Not saggy."

Jesse said, "Where's your ex?"

"Richie and his son are in Los Angeles, visiting the boy's

sainted mother. They were supposed to stay a week. They've stayed two."

"How's it going with the three of you?" Jesse said. "Or four, counting Rosie."

Rosie was Sunny's dog.

"Love the boy," she said. "Still love the father. It's that thing about the three of us that's the problem."

"Ongoing," Jesse said.

"Ongoing," she said. "I'm good at a lot of things. Stepmom isn't one of them and might not ever be. And he's talking about marriage again."

"Love is lovelier," Jesse said.

"Theoretically."

"Are you and Richie currently, ah, together?"

"If you mean *together* in a carnal sense, no. He needs time to figure out how to be a dad."

"So the two of you aren't doing it in the changing room of boutiques the way we did that time in Beverly Hills?"

"That was more a one-off," she said.

"Two-off, as I recall."

There was a silence now, from both of them. Neither, Jesse knew, was uncomfortable with this kind of silence.

Finally Jesse said, "Change of subject?"

"And stop talking dirty to each other? Is this really you?"

"Caught a dead body today at the lake," Jesse said. "Or Suit did."

"Do tell."

He did. When he finished, Sunny said, "I'm sorry for the dead fellow. But maybe this is a good thing for you. Maybe even better than sex."

"Speak for yourself," he said. "If I use the blue light *and* the siren, I could still be there in half an hour."

"I thought we were going to hit the pause button on being friends with benefits," she said, "and just try being good old friends."

"Thinking that's starting to get old," he said.

"Maybe we should put our therapists in a room and let them figure out where this relationship should go," Sunny said.

"It's a relationship again?"

"Always was," Sunny said.

"Dr. Silverman and Dr. Dix, fighting for the title," Jesse said.

"We could make it pay-per-view."

There was another silence and then Jesse said, "You said you still love Richie. What about me? Am I still first runner-up?"

"Let me get back to you on that."

Jesse said, "Do you really have goop on your face?"

"I might have lied about that," she said.

Then she told him what she was really wearing. Or, more accurately, not wearing.

Then they did talk dirty to each other. It was, Jesse decided, better than baseball.

# Nine

Molly Crane stood in her living room, having pulled back the draperies a couple inches after turning out the lights, unable to shake the feeling that she was being watched.

She'd had the feeling all night.

She was alone in the house. Michael was just a few days into the Great Pacific Race, which used to start in May but had been pushed back to July this year, rowing from Monterey to Honolulu with a rich friend, something for which he'd been training for a year, 2,400 miles, no engines, no sails, four to a boat, two hours on and two hours off for a month. Or more. Like his version of the Boston Marathon, just across the Pacific. He'd been dreaming about a boat like this, this race, his whole life. But any kind of boat made Michael Crane happy. He'd been working on them since high school, the same as his father had.

Molly knew Jesse's father had been an L.A. cop.

*Boys and their daddies,* she thought.

But being on a boat, being in the water, did make her husband happy. *Happier than he is with me? Now, that was a damned good question,* she thought. She knew they loved each other. That had never been in doubt, from the time they started dating in high school when both of them were fourteen. As far as Molly knew—and she was a cop, after all—he had never cheated on her. To this day, she didn't completely understand her one and only indiscretion with a career criminal named Wilson Cromartie, known as Crow. Why she had wanted him the way she did. Wanted him and needed him. She had told Jesse once that it *had been* a need for her at the time, the way his drinking had been.

"But you stopped after one," Jesse said.

"It wasn't easy, let me tell you," Molly said.

"Booze is always around," Jesse said. "Maybe a good thing for you Crow isn't."

But she had given in to it. Or let herself be carried along by it. She had cheated on Michael. The next day, she knew that Jesse knew before she told him. They knew things about each other that way, things that Michael didn't know about her and that Jenn, Jesse's ex-wife, didn't know about Jesse. Maybe Sunny knew Jesse that way. Sunny's relationship with him, Molly had always thought, was closest to the one Molly had shared with him, almost from the day he'd showed up in Paradise.

Just without sex. Not with Jesse. They'd never had any interest in making it physical, despite the jokes and comments and fake flirtation. Even with the times in the old days when they'd gotten drunk together, it was understood between them, no discussion necessary. When Jesse had most needed taking care of, when he'd tried to disappear into the bottle, Molly felt more as if she were taking care of a brother.

If she loved Jesse, and she knew she did, it was like that.

Molly Crane was a caregiver, through and through. She always had been. A good Catholic girl, except when she'd been bad with boys in college, during the period when she and Michael decided not to be exclusive. But she did the most to take care of their marriage and their four daughters. The youngest was going off to college in the fall. University of New Haven. She was going to study criminology.

The thought of it made Molly smile.

*Girls and their mommies.*

At the department, Molly didn't just take care of Jesse. She took care of Suit and everybody else. Managed the things that Jesse had no interest in managing, as if managing one more household.

Starting with the chief.

Now she felt as if she were taking care of him as much as she ever had, whether he realized it or not, even though he had stopped drinking, at least for now. Day at a goddamn time, as he kept telling her.

Molly knew enough about alcoholism. There'd been enough of it in her own family, starting with her own father. She knew things were supposed to get better once they stopped drinking, even though her father never had. But these days Jesse seemed as sad as he ever had. And as distant. Even with a son in his life. She'd come into his office and he'd be sitting behind his desk, pounding that stupid ball into his mitt. He'd have that faraway look on his face, as if things were supposed to have turned out better for him.

Drunk or sober.

At least today had been different. This victim *was* personal for him, dying, as he had, so soon after getting sober. She could see it in Jesse's eyes, mostly. Something flickering in there. A candle slowly coming to life.

Like having a problem to solve, a killer to find, was a need with him, replacing his need for drink.

The things you thought about when you were the one alone in the night.

She stared harder at the street. Emma was spending a couple weeks with her best friend's family in Nantucket. *Christ,* Molly thought, *what is it going to be like when she was off to college and Michael was away again at another race and the house was empty and quiet like this all the time?* When she was officially— *Oh, kill me now for even using the expression; oh, fuck me*—an empty nester.

Not much scared Molly Crane. But that scared the holy hell out of her. She knew herself and her husband well enough by now to know how little care Michael required from her.

So who was she going to take care of when she got home from the office at night?

Maybe that was why she was the one feeling restless last night, even if she never would have admitted that to Annie. Even if she hadn't gone to the Scupper looking to pick up a man, the way Annie so clearly had.

"I'm bored and I'm horny," Annie had said after her second drink, or maybe it had been her third.

"Not a good mix," Molly had said.

"Speak for yourself," Annie had said.

Then she had nearly been raped. It made Molly, the caregiver, feel guilty as sin afterward. *Was* guilt a sin? She couldn't remember whether the nuns had ever addressed that. Just the guilt part, for doing dirty things and thinking dirty thoughts.

*I shouldn't have left her in that bar by herself.*

Maybe somebody had been watching her—them—at the Scupper.

She knew why Annie had been there. *But why was I there, really?* Molly prided herself on her honesty, starting with being honest about herself. Was she already starting to worry about what might happen to her marriage when it was the two of them alone in the house, when they were both in the house?

She wasn't feeling what she'd been feeling with Crow that time. The ocean itself couldn't have stopped what happened between them, just that one night, but one she remembered as vividly as if she had it on tape.

She'd been thinking about Crow lately.

She *was* feeling restless these days, as if there were some kind of hole in her life that even a job she loved, one that involved working with people she loved—starting with the chief—couldn't fill.

Maybe she was the one who needed to start seeing Dix, Jesse's shrink.

She knew that even with a son in his life now, and Sunny always on the periphery, the job was all Jesse really needed. He still didn't know how to be a dad to Cole. If anything, he acted more like an older brother. Or friend. Maybe they'd be drinking buddies if Jesse still drank.

But Jesse knew how to be a cop. He knew how to be chief. Molly heard the way he talked about being a ballplayer. There was no way he could have been better at that than being a cop. Even being a cop in a small town like theirs.

It did everything except make Jesse happy. That was Molly's fantasy about Jesse. Not being in bed with him. Just that he'd find some happiness. Maybe peace along with it. Jenn had never made him happy, at least not for very long. Diana never had. Molly still thought Sunny had come closest. But maybe that was because Jesse couldn't have her, at least not completely. At least not yet, and maybe not ever, Sunny's job being as important to her as Jesse's was to him.

He was just so fucking sad sometimes.

Molly felt sad tonight.

She kept looking out the window at the quiet cul-de-sac that had been part of her world for her entire marriage, a few blocks from the other quiet street on which she'd grown up. This was the house in which they'd raised their children. Now the three older daughters had left Paradise, for good, Molly was certain of that. Emma was on her way to college.

Maybe, Molly thought, her unease tonight, the wariness she was feeling, was because of what had happened to Annie last night. And not just to Annie. To Jesse's acquaintance from the AA meeting.

Usually when one or more of the girls were in the house, she'd lock away her gun, the Glock .40 like the one Jesse carried, the gun he'd brought with him from Los Angeles.

Tonight she would keep the gun on her nightstand.

She did not feel safe tonight.

She put the living room lights back on as she headed upstairs for bed, having no idea how right she was.

She was being watched.

And wasn't the only one.

# Ten

They caught one small break. There turned out to be security footage in Marshport of Paul coming out of the First Episcopal Church on Saturday night. Jesse had called the chief there, Captain John Kyle, who told Jesse they had a camera set up at one of their new substations across the street. The picture of Paul's face was clear enough that Jesse allowed Nellie Shofner to put it up on the *Crier* website on Wednesday night. Trying to make something happen. Get them in the game.

Now it was Thursday afternoon, and they still had no hits from any of the agencies Molly and Suit had contacted. No missing-persons report filed on a white male in the whole state since Sunday.

"We're reaching the point where we may need some help from the universe," Molly said.

"Is there a number we can call for that?" Jesse said.

"On it," Molly said.

They had been eating lunch at his desk, just the two of them. *Like an old married couple,* he thought. Molly said that Nellie Shofner had called again an hour before, asking if there were any developments in the case. Nellie still didn't know they had a first name on the victim, and was still calling him John Doe. Molly asked Jesse now if he knew the expression had started with plaintiffs in property cases. He told her he did not.

"Your head ever feel full, all that useless information stored up there?" he said.

"Just because you didn't know doesn't make it useless," Molly said. "You're just jealous."

"Often," Jesse said. "What did you tell Nellie?"

"That the investigation was ongoing," Molly said. "She told me that I was getting almost as good at saying nothing as you are."

"Less is more," Jesse said.

"A lot less, in your case," Molly said. "A *whole* lot less."

Jesse knew how these things worked. You just kept pulling on strings. Occasionally the universe did intervene and a string got pulled for you. He remembered another case, a floater they'd found off Stiles Island, a woman who'd been in the water awhile. Florence Horvath, her name was. It took some time identifying her, too. Turned out she had rented a boat at Ned's Cove and never returned it. But the owner had a credit card on file, and a picture of her driver's license. Then the boat turned up at another yard in the harbor. It turned out to be one of the saddest cases he'd ever worked, the woman killed by the father who'd been abusing her since she was a child. There was your fucking universe for you right there.

But the finding out, the figuring out, the grunt work and grind, sometimes started with something as random as the guy from the boatyard showing up at the station. And then you were in the game.

Jesse had met the victim this time but didn't know *who* he was. Somebody did. *Matter of time,* he kept telling himself. Even as he felt they were losing valuable time.

Things got late early. But he'd done this kind of work plenty of times before. He knew how good he was at it. Wondered sometimes where his skill set could have taken him in L.A. if he hadn't drunk himself out of town. Or maybe he was supposed to end up here. Maybe this was who *he* was and all he was and where he belonged.

It was nearly five in the afternoon. His door was open, as usual. Molly still gave a rap on the frame to announce herself before poking her head in.

"Got a woman to see you," Molly said. "She saw the picture of Paul on the website. Says she knows him."

Her name was Ellen Chagnon. She said she was up in Boston from Florida, attending a bachelorette party for an old friend.

"Where in Florida?" Jesse said.

"Wellington."

"Where's that?" he said.

"West of West Palm."

She wore her red hair short, had a lot of freckles that she didn't try to hide with makeup, was small, but with a nice figure. More than a nice figure. Her pale green T-shirt showed off what Jesse, as a trained investigator, thought were amazing breasts. They looked real, even though it was getting harder and harder for him to tell. The T-shirt also set off the red hair nicely, a darker shade of green than the eyes. She wore white jeans tighter than the T-shirt, which was saying plenty, and sandals. Apple Watch. No rings. He thought she was in her twenties, maybe thirties. Young, anyway. But the whole world was looking younger and younger to Jesse. Sunny said it was happening to her, too. She said you woke up one day and the kid from UPS was m'am-ing you.

"I bartend in Wellington, a place called Oli's," she said. "Paul used to come in, a couple nights a week. Sometimes more."

"You ever get a last name?"

She shook her head. "He was just Paul."

*Like an AA meeting,* Jesse thought. *Just in a bar. First names only.*

"How'd he pay?"

She let out some air. "Wow," she said. "It was last winter. I think cash."

"Never a credit card?"

"Might have," she said. "There's probably a way to check, even though nobody ever asked me to."

"I can," Jesse said.

She was in one of the chairs across from Jesse. And nervous, Jesse could see, busy with her hands, giving the appearance of constant motion even sitting down. Her fingernails were an even brighter green than her T-shirt. A couple times he saw her stop herself from chewing on a thumbnail. Probably worried it would ruin her manicure. He'd asked Sunny Randall once if she'd ever chewed her nails and she put out her hands, showing off her own latest manicure, and said, "Not anymore."

Most people, Jesse knew, went their whole lives without ever sitting in a police station for a conversation like this about a murder. It was showing now with Ellen Chagnon.

"How did he die?" she said. "It didn't say in the story."

No reason not to tell her.

"He was shot," Jesse said.

"Jesus," she said. "Somebody shot him?"

"They did."

"Was it, like, a robbery or something?"

"To be determined," he said.

He smiled. Amiable Jesse. Small-town chief, putting his visitor at ease. And a pretty hot visitor at that.

He asked if she had any idea what Paul did for a living.

"He said he worked with horses," she said. "A groom, maybe? Wellington is pretty big horse country."

"I thought Central Florida was horse country," Jesse said.

"It is," she said. "But we've got one of the biggest equestrian festivals in the country. In Wellington, I mean. Starts in December and goes all the way to April."

"So there's barns there."

"A bunch. Most of them over near the show."

"He ever mention which one?" Jesse said.

She shook her head.

"He ever mention whether he lived in Wellington or just worked there?"

"He actually did one night," she said. "He said he lived *where* he worked. Said it was a short commute to the stalls every morning."

"But not which barn."

"It wouldn't have meant much to me if he had," she said. "One ear and out the other. The only horses I care about are the ones carrying around polo players with accents. And riding pants."

She smiled. Jesse smiled.

"He drink a lot when he was at your bar?" Jesse said.

"It's not a juice bar," she said.

"The reason I ask," Jesse said, "is that I happened to meet him at an AA meeting the night he died."

"You're AA?" she said.

"I am," she said.

"But you're the chief of police."

"They like me a lot better now that I'm sober."

She tilted her head and smiled again. More with her eyes this time. "And me a bartender," she said.

Jesse smiled. "You ever remember seeing Paul drunk?"

"He'd come in on Fridays sometimes," she said. "Happy hour. I told him one time he didn't seem too happy. But drunk? I don't ever remember him falling out of there, if that's what you mean."

"Anything else he ever said that you think might help me find out more about him?" Jesse said. "Find out who he really is? Or was?"

She steepled her fingers under her chin. She had nice hands. Jesse noticed people's hands. Sunny had beautiful hands.

He was thinking about her more and more these days.

"It was usually crowded," she said. "He was just one of those guys. You know? He acted alone even with people all around him."

"I know the type," Jesse said.

*I* was *the type,* he thought.

"I wish I could help more," she said.

"You've helped more than you realize," Jesse said. "It was nice of you to make the trip up here."

"I guess I just didn't think it was something you just called in," she said. "Man, it's creepy, seeing a picture of someone you know like that, and finding out he's dead."

Jesse stood and came around his desk. She stood. He thanked her again for calling. She was smiling at him again. They stood facing each other. Someone walking into his office—like Molly—might have suggested Ellen Chagnon had invaded Jesse's personal space. It just didn't feel like an invasion.

"I was going to offer to buy you a drink," she said. "But that's kind of off the table, huh?"

"It's a nice offer," he said. "But it looks like I'm going to be jammed up on this for a while."

"Can't blame a girl for trying," Ellen Chagnon said.

"I never have," Jesse said.

# Eleven

Jesse called the chief of police in Wellington after Ellen Chagnon left, told him he was working a homicide and that the victim was someone who'd worked with horses there. The chief asked if he had a name, and not for any of the horses. Jesse said all he had was a first name.

"That ought to narrow things down considerable," the chief said. "You and me working together, we'll probably crack the case no problem."

His name was Ed Johnson. It was a southern accent, but one that Jesse thought could have come from anywhere south of Baltimore. Johnson said he'd be happy as a pig in slop to help out any way he could. He asked Jesse how many people lived in his town. Jesse told him. He asked Jesse how many he had on his force. Jesse told him. Chief Ed Johnson told him he had eight cops on his force, nine counting himself.

"It's like we're in a special club of small-town po-licing," he said to Jesse. "We should have decoder rings and a secret handshake."

Then he told Jesse that there were a "pantload" of barns in Wellington, but a lot of them were empty in the summer, the owners and the trainers and the grooms traveling to shows around the country and as far away as Canada. But he could probably wrestle up a list. Jesse said he'd be grateful.

"You fixing on coming down here?" Johnson said.

"Thinking about it," Jesse said. "You find an app yet that solves this shit for you?"

"Still lookin'," Johnson said.

"Think there's any kind of app better than you?" Jesse said.

"Fuck no," Johnson said. "Where'd be the fun in that?"

"You ever do cop work anyplace except where you are?" Jesse asked.

"SID in Miami," Johnson said. "Did a full twenty."

"You miss it?"

Johnson snorted. "Depends on the humidity, and whether another one of those El Chapos has shot up another El Fuckhead."

He said he'd send along a list in the morning. Jesse thanked him. Johnson said to give him a shout if he came down, he'd buy Jesse a drink.

Jesse said he'd like that. It was easier that way. Not everybody wanted to hear his life story.

Before Jesse left the office he stopped by Molly Crane's desk.

"I've been forgetting to ask," he said. "How you doing with your friend Annie? She ready to come by and talk to me?"

Molly shook her head. "I think she's sorry she even talked about it with me," she said. "She basically just wants to forget it ever happened. She says she hasn't touched a drink since Saturday night. Who knows? Maybe she'll end up going to meetings with you."

"Keep trying," Jesse said. "Before this guy tries again. Or does more than try."

"Yes, boss."

Jesse smiled at her. "You ever wonder which one of us is really the boss of this place?"

She smiled, even more wickedly than usual.

"I never wonder, actually," she said.

Jesse thought about calling Sunny when he got home, even thought about asking her if she wanted to make a quick road trip to Florida with him. But he did not. He wanted to give himself some quiet time to think about what Ellen Chagnon had told him. Ellen, the smoking-hot bartender. He didn't remember many who looked like her when he was still drinking, at happy hour or any hour. But then Jesse had never been a happy drunk. Just a drunk.

*Buy you a drink,* the chief in Wellington had said.

*I'd like that,* Jesse had said.

He baked a small swordfish steak he'd bought at the fish market off Geary Street, green beans on the side, sprinkled with some Parmesan. Fixed himself a small salad. He used to eat out a lot more, but that had meant a drink before dinner and then maybe some wine during. Maybe a scotch for dessert. And not just one. He was better off at home now. Getting better at cooking for himself.

When he finished eating, he washed the dishes by hand, brewed some coffee, stayed at the table. He still didn't have a last name for his victim, but he had an occupation. He had a bar in Wellington, Florida. If Ellen knew him, maybe some of the other bartenders did. Maybe they had a last name.

Jesse had a yellow legal pad in front of him. The pads always helped him think better. He wrote:

WHY?

Why was Paul in Paradise? Why the stop at Whit and Lily Cain's home? Whit Cain spent a lot of time in the same part of Florida. Did the Cains own horses? Lily had never mentioned it if they did. If he didn't fly to Florida, he could stop by and ask. But horses would make sense as a hobby for a wealthy man. Jesse had seen a piece on *SportsCenter* one time, just wanting ball scores, about how Springsteen's daughter was a rider, and had even gone to the Olympics.

Jesse looked at his watch. It was still just nine o'clock, too soon for bed. The rest of the night stretched out in front of him. The faint hum of the air conditioner was almost impossible for him to hear, as if drowned out by the quiet of this place. His new home. The one without a bottle of scotch in it.

He didn't want a drink tonight as much as he wanted something to happen. Maybe needed something to happen. Maybe that was why he was thinking of going to Florida. He had a travel budget, one he hardly ever used. Nora Hayes, big boss at the Board of Selectmen now, had even kicked in more money this year. Molly said Nora probably thought of it as a tip. Nobody would complain about him spending the money to go down there if it helped him clear a murder in the middle of the summer season.

He took his coffee cup and turned on the television and put on the Red Sox game. It wasn't that he felt like watching the game as much as the sudden urge he had to drown out the quiet around him. As if he were asking the announcers, Dave O'Brien and Jerry Remy and Dennis Eckersley, if they'd mind keeping him company.

But he couldn't focus on the game. He was impatient with his lack of progress, even though he'd made minor progress today. He felt as if he were missing something.

Now he wanted a drink.

He walked over to the table next to the Ozzie Smith poster where he kept the glove he'd worn in the minors. He'd had it restitched a few times and still used it for softball, even though it was an infielder's glove that was really too small for softball. He used it anyway. Maybe because of vanity. *Probably* because of vanity. And memory, a way of reminding them—reminding himself—that he'd been a real ballplayer once. The new glove, the one Cole had bought him, didn't feel like this on his hand. Jesse knew it never would.

The signed Ozzie ball was in the pocket.

Jesse took the ball and glove with him out onto the terrace. He felt the ocean breeze on his face immediately, sensed the vast and powerful expanse of it out past Lighthouse Point, a few lights from big boats in the distance. There were clouds tonight, a lot of them. Jesse had heard on the car radio on the way home that a late storm had been forecast, sometime before midnight.

He began to toss the ball into the pocket of the glove. Better a ball in his hand than a drink. He was thinking about the Cains again, what possible connection Paul could have had to them. Throwing the ball harder now into the glove, the sound as sweet and familiar as the crack of the bat.

There was a sudden, bright flash of lightning out over the water now, the attendant and immediate clap of thunder to go with it, startling him.

Jesse didn't close the glove in time and the ball fell to his feet.

"Error, shortstop," he said. "E six."

It was when he was turning to reach down for the ball that he heard another sharp explosion in the night sky. For a moment, less than that, Jesse processed it as another part of the storm over the water.

Then the bullet caught up with the sound of a gun having been fired, and shattered the glass in the door behind him.

# Twelve

Jesse scrabbled back through the door, staying as low as he could without putting his hands down into the broken glass. He crawled through the living room, on elbows and knees, pulling on the string of the standing lamp next to his chair to throw the room into darkness, reaching up to grab his Glock where he'd left it on the table next to the front door. Then he was through the door and down the two flights of steps, out the side door, and into the rain.

The rain hit him like a flurry of punches, the wind blowing hard off the water, the storm already seeming to be at full force. The lightning still splashed across the sky, the sound of the thunder mixing now with the roar of the rain.

Jesse could only guess the exact angle of the shot. There had been no time for him to look through the iron rails of the terrace for movement in the street, or in the distance. The harbor was to the left. Too many possible witnesses there, even late at night, at least before the storm had come. The beach was at the end of Front Street, to his right.

The shot could have come from the street, the shooter finding enough cover to hide himself. Or maybe just not giving a shit. Maybe he'd been watching Jesse's condo and there he was, standing on the terrace, and he'd seized the opportunity and taken the shot.

Jesse had been standing there, pounding the ball into the glove.

But then he'd moved.

The dropped ball maybe saving his life.

He moved along the end of the building, still not sure if the shooter was out here and still close. Maybe he thought he'd hit Jesse and put him down, and was gone.

With a rifle, the shooter could have set up at the end of Front Street, or the beach. Jesse came into the open now, gun pressed to his right leg, and ran as hard as he could toward the water, a high, singing sound in his ears, like a siren, as loud as the storm.

Somebody had taken a shot at him.

The fucking chief of police.

He couldn't throw a baseball the way he once could, his right shoulder having turned to shit a long time ago. But he could still run. He'd started running again, a few miles a few days a week, a few months after rehab. Again. Dix said it was another way for him to feel as if he were doing something more than running in place.

He zigzagged across Front Street and through the rain, in and out of the flashes of light from the sky, like spotlights being turned on and off. The wind slapped against his face all the way to the beach, Jesse running with his gun now pressed tight to his chest, the way he'd been taught as a rookie, finger off the trigger but against the frame of the gun. Indexing, they'd called it at the Academy. The finger was braced, but off the trigger. Preventing what they called a "sympathetic reaction" from the trigger while you were running. Lessons learned, and remembered.

*If it was me,* Jesse thought, *and I hadn't driven a car into the neighborhood where I was going to take the shot, I would have run this way, to the beach and then away from the harbor, in the general direction of Stiles Island.* Jesse faced in that direction now. There was one more flash of light in the sky. One last muted sound of thunder in the distance, to the north.

Then the storm was gone as quickly as it had come, as if it had gone crashing to the bottom of the sea.

Jesse stood there, soaking wet, chest still heaving, gun back at his side.

Then he turned and walked off the beach, looking around him and behind him every few steps, walked back up Front Street until he was home. Once inside, he picked up his cell phone where he'd left it in the kitchen and called his own police department.

"This is Jesse Stone," he said to Jeff Alonso, working the overnight shift tonight. "I need to report a shooting."

"Where?" Jeff Alonso said.

"My house," Jesse said.

# Thirteen

The official description of the bullet Jesse found lodged in the wall near the television set was "projectile evidence." He put on the crime scene gloves he kept in a drawer in his bathroom, carefully dug out the bullet, and bagged it. In the morning he would have one of his cops on duty drive it to the state lab, where they'd measure the lands and grooves that cut into bullets as they spun through the barrel— essentially a way of fingerprinting the gun that had fired it— and compare the results against the larger database to determine if the gun had been used in a previous crime.

Jesse had already applied his own eye test to the bullet, and would have placed a significant bet on it being a .223, which meant the gun that fired it was likely an AR-15.

"I love it when they call them 'sport rifles,'" Molly said.

"Tonight somebody was hunting me," Jesse said.

He'd collected his glove and ball from the terrace. When

Jesse had told Molly what had happened she'd said, "I'll never make fun of baseball ever again."

"Finally," he'd said.

He had called her after calling the station because he knew he was just opening himself up to a world of hurt if he waited until morning to tell her about the shooting. He'd asked her if they should awaken Suit, too. Molly told Jesse there was no need. If the two of them couldn't find the bullet they should think about doing something else for a living, maybe opening a bowling alley.

By now Jesse had changed into dry clothes and brewed a pot of coffee. He was still riding an adrenaline high, and now so was Molly, who had come to like police work as much as Jesse did. A late bloomer.

Molly wore a gray sweatshirt that miraculously had no writing of any kind that Jesse could see, or logo. Jeans. Running shoes. A PPD ball cap. It was one of those moments when Jesse could see clearly the girl she had been, but what she would look like when she was old at the same time.

"So we have now had two shootings in our little town in less than a week," Molly said. "We both know what the chief of police always says about coincidence."

"No way God would leave that much to chance," Jesse said.

The clock on the kitchen wall said it was 12:45. Nearly three hours since whoever tried to shoot Jesse had taken the shot.

"It was a long gun with me," Jesse said. "A .22 with Paul."

"The guy could own more than one," Molly said.

"There's no connection between Paul and me."

"Other than AA."

"Totally random."

"Or not," Molly said. "I'll refer you back to what you just said about coincidence."

She looked at him. Big brown eyes, alive and alert despite the hour and circumstances.

"You were lucky tonight, Jesse," she said.

"And me, usually with the surest hands in the men's softball league."

"It's not funny, damn it!" she said. "And then you go chasing after the guy in the storm?"

"I remember reading something once about why this guy loved *Gunga Din*," Jesse said. "He talked about stupid courage."

They both drank coffee. Maybe they both knew they weren't going to do much sleeping.

"Really stupid," she said.

"Good thing Suit's not here," Jesse said. "You know how he hates it when Mom and Dad fight in front of him."

"I'm not his mom," she said. "Or your wife."

He smiled.

"I tell Suit all the time I don't need another wife," he said. "I've got you to tell me what to do."

"Shut up," she said.

"See there?"

But she was smiling back at him. They sat across the butcher-block table from each other, just a few feet but all of their shared history between them, history and love and respect and friendship. He had left the terrace door open a crack. The sound of the ocean was much fainter than it had been a few hours before, the east wind barely more than a whisper.

"Maybe the guy who shot Paul thinks he told me something, or thinks I know something I shouldn't," Jesse said. "Even though I really don't know shit at this point."

"You're assuming the shooter is a guy," Molly said.

"Figure of speech."

"But if it's not the same shooter," Molly said, "you're telling me some rando tried to shoot the chief of police tonight?"

"If it's someone I previously pissed off," Jesse said, "we'd be talking about a pretty long list."

"Most of the ones you've pissed off the most are either dead or in jail," Molly said.

"It's where AA tells you drunks end up if they don't stop," Jesse said.

"We can still start compiling a list of possibles in the morning," Molly said.

She took her cup to the sink, emptied the last of the coffee, rinsed it, opened the door to the dishwasher and placed it inside. Then she told him not to get up, leaned over and kissed him on the cheek, and left.

Jesse sat there for a few minutes after she was gone, staring at the bullet in the Baggie on the table in front of him. Picturing himself dropping the ball and turning to reach down for it. He got up and shut off the kitchen light and locked the terrace door and headed for his bedroom, thinking:

Maybe there was shit God left to chance after all.

# Fourteen

**M**olly and Suit and Jesse were in his office early the next morning when Molly suggested that they should put a protective detail on Jesse, maybe in three eight-hour shifts, now that somebody had used him for target practice with an assault weapon.

"Hard no," Jesse said. "We don't have the numbers. That's one thing. And I don't need somebody to hold my hand."

"I'm not talking about somebody holding your hand," Molly said. "Just watching your back in case this guy tries again."

"I'd be happy to do it," Suit said.

"I know you would," Jesse said. "I just think it's bad optics for the chief of police to need a bodyguard."

"The way I see it," Molly said, "it would be much worse optics if the next time somebody took a shot at you they hit what they were aiming at."

"If you don't want one of us to do it," Suit said, "we could ask Sunny."

Molly grinned. "And she'd probably do it for free," she said. "Guard Jesse's body, I mean."

"She'd have to do it in Florida the next couple days," Jesse said.

"You're going down there?" Suit said.

"So far what the bartender told me is the best lead we got," Jesse said.

"The chief in Wellington would probably be willing to put one of his people on it and save you a trip," Molly said.

"But they wouldn't be as good as me," Jesse said.

Now Suitcase Simpson grinned. "Nobody better," he said.

"Just ask him," Molly said.

"He's the chief, after all," Suit said.

Molly asked if Jesse needed her to make a flight reservation, and book a hotel. Jesse said he already had, that he was leaving in the late afternoon for West Palm Beach and had booked himself into a Hampton Inn in Wellington. She asked if he'd booked a rental car. He said he'd forgotten. She said she'd take care of it.

Jesse called Cole on his way to the airport, told him where he was going and why.

"Old-fashioned police work," Cole said. "What did they used to call you guys back in the day, flatfoots?"

"Even if we had high arches."

Jesse had gone back and forth inside his own head about telling Cole that somebody had tried to kill him. But told him now. Molly and Suit were like family, but Cole was the only real family he had. Jesse sometimes thought of their relationship the way he thought about himself:

Work in progress.

"If he tried once, he could try again," Cole said. "Maybe you need to catch this guy before you do anything else."

"Thought about it," Jesse said. "But for now I'm staying with the real murder and not the attempted one."

"When you get back from Florida, I'll come for dinner," Cole said.

"Molly thinks I need a bodyguard when I get back."

"I volunteer," Cole said. "I'm already great at surveillance."

"Did one of your commanding officers tell you that?"

"It was more something I intuited."

"Being the cocky bastard you are."

"Where do you think I get it from?"

Jesse said he'd call in a couple days. Cole told him to watch his ass.

"That's my line," Jesse said. "Now that you're a statie."

"I love you," Cole said.

It was something he'd been saying lately when they'd get off the phone, as if it were a new jacket he was trying on for size.

"Yeah, well, don't make a big deal out of it," Jesse said.

He had satellite radio in the Explorer. He put on the channel for Sinatra, who used to say he was sorry for all the people who didn't drink.

Frank was finishing up "Angel Eyes."

*'Scuse me while I disappear.*

Jesse wasn't disappearing. Wasn't running away from anything, including whoever had taken the shot at him last night. He was just being a cop. Working a case about an ex-drunk who hadn't been as lucky as Jesse had been on his terrace.

He knew he could have asked for help in Florida. He'd

worked with Kelly Cruz, a kick-ass detective out of Fort Lauderdale, on the Florence Horvath case. They'd made a good team. But he didn't want to hand this one off. Kelly Cruz was damn good. Just not as good as he was. He hadn't been bullshitting Molly and Suit in the office. He'd never thought anybody was better than he was, whether he'd ended up in Paradise, Massachusetts, or not. Had thought that even before he got sober.

Jesse had booked himself an aisle seat close to the front of the plane with extra leg room. When they'd reached their cruising altitude a pretty blond flight attendant came along with the cart and asked if he wanted something to drink.

"Always," he said.

She smiled at him with a lot of white teeth and said, "I meant right now."

"So did I," Jesse said.

He asked her for a bottle of water. It was one of the small ones you got on airplanes. Jesse finished it in about three gulps. Then he put the seat back as far as it would go and stretched out his legs as far as they could go and closed his eyes. He was still tired because of all the sleep he'd lost the night before.

He didn't wake up until the pilot made the announcements about final preparations for their landing at West Palm Beach.

# Fifteen

**C**hief Ed Johnson's list of local horse barns was waiting for Jesse when he checked into the Hampton Inn, along with a note that read: *Call me if you want a ride along. Just thinking about a real-live murder investigation almost made my dick hard.*

Jesse called and thanked him for the offer.

"What you're doing, we could have done for you," Johnson said.

"It's not the same as doing it yourself," Jesse said.

"Never was for me," Chief Johnson said.

"Anything pop yet on the shooting down here you told me about?" Jesse said.

"Need some luck," Ed Johnson said.

"Don't we all," Jesse said.

Jesse had asked at the front desk where the nearest pizza place was and was told the Mellow Mushroom was within walking distance. He went and came back with a small mushroom and green peppers pie, got a couple Cokes from the vending machine off the lobby, and sat and looked over Ed Johnson's list while he ate pizza.

The barn names meant nothing to him. The only thing Jesse really knew about horses was that he'd watch the Belmont Stakes if one of them had a chance to win the Triple Crown. Johnson had included a map of Wellington with the list, but the geography meant nothing to Jesse, either, other than showing him that the barns formed a perimeter around the grounds for the Wellington horse festival on Pierson Road, which Waze told Jesse was only ten minutes away with no traffic. He couldn't imagine there would be much in Florida in the middle of July. When he was on the jetway after the plane door opened, he felt as if he'd walked into a melting furnace.

When he finished eating he got into his rental car and took the short drive to Oli's, in the big outdoor mall next to the hotel. He took a seat at the bar and ordered a club soda. The woman bartender, dressed in a black tank top and with sleeves of tattoos on both arms, asked if he wanted a lime with it. Jesse told her sure. Live it up.

When she brought his drink back he got right to it, telling her who he was and why he was here and what Ellen Chagnon had told him.

She said, "The guy got murdered? Holy holy."

"You recognize him?"

She held the picture up and studied it, then shook her head.

"Let me go ask Alex," she said. "The manager."

She walked back to the kitchen. A couple minutes later the manager came back with the bartender. He said he didn't recognize Paul and that he'd asked the waiters, and none of them recognized him, either.

"But you gotta remember something," Alex said to Jesse. "If he was in here drinking when Ellen said he was, it was the season."

He made "the season" sound as if it explained everything except interest rates.

Jesse thanked him and made the short drive back to the Hampton Inn and watched a ball game on ESPN from his bed until he was asleep and the ball game was watching him. Big night in horse country.

The next morning he started out in an area called Palm Beach Point. There were a lot of barns there. No one recognized Paul at any of them, nor at the barns in what was called Grand Prix Village.

Someone finally did in the afternoon, at Stony Hill Stables on Appaloosa Trail.

The manager, a short, sturdy-looking woman in riding clothes with vivid blue eyes and a straw-colored braid that went all the way down her back, introduced herself as Karen Boles. Jesse introduced himself, showed her the badge, showed her the picture of Paul, and asked if she knew him. She said he'd worked for her until the end of January.

"Paul Hutton," she said. "Did he do something?"

"He was murdered," Jesse said.

"Oh no," she said.

Her legs seemed to buckle slightly. She put a hand to her

mouth. Her reaction was genuine, Jesse thought, unless she was a better actress than Meryl Streep.

"How did he die?"

Jesse told her that he'd been shot.

"Sweet Jesus," she said. "I wondered what happened to him after he left."

"What did he do for you?" Jesse said.

"He was one of our grooms," she said. "Lived in the apartment over the barn." She jerked her head toward a large wooden structure. Jesse wished they were inside. He would have offered to buy one of her horses to get out of the sun.

"You ask for any references when he got here?" Jesse said.

"There was one place, over in Ocala," she said. "Closed up about six months ago when the owner went back to Buenos Aires. But it's a transient world, Chief. Trainers got vetted. Grooms not so much, especially when one leaves in a hurry and you need to replace them."

"He ever talk much about his life?"

"Not much," she said. "Not much of a talker, our Paul. He said that he was an orphan, that he'd been abandoned."

"You ask him where?"

"I did," she said. "He said he didn't want to talk about it. Just told me one time that it was no accident that his life had turned into a dumpster fire. I remember asking him what he meant by that, but he shut down. We never had the conversation again."

Jesse said, "Why did he leave?"

"He was asked to," she said. "Or told to, that would be a more accurate way of putting it."

"By you?"

"By me and the owners," she said. "Mr. and Mrs. Packer."

"He wasn't good at his job?" Jesse said.

"He was fine with the horses, great with them, actually," she said. "He just turned out to be way better at being a fall-down drunk."

Everyone at the barn knew he drank, Karen Boles said. Paul Hutton never went out with the other horse people on Sunday nights, which she said was the biggest party night during the festival, because the place shut down on Monday. A friend of hers, another trainer, said he spotted him at Oli's a few times and said hello, but that she just assumed he did most of his drinking in the apartment. But she could smell the alcohol on him a lot of mornings. There got to be too many mornings when the other groom would have to go bang on the apartment door to wake him up. Finally one morning they found him passed out in a stall next to one of the horses, and let him go.

"How did he take it?" Jesse said. "Getting fired."

"He was as polite as ever," she said. "Said he'd finally hit bottom, and that it was time to get better. Left in a hurry. I told him that if he ever got himself straightened out, to give me a call. I kind of liked the guy. He just finally couldn't control his drinking."

Jesse told her there was a lot of that going around.

"He say where he was headed when he left here?"

"No," she said. "Kept to himself till the end."

They stood in the open area in front of the barn entrance in the afternoon heat. Jesse could occasionally hear the sound of the horses from inside. At least they were out of the sun. He thought it might be hotter than it had been when he got off the plane yesterday, but it would have been like trying to compare two flames on the same stove. He'd always heard people talking about what it was like in Florida in the summer. Now he knew. Before long he imagined sweat would be spilling down his arms and off his fingertips and creating one more man-made lake in Florida.

"He have any friends?" Jesse asked.

"We have a pretty small operation here," she said. "Not like the bigger, fancier barns. I guess he was closest to the other groom, Hector."

"Could I talk to him?"

"He's the one who left in a hurry," Karen said. "He got wind of an ICE sweep. Then he was the one in the wind."

"Paul leave anything behind?" Jesse said.

"After he was gone I cleaned out the apartment, even though the guy who ended up replacing him lives with his wife over in Royal Palm," she said. "He only left a few things. Some clothes, a couple books."

"Laptop?"

She shook her head.

"You throw his stuff out?"

"Nah, I just put stuff in a box. I figured if he ever came back, it would still be here for him."

"Still got it?"

"Storage room in the back of the barn," she said. "Come on, I'll show you."

She walked him past the horses and to the back of the

barn and showed him the small storage area. There were some saddles stacked against the wall, bridles hanging, spurs. Old boots lined up under the bridles.

There wasn't much in the box. A pair of jeans, a few T-shirts. A faded green University of Miami sweatshirt.

"This all of it?" Jesse said.

Karen Boles nodded. "Almost like he was never here at all," she said.

"Then he was in the wind until he showed up in my neck of the woods," Jesse said.

"When you find out what happened to him," she said, "will you give me a call?"

"*When* I find out?" Jesse said. "Not if?"

"I'm good at reading people," she said. She smiled. "Even if you missed a few jumps, you're the type that would finish the damn course."

She was still smiling.

"Or you can just give me a call if you're ever back down here," she said. "You ever get up on a horse?"

"Only on carousels."

"Maybe I could teach you how to ride."

Jesse said he'd take her up on that if she promised he wouldn't fall off. Karen Boles said that nobody had fallen off her yet. She laughed. He laughed. Then headed for the rental car. He didn't have much of a love life back home. But first Ellen the bartender had come on to him. Now the horse trainer. A small sampling, but he still seemed to have it with the women of Wellington, Florida.

# Sixteen

Molly was getting ready to leave the office at around six when Jesse called to tell her that the 8:30 flight from West Palm was booked and that he'd made a reservation on the first one out tomorrow morning.

He'd called earlier to give her Paul Hutton's full name. Molly told him she would run it through the National Crime Information Center before Jesse got the chance, see if she could find a date of birth and driver's license if he had one, and even a last-known address before the apartment above the barn on Appaloosa Trail, especially if someone anywhere in the country had reported a Paul Hutton missing.

She'd had success using NCIC before and knew she might know as early as tomorrow how many hits there'd been on the name, just in Florida alone. She was excited at the prospect. At the chase. Molly knew how good Jesse was at police work, even when it was a grind. But she knew she was good, too, and getting better all the time.

She was a work in progress, same as her boss.

"Provided it's the guy's real name," Jesse said.

"You know you're getting more cynical as you get older, right?" Molly said.

He made a snorting noise at his end of the phone.

"Hardly breaking news."

"I'm Catholic," she said. "We come by it naturally. What's your excuse?"

Michael was in the middle of the ocean somewhere. He had asked her before leaving if she was going to mind him being away for as long as he would be. She'd told him that if he didn't do this race now, he might never. He told her again how much he loved her. She knew she loved him the same way. But still wondered, all this time into their marriage, if they'd both become complacent.

Another night for Molly in the house alone. She was getting used to cooking for one, the way single women did all the time. But it was different with Molly. She had never been a single woman, not really. She and Michael had started going steady in high school. She'd never had a serious relationship with any other man in her life, even when they *had* tried seeing other people.

Maybe that was the problem, if it even was a problem. She was feeling more and more like a single woman lately.

Sometimes, when she was alone, she worried that she was just like Annie. Maybe she wanted to kick up her heels, whether she could admit that to herself or not.

Jesse was right: The things you fixated on when you spent too much time alone.

She defrosted a leftover turkey burger and indulged herself with waffle fries, and put together a small chopped salad with romaine, feta, cucumbers, and a garlic dressing she could buy only online.

She set the kitchen table for one. Poured herself a glass of Whispering Angel and ate dinner while watching the *CBS Evening News* on the small TV set on the counter. Norah O'Donnell was the anchor now. *Sisterhood,* Molly thought, and raised her glass.

She took a long bath after dinner, in the oversized tub Michael had put in for them himself. She wasn't ready for bed when she finished, it was too early, so she put on some sweatpants and the University of New Haven T-shirt Emma had gotten her on her official visit there and went downstairs and then out into the backyard to see if there were fireflies tonight, and to look up into the stars. She'd always loved this time of night, darkness having just fallen, as if God had pulled down a shade.

There were fireflies tonight. As always, the sight of them, the *existence* of them, made her as happy as she had been chasing them around the yard when she was a little girl.

*But am I?*

*Happy?*

She knew that her job, all the new responsibilities that came with being deputy chief, made her happy. Gave her purpose, beyond being a wife and mother, more of a purpose than she'd ever felt in her life. They had a murder investigation now, a mystery to solve. And even though Jesse was the one in charge, she knew her contribution was essential.

Like she was crewing for him.

She still couldn't shake the thought that somehow the two shootings, Paul Hutton and the attempt on Jesse's life, might somehow be connected. During her lunch break today she had driven over to Jesse's and walked up and down his street, finally following the path the shooter would have taken to the beach, if he'd been running for the beach.

Maybe they'd missed something when they'd all walked along the water the next morning, even knowing that the storm had likely washed away footprints or anything else.

Jesse was the one who always said to rely on yourself with cases like these, trust that you might see something nobody else did.

But she hadn't seen anything resembling a clue.

All she saw now in the night, head tilted back, were the stars.

Then she was being grabbed from behind, a hand clamped over her mouth, and in a blink she was on the ground and he was on top of her.

Molly tried to twist loose. But she was on her stomach and she could feel the full weight of him on her, all the air coming out of her at once as she could feel his free hand start to pull down her sweatpants.

Her gun was in her purse, on the table in the front hall.

In the empty house.

She tried to scream and couldn't. She could barely breathe. She tried to bite his hand but couldn't get her mouth open.

*I cannot let this happen.*

*Not to me.*

*I will not let this happen.*

"How do you like it, bitch?" he said into her ear.

She kept trying to twist away, to get out from under him as she tried to keep her legs pressed together at the same time.

The sweatpants were at her knees now.

She could feel him fumbling with his own pants.

"Bitch," he said again.

He took his hand away from her mouth just long enough to punch her hard on the side of her head, dazing her. Then he hit her again, with even more force behind the blow the second time, and Molly thought she might go out.

But as he'd hit her, Molly managed to get her right hand out from beneath her.

She tried to slap at him with her free hand, but her blows had nothing behind them.

It was when her right hand fell back into the grass, near her new rosebushes, that she felt the trowel that she'd forgotten to bring inside after gardening the day before.

Molly gripped the handle as he pressed her face into the wet grass.

*Now.*

She used what strength she had and stabbed him in the leg with the pointed end of the trowel. Then again. She heard him cry out in pain. He tried to reach for her hand, but as he did Molly rolled out from underneath him, a few feet away, trying to get to her feet.

He was trying to do the same.

He was wearing some kind of black windbreaker, a black ski mask.

They faced each other, Molly whipping the trowel in front of her, wanting to call out so one of her neighbors might hear, but no sound came out of her at first.

Finally, she screamed.

*"Someone help me!"*

Chest heaving, eyes on her attacker, backing away from him.

*"Someone call nine-one-one!"*

The guy was pulling his jeans up when he heard voices from next door. Then they both saw lights splashing across the backyard next to Molly's. The Thompsons.

The guy turned and ran toward the low, white picket fence, nearly going down as he caught his trailing leg jumping over it.

Molly ran back inside the house, grabbed her gun from the bottom of her purse. As she ran across the yard she saw Jack Thompson coming through the hedges with a baseball bat.

"Guy tried to rape me," Molly shouted as she ran past Jack Thompson. "I'm going after him."

Then she was over the fence in her bare feet, chasing the bastard even though it was too late, he'd had too much lead time and was gone. Molly kept running anyway, across one yard and then the one next to it, until she was in the street and could hear the first sirens in the distance.

Like Jesse had said.

Stupid courage.

# Seventeen

"ichael told me how to get a message to him if there was an emergency," Molly said. "But I'm not doing it."

"This isn't an emergency?" Jesse said.

"It's over," she said. "And I've got you to protect me."

"So you'll let me?" Jesse said. "Protect you?"

She smiled.

"The way you let the rest of us protect you?"

"It's different," Jesse said.

"Because I'm a woman?" Molly said.

They were standing in the middle of Molly's backyard. Jesse had driven straight to her house from the airport. She'd called him the night before, after Suit and Peter had bagged the clothes she was wearing and the trowel and even clipped her fingernails, even though Molly couldn't remember whether she'd scratched him or not. They were already going over the trace evidence at the state crime lab, looking for DNA.

Jesse was here because he wanted to hear Molly tell it. He knew she'd taken Suit and Peter through it, from the time the guy had grabbed her. Jesse wanted to hear for himself. His crime scene now. In Molly Crane's backyard.

"If Michael found out he'd want to fly back and then go door-to-door looking for this guy," Molly said. "And then beat him to within an inch of his life."

"Why stop there?" Jesse said. "I say go the extra inch."

"You know better than anyone that this comes with the job," she said.

"Bullshit it does," Jesse said.

"I was a decoy that time for the Peeping Tom," Molly said.

"Suit and I were outside," he said. "Guns drawn."

"I still did all right for myself," she said.

"You were lucky with that trowel."

"What's that line you always use from the old baseball guy about luck?"

"It's the residue of design," Jesse said. "But there was no design in you leaving a garden tool in the dirt so it would be there if you ever needed it."

"God looks out for good Catholic girls."

"Good?" Jesse said.

She took in a lot of air and let it out. "First somebody shoots at you," she said. "Now this. It's like somebody's coming for us."

He told her to take him through it. She knew him well enough to know why. He always thought he would pick up on something the others had missed. Molly started at the beginning. She even included the part about the fireflies. She told her story in an organized way, not rushing, until she was running after the guy and into the night, knowing she was wasting her time, wondering as she ran what she would do if she caught him.

"He came to my goddamn house," Molly said when she finished. "My kids grew up playing in this goddamn yard."

"You need to talk to Annie again," Jesse said. "Or we talk to her together. We need you to compare notes. Get her to tell her story, see if there's anything she forgot. Or some detail she might remember. Even ask her what happened to the clothes she wore that night."

"She said she burned them," Molly said.

"Tell her to talk to me."

"You're the one who's always telling me that people don't ever have to talk to the police if they don't want to," Molly said.

"Let's keep that our little secret."

"You think it's the same guy?"

"Maybe he wasn't after Annie that night," Jesse said. "Maybe it was you, until you went home with Suit and Elena."

"If he was after me," Molly said, "do we think he might be the same one who took the shot at you?"

"Somebody with a grudge against the members of the Paradise Police Department?" Jesse said.

Molly slowly nodded.

"It would mean going through anybody and everybody we've ever put away," Jesse said. "And friends. And family."

"How far back?"

"All the way back to when I showed up here and we first

started working together," Jesse said. "I know you remember the day. It was like stardust fell from the sky."

Molly looked at him as if he'd suddenly started speaking in tongues.

"Poetry from Chief Stone?"

"Sinatra," he said.

"So we've got to do a read-back on everybody we've ever pissed off who's still aboveground?" Molly said.

Jesse grinned. "I know," he said. "We may need to put on more people."

They were back inside, in Molly's kitchen. Jesse told her that they wanted frequent check-ins from her during the day, either with him or Suit or Gabe or Peter. He told her he was going to have her house watched at night, whether she liked it or not. She wanted to know if he was going to do the same with Suit, who'd been working with Jesse as long as she had. Jesse told her yes.

"Who's watching you?" Molly said.

"My Higher Power," he said. "Even though I'm not a good Catholic girl."

Then he kissed the top of her head and said that if it was just the same with her, he wanted to get back to trying to solve a murder.

"Oh, that," Molly said.

"We never close," Jesse said.

# Eighteen

Suit had spent a lot of the last couple days on various free credit reporting sites, trying to get a hit on "Paul Hutton" even without a date of birth or Social Security number. If he found anything, maybe they could begin to learn how he spent his money and where he spent it when he wasn't working with horses.

"It would have been nice if that barn woman hadn't been paying him off the books," Suit said when Jesse was back in the office.

"She said it was the way he wanted it," Jesse said. "Said there's a lot of that going around in the horse business down there."

"I thought that was for undocumenteds," Suit said. "Or illegals. Or whatever."

"All sorts of ways to live on the margins," Jesse said. "Or be anonymous."

"And the rich people they work for go along to save a few bucks," Suit said.

"Until they get caught," Jesse said.

"What's the country coming to?" Suit said.

Suit went back to work. Jesse sat behind his desk, happy to be back there. It was the place where he felt in control. As if there was still one place where he was chief of himself.

Jesse had called Marshport Taxi, gotten the name and number of the driver who'd dropped off Paul Hutton at the Cain estate, got in touch with him and asked him to come in.

"I'm working," Luis Andujar said.

"Me, too," Jesse said.

Andujar showed up half an hour later, on time. He was short, dark, built like a Jeep, handlebar mustache. And clearly nervous as hell to be anywhere near a police station.

"I am not comfortable talking to the police," he said when he sat down across from Jesse.

"Hardly anybody is," Jesse said. "Talking to cops frankly wears *my* ass out a lot of the time."

"My wife and my two boys and me, we keep to ourself," Andujar said. "I drive for Uber when I do not drive for the cab company."

Jesse leaned forward and smiled, trying to put him at ease.

"Where you from, Luis?"

"Guatemala," he said.

"I'm not interested in your immigration status," Jesse said. "You could say I'm with the government. Just not like that."

"We think anybody with a badge is your government."

"Here, we preserve and protect," Jesse said. "We're big on the protect part. Okay?"

"Okay."

"Tell me about that night," Jesse said.

Andujar checked his phone, told Jesse he'd picked up Paul Hutton in Marshport about 8:45, outside a Five Guys burger place.

Jesse asked how Hutton seemed.

"He seemed like a passenger," Andujar said.

"In a hurry to get over there?"

"No."

"When he gave you the address, did you know where you were taking him?"

"To one of the *muy grande* houses in your town? Yes."

"*Muy grande.*" Jesse smiled. So did Andujar for the first time.

"*Big-ass* in your language," he said to Jesse.

"You'd had fares there before?"

"Not so much."

"Did you know who owned the house?"

Andujar shook his head.

"Did he say whether he was there to see a man or woman?" Jesse said.

Andujar frowned, then closed his eyes. Jesse didn't want him to feel rushed. It was always the same, whether here or in Molly's backyard. Let them tell it their way.

"I remember this," Andujar said. "I was just trying to make conversation, and asked if it was his first trip to Paradise. And he laughed, the man did. He said he wished. And I said, 'Wish what?' And he said, 'That it turned out to be a trip to paradise.'"

They sat there in silence until Andujar said, "That's it. I don't remember anything else. We pulled up to the gate and he paid me and I left him there."

"But he never gave you a name."

"No."

"And you didn't ask him what business he might have in that neighborhood?"

"He was just a fare on a Saturday night," Andujar said. "I was happy to have one who was sober. I get the drunk kids later when I'm driving for Uber."

"He's the fare who ended up dead."

*"Madre de dios,"* Andujar said.

He quickly made the sign of the cross.

Jesse stood. He stood. Jesse came around the desk and shook his hand and thanked him for coming, walked him out, watched as he got into what looked to be an ancient green Subaru Outback. He didn't look back. Jesse thought it might be the only time all day that he wasn't looking over his shoulder.

Then Jesse drove over to the Neck. Lily and Bryce Cain had told him they had no idea who Paul Hutton was, or why he'd gone to the house that night. Maybe one of them was lying. Or both.

*And to an officer of the law,* Jesse thought.

Suit was right.

What was the country coming to?

# Nineteen

**B**ryce Cain was waiting on the front porch after he'd buzzed Jesse in through the front gate. He was wearing running shorts. Jesse knew he was a runner. Half-marathons, Lily had told him once, same as she used to run. No wonder he always looked as if he needed a hot meal.

"You ever call before you just show up?" Bryce said.

"I called your mom's cell," Jesse said. "No answer."

"She doesn't always have it with her," Bryce said. "She's funny that way."

"So she's not here?"

"She's not and I'm leaving. I just came over to look in on my father."

"How's he doing?"

"She pushes his chair over to the window and he looks out at the water. Or maybe infinity. He doesn't talk much, at least not to me."

Jesse thought, *I wouldn't, either, if I didn't have to.*

"Mostly," Bryce continued, "he just sits there while she holds his hand."

"Your mom?"

"Karina. His nurse. Or caretaker. Whatever."

"She up there with him now?" Jesse said.

Bryce had given no indication that he was going to invite Jesse inside. His phone was in his hand, like a security blanket. Jesse imagined he'd burst into tears if he reached over and took it away from him.

"The only time she leaves his side is when she sleeps," Bryce said. "She's got a room down the hall."

"She a citizen?" Jesse said.

He was thinking about Luis Andujar.

"Did you come over here to ask me about Karina?" Bryce said.

Jesse didn't want to be talking to him about any of this. Bryce was one of those people who made you wonder who *they* thought were assholes. But Lily wasn't here. He was. Jesse had questions.

"The guy who got killed said he was hoping his trip over here really was a trip to paradise," Jesse said. "Any idea what that would have meant?"

"From a dead drunk I never met?" Bryce said.

His shirt today was the color of Molly's roses, and had a whale on the front.

"Ex-drunk," Jesse said.

"Whatever," Bryce Cain said.

"I was going to ask your mother this, but I'll ask you," Jesse said. "Is there any possible connection you can think of between this guy and your family?"

"None," he said.

"Any possible connection between your family and the horse business in South Florida?"

He could hear Bryce Cain's phone buzzing. Bryce turned his palm up so he could see the screen, and quickly glanced down at it. He was absolutely the type. One of those who thought a missed call or text or email might alter the order of the universe.

Bet he never leaves the house without his phone.

"I think my father might have owned horses at one time," Bryce said. "Back in the day. And used to like to bet them at Hialeah. But I don't think he's done either for years."

"Paul, the guy who died, worked as a groom in Wellington," Jesse said. "It's close to Palm Beach, and I know your father spent more and more time down there."

"Wait, you think *that* might be a connection between my dad and this Hutton guy?" Bryce said.

"I'm not sure what I think," Jesse said. "I'm just looking to figure out why a cab dropped him off here the night he died."

"Look somewhere else," he said. "And stop bothering my mother."

"I wasn't aware I was bothering anybody."

"She's too polite to tell you to fuck off," Bryce said.

Jesse grinned. He couldn't help himself.

"Actually," he said, "she's not."

"We went over this before," Bryce said. "My father's dying. We don't need any other distractions around here right now."

The phone buzzed again. Bryce looked at it again.

"Are we done here?" he said to Jesse.

"Just one more thing."

Bryce blew out some air.

"Go ahead," he said.

"The last time I was here you said I forget sometimes that I work for you," Jesse said. He casually took a step closer to Bryce, smiling. "You weren't talking about yourself, were you?"

Bryce opened his mouth, then closed it before turning and walking into the house. Jesse walked down the front steps to where he'd parked the car. Still smiling. Wondering how Bryce Cain knew Paul Hutton's last name.

# Twenty

Jesse and Molly met back at the office. She'd been to Annie's house and said that Annie's recollections of the night hadn't changed. Before Molly had left, Annie told her that she really hadn't been kidding, she had burned the clothes she'd been wearing that night, jeans and shirt and underthings and even her shoes. She said she didn't want to talk about what had happened ever again, with Molly or Jesse or anyone, that the more she talked about it the better the chance that her husband would find out.

"She does know she was the victim, right?" Jesse said. "Or attempted victim."

"You say 'victim,'" Molly said. "She feels guilty, like she somehow had it coming."

Jesse shook his head.

"She's still being an idiot."

"What did she say about what happened to you?" Jesse said.

"That she wished she could have been the one to stab the fucker, if it was the same guy," Molly said. "And not in the leg."

They were in the conference room, just the two of them. Suit was at his desk, still looking for any possible financial information on the late Paul Hutton. Jesse and Molly were going over old case files. Not long after he'd become chief in Paradise, all the police departments in Massachusetts had changed over to electronic report systems. The shorthand for them was RMS. Records Management Systems. They were sorted by modus operandi: murder, gun crimes, and domestic violence. It was a long list, more than two dozen possible boxes to check. There were separate categories, case by case, for "interested parties," people with a nexus to a particular crime, just not as victim or suspect.

There was no box, Molly said, for people you had pissed off along the way.

Before RMS, it was all paper, in two boxes at the other end of the table. Molly had already gone through the first one when Jesse had arrived back at the office from the Cains'.

"I could do this myself," Molly said. "And you could stay on Paul Hutton."

"I'm still not convinced they're not connected somehow," Jesse said.

"Because you don't believe in coincidence," Molly said.

"Neither do you."

"Words to live by from the chief?" Molly said.

"You can drive yourself crazy with what-ifs," Jesse said.

"Not just them."

"A guy got shot," Jesse said. "Somebody took a shot at me not long after."

"We haven't found one thing connecting the two events," Molly said.

"Doesn't mean there isn't one," he said.

He'd told her about Bryce Cain knowing Paul's full name. Molly said that maybe somebody in the department had said something to somebody, and it had gotten back to him, the way things did in a small town. Jesse told her she didn't believe that and neither did he.

"You going to call him out on it?" Molly said.

"Not just yet," Jesse said. "I'll wait for that perfect moment."

"I'm guessing it won't be a perfect moment for him."

"Probably not."

"You sure you don't want me to focus on coming up with a list of possibles out of the past so you can focus on your vic?" Molly said.

"I've multitasked before," Jesse said, and nodded at the boxes.

Molly had made a list of possible suspects after going through the first box. They began to sort through the next box, case by case. They could both feel the almost kinetic energy in the room, even though this kind of work was always a grind. But cases like these, personal or not, made them forget all the times when the biggest crimes in Paradise involved bar fights, or underaged drinking at the beach, or graffiti on the bridge to Stiles Island, or noise violations when a party at one of the *muy grande* houses got too loud.

This was for all the times when being chief, as much as he loved being chief, felt like early retirement, when boredom would set in.

And could drive a guy to drink.

The very first name on the list was Hasty Hathaway, former president of the Board of Selectmen who'd hired Jesse thinking he was hiring a drunk he could control. Jesse ended up putting him away for murder and racketeering and a lot of other bad shit produced by the secret militia group the crazy bastard had going for him on the side.

"How long will Hasty be at Concord?" Molly said.

"Until the twelfth of never," Jesse said. "But my math could be slightly off."

"Could he still be harboring his grudge against us?" Molly said.

"I was over there not long ago at his parole hearing," Jesse said, "telling them that I didn't think this asshole would ever be rehabilitated, and reminding them that he would have had me killed if I hadn't taken him down."

"Whatever happened to the frisky Mrs. Hathaway, by the way? Have we lost track of that little minx?"

"I assume she is still looking to bang every guy she can get to stand still long enough," Jesse said.

"I'm still amazed she missed you," Molly said.

"Not for lack of effort," Jesse said.

"Even when your steely will was weakened by drink?"

"Even *I* never drank that much," he said.

They finished with the second box of paper files and moved on to electronic. When they did, Jesse said, "What about the Marino kid?"

Bo Marino and a couple of his dumbass high school buddies had raped a Paradise High School girl named Candace

Pennington. One had taken naked pictures of her while the other two held her down. But Bo Marino, a jackwagon and son of a jackwagon, had been the ringleader. He had escaped doing time only because he was a minor. Somehow he and his friends had even been lawyered off the sex offender list.

"I lost track of Bo after he did his community service for me," Jesse said. "But put him high up on our list. Sunny says that if you're born round, you don't die square."

"You reference Sunny quite a lot," Molly said. "Have you noticed that?"

"She has a lot of interesting things to say," Jesse said.

Molly grinned.

"With or without her clothes on?" Molly said.

"Hey, she's your friend, too," Jesse said.

"Just without benefits."

"I haven't been the beneficiary of those for a while," he said.

"At least outside your dreams," Molly said.

They worked through the afternoon and into the early evening. They talked about cases and perps and victims they had forgotten. They remembered the two serial killers, Tony and Brianna Lincoln, who'd finally been caught in Canada after killing Jesse's friend Abby Taylor and Anthony D'Angelo, a good kid who'd been one of Jesse's Paradise cops.

It was past six o'clock when they stopped and decided to go over to the Gray Gull and have an early dinner. When they got to their table, Sunny Randall was waiting for them.

"Say hi to your new roommate," Jesse said to Molly.

"You're kidding, right?" Molly said.

"Not even a little bit," Jesse said.

They were still going around and around on that during dessert when Jesse got the call that somebody had left a pipe bomb at Suit's front door.

# Twenty-One

**S**uit had immediately called the State Police Bomb Squad when he saw how the package looked, so they'd arrived before Jesse and Molly and Sunny had.

"I remembered the pictures of those packages when that wingnut was sending pipe bombs to politicians a few years ago," Suit said to Jesse.

"You did right," Jesse said.

"See something, say something," Suit said.

Suit and Elena lived at the end of Cypress Lane. Elena had already left for her sister's house in Salem. Suit had known enough to have the houses closest to his, on both sides of the street, evacuate even before the bomb squad arrived. The neighbors were now milling around outside the yellow crime scene tape, even though the show was over. They'd used a robot to remove the package from Suit's front porch, place it on the flatbed truck they'd brought with them. The truck was already gone.

"What the fuck, Jesse?" Suit said.

"How's Elena?"

"Freaked," Suit said.

Suit said the bulging envelope was just big enough not to fit in their mailbox, so it was on top of the rest of the mail in the white container their USPS guy had left at the front door. The mail, as it turned out, had come late in the day, after Suit had taken Elena to an early dinner at the Chowder House. When they got home, Suit didn't like the looks of the envelope. He was on high alert already, because of what had happened to Molly and Jesse.

"You always tell me that being careful never got anybody killed," Suit said. "But not being careful could."

"Words to live by," Sunny said.

"Literally," Molly said.

They were standing in the middle of Suit's front yard.

"You were right not to wait to call the bomb squad," Jesse said.

Jesse's phone rang. He saw that it was Brian Lundquist, telling him that his guys hadn't fucked around, they'd already water-blasted the contents, a six-inch bomb filled with shrapnel that had failed to detonate.

*First me,* Jesse thought. *Then Molly. Now Suit. Suit was right. What the fuck.*

"Did this SOB just want to scare Suit," Lundquist said, "or did he screw up his homemade bomb?"

"You save the packaging?" Jesse said.

"My guys do this for a living," Lundquist said. "It was mailed two days ago. From Paradise."

"Prints?"

"Lots," Lundquist said. "Dusted it before the water blasted. Whoever it was must have worn gloves. None of the other prints are in the system. Probably USPS people down the line."

"Bad bomb," Jesse said. "Still bad intentions."

Jesse had walked to the street to take Lundquist's call.

"What the hell *is* going on there?" Lundquist said.

"Beats the hell out of me," Jesse said.

"You need reinforcements?"

"Got Sunny Randall," Jesse said.

"I meant from law enforcement."

"I know," Jesse said. "But I've got this for now. I can protect my people."

"You sure?"

"Day at a time," Jesse said.

"I've heard that one," Lundquist said.


Jesse put a car in front of the house. Suit didn't argue. When they were back at Molly's, she agreed to have Sunny stay with her until Michael was back.

"I'm fun at sleepovers," Sunny said.

"So I've heard," Molly said.

Jesse and Molly and Sunny were in Molly's living room. Molly and Sunny were sipping Irish whiskey. Jesse had a club soda. He knew Sunny liked an occasional Irish late at night. There was a time when he'd have joined her. As always, he watched her, fascinated, as she took small sips. Sipping whiskey had always been a skill out of his reach, like playing a musical instrument.

"He'll make a mistake," Sunny said.

"They always do," Jesse said.

She was wearing a black T-shirt, faded jeans, sandals. Her hair, he'd noticed, was shorter than it had been the last time he'd seen her. Jesse had always loved the smell of her hair, no matter how long or short she was wearing it.

He stared at her. She stared back and smiled, as if everything they knew about each other and everything they felt, whatever they still felt, was in the air between them.

She sipped some of her whiskey and winked at him, as if telling him that everything he knew, she did, too.

"If it's the same guy, he's no criminal genius," Jesse said. "He's missed with two women now. Missed with his bomb. Missed with me."

"By sheer chance with you," Molly said.

She sipped some of her whiskey. There hadn't been much in her glass to begin with, but it was still half-full.

"He's like this mutt terrorist," Jesse said. "Just one who hasn't killed anybody yet."

"Can't let him win," Sunny said.

The three of them sat there in silence until Molly said, "I could stay with a friend, Sunny, if you've got another friend you'd like to stay with tonight. I have to take orders from the chief of police, but you don't." She grinned. "Unless you want to, of course."

"I'm not here because he wants me to be here," Sunny said. "I'm here because I want to be here. You're my friend, too, girlfriend."

Sunny turned to Jesse now and said, "And I can do more than just sleepovers. I can help try to catch the stalker while you catch your killer. Okay?"

"Okay," he said.

Molly said, "You're absolutely certain you wouldn't rather Sunny guard you?"

"We've tried it multiple times," Jesse said. "Somehow she manages to keep losing me."

"And yet," Sunny said, "here we are."

Molly finished her drink, put it down, said to Jesse, "Go home now. If this is going to be a sleepover, Sunny and I need to start dishing about boys."

Sunny walked Jesse out, neither one of them saying anything, as if they didn't want to disturb the night hush around them, until Jesse said, "You think this guy worked out some kind of plan? Or is he just making it up as he goes along?"

"When a guy shot Richie and then started going after members of his family one by one," she said, "my therapist told me that whatever he was doing made perfect sense to him."

"In the middle of it," Jesse said, "he came after you."

"Only because I dropped my guard," she said.

"Got it up now?" Jesse said.

"Would it be somewhat less than ladylike," Sunny said, "for me to tell you that ought to be my line?"

They were on the driver's side of the car. Suddenly quite close to each other. Close enough for him to smell her hair.

They were kissing then, like teenagers, outside a parked car. *Here we are,* Sunny had said. Here they were, under the streetlight in front of Molly Crane's house, lost in the moment, oblivious to whether Molly or anybody else was watching them until Sunny pulled back, still smiling but out of breath now, saying, "To be continued."

"It's wrong to lie to the chief of police," he said.

"Not lying," she said, and kissed him again, as fiercely as before.

She turned and walked back into the house then. Jesse watched her go, sure there was an extra swing to her hips in her tight jeans.

He was the chief, after all.

Paid to notice everything.

# Twenty-Two

In the morning Jesse called Vinnie Morris at the office he kept above his bowling alley on Concord Turnpike.

"You need somebody capped?" Vinnie said.

"Capped?" Jesse said.

"I was binge-watching some *Sopranos* last night," he said. "So shoot me."

"I see what you did there," Jesse said.

Vinnie Morris was a legendary shooter, all the way back to his days working for Boston crime bosses Joe Broz and Gino Fish when they were still alive. It was, Jesse knew, a stretch to say that Vinnie had gone straight. He just wasn't as crooked as he once was. And more on the right side of things, since Gino died, than not.

They had each done favors for the other in the past. There had been a time when Vinnie had crossed lines that Jesse would not, knowing that Jesse would not. On top of that, he was a friend of Spenser's and Sunny's. If Jesse and Vinnie

Morris weren't friends, they had a relationship now with some history to it, based on respect and trust.

And Jesse knew that if the situation called for it, Vinnie Morris could shoot the seams off a baseball.

"You busy these days?" Jesse said.

"I just finished a thing in Miami."

"A thing."

"Yeah," he said. "A thing. For a guy needed one."

"You mind me asking what kind of thing?"

"I do."

"And for whom?"

"Guy I owed a favor."

"You have to cap anybody?"

"No," Vinnie said. "Was more an *implied*-type thing that I could if necessary. Turned out it wasn't."

"Necessary," Jesse said.

"Whatever," Vinnie said. "An accommodation was reached."

"I'm always a sucker for a happy ending," Jesse said.

Jesse had been to the bowling alley. He'd always thought that Vinnie owning it was like some kind of private joke with himself. Jesse could picture him behind his desk, the shooting-range target on the wall across from him. Something else to amuse Vinnie, even though not much did.

"What do you need?" Vinnie said.

"A favor for which I am willing to pay you," Jesse said. "Out of what I think of as my discretionary fund."

"You don't have to pay me," Vinnie said. "We owe each other. I do something for you, you do something for me someday."

"Something legit?"

He thought he heard Vinnie make a snorting sound.

"I didn't suddenly forget who I was talking to," Vinnie said.

Then Jesse told him what he needed. Vinnie said, "I can do that. How long?"

"Hoping not very," Jesse said.

"What if I need to shoot somebody?"

"This one I'd like to have alive," Jesse said.

"Wasn't like that the other time," Vinnie said.

"I know," Jesse said.

"And Sunny's got Molly?"

"She does."

"You sure you don't need me on them?"

"If I put you on them and Sunny finds out," Jesse said, "we're both opening ourselves up to heartbreak. And if I decide I need more backup, I can always get Spike into the game."

"He's good," Vinnie said. "For a gay guy."

"Most straight guys wish they were as good as Spike."

"Not this straight guy," Vinnie said. There was a pause and then he said, "While all this watching is going on, who's watching you?"

"See, there," Jesse said. "You *did* forget who you were talking to for a second."

# Twenty-Three

Lundquist had called before Jesse went to bed, and convinced him to let him send some backup to Paradise, at least in the short run.

"Maybe four guys during the day, another four at night," Lundquist said. "I'll tell 'em to flash their lights and badges every chance they get."

"Show of force," Jesse said.

"Exactly."

"No," Jesse said.

"Why not?"

"I told you," Jesse said. "I got this."

"Unless this maroon finds a way to dial things up."

"Maybe I'll bring back stop-and-frisk if my guys see somebody suspicious," Jesse said.

"Boy, those were the days," Lundquist said.

In the late morning, Jesse called Molly and Sunny and Suit into the conference room.

"Suit and I will stay on the Paul Hutton case," he told them. "Eventually we're going to start filling in the blanks on his past. I'm going to find out the connection between him and the Cain house. There had to be a reason why he went there that night."

He turned to Molly then and said, "And you keep going through those files to find out who's put a target on us."

"Still could turn out to be the one who put a target on Hutton," Molly said.

"Feeling a little left out here," Sunny said, "other than my responsibilities for watching Molly's ass."

"My very well-conditioned ass," Molly said.

"Thought that went without saying," Suit said.

"Shut up, Luther," Molly said.

"Not leaving you out," Jesse said to Sunny. "It can't hurt to have a fresh set of eyes on Molly's list of suspects."

"My pleasure."

"How long can you stay?" Jesse said.

"Long as it takes," Sunny said. "I've got no need to be in Boston right now."

"What about Rosie?"

Her dog.

"With Spike," she said. "I'll bring her up if I decide to extend my stay."

"You know I plan to pay you," Jesse said. "And don't try to talk me out of it."

"Wasn't planning to," Sunny said. "I lost my amateur status a long time ago."

Suit grinned.

"How old were you when you turned pro?" Suit said.

"Shut up, Luther," Sunny said.

Suit went back to his desk. Molly said she was going to make more coffee for her and Sunny. Just Jesse and Sunny in the conference room now.

In a low voice, Sunny said, "You need to make a plan for us to get some alone time."

"You sure?" Jesse said. "The 'us' part?"

"Hell no," Sunny Randall said.

# Twenty-Four

Jesse got ready to leave the office at a little after six o'clock. Molly and Sunny and Suit were on their way to have dinner at Molly's house. Jesse told them he might stop by for dessert. Molly said he hadn't asked what they were having for dessert. Jesse said it didn't matter, the worst he ever had was great.

"Where are you going right now?" Molly asked.

"Marshport," Jesse said. "I want to go back to where it started and then hope something develops."

"Always one of your best strategies," Molly said.

He parked across from the First Episcopal Church, and pictured Paul Hutton coming out and getting into Luis Andujar's taxi that night. He knew they were halfway through the six o'clock meeting, and wondered if his friend Laura was in there. Jesse had found her smart and attractive. But now Sunny was back. Maybe in a bigger way than he could have anticipated.

He thought: *Down, boy.*

He drove from there to Lily Cain's house, as Andujar had that night with Paul Hutton in his backseat. Who *had* he gone to see? What had Hutton been thinking on his way to the mansion at the edge of the water in the last few hours of his life?

*Just another dead drunk,* Bryce Cain had said.

As Jesse sat in the Explorer across from the front gate to the Cain house, he thought about how hard it had been for him to get sober. All the times he'd gotten sober. Another old joke: *Of course I can quit drinking, done it plenty of times.* This time he had made it stick, at least for now. Paul had been making it stick. Had thought his whole life—his new, sober life—was ahead of him.

*Yeah,* Jesse thought to himself now, car windows down, listening to the sound of the waves in the distance.

You want to make your Higher Power laugh His ass off?

Tell Him about your plans.

How *did* Paul Hutton get from here to the lake?

Suit had checked all of the car services around, including Luis Andujar's, even one town over. He'd check with Uber and Lyft. There had been no pickup here that night. There had been seven pickups in town, all kids who'd been drinking, according to the drivers. Two had been dropped at the lake, probably to party. Neither fit the description of Paul Hutton.

Jesse set the trip odometer and drove to the lake now, taking the most direct route through town. The distance was 2.7 miles. So Hutton could have walked. If he had walked, he was going into town to meet somebody.

Maybe there had been a change of plans with whomever he thought he was meeting at Lily's house.

But who? Lily herself? Bryce? Karina, the nurse?

"Fuck," Jesse said.

He was out of the car now, having walked down near the water to where Christina Sample had discovered the body. Darkness had come early tonight.

Had it been the killer who set up the meet? Was it a setup or a random killing? But if it was random, what was Paul Hutton doing at the lake in the first place? Then whoever put one in the back of his head knew enough to take his phone, if indeed he'd had one in the first place. Phones had SIM cards. They had memories. They told stories.

"Fuck," he said again.

No phone. No credit card, at least not yet. But who didn't have a credit card in the modern world, where people even used them to buy a cup of coffee?

Maybe a guy who didn't have a phone or credit card was one who liked living off the grid.

But looking to connect with someone that night.

Or something.

*Maybe I should give this up,* Jesse thought. Focus on our would-be rapist, would-be shooter, would-be Unabomber.

Because who was the bigger threat in Paradise right now? Easy.

That asshole was.

Jesse heard something then from the woods behind him.

As soon as he did, he dropped to the ground and rolled to his right, clearing his gun from the holster on his hip as he did.

Jesse waited.

There was just the sound of the wind in the trees now, and the soft lap of the water on the shore behind him. Had it been footsteps he'd heard, or a small animal?

Like he always told Suit: Nobody ever died from being too careful.

Jesse quieted his own breathing. Waited and listened.

But then he did hear footsteps from the woods, twigs snapping, somebody running away from him, in the direction of the softball field.

Jesse was up then, gun out, into the darkness of the woods, wondering where a big moon was when he needed it. There were lights at the field when they had a game. Just not tonight.

Jesse couldn't tell how close he was to the runner ahead of him.

Maybe close enough.

He had his gun in his right hand and shielded himself from branches with his left as he ran. He knew there was a small clearing up ahead, then more woods. Then the ballfield.

He fired a shot into the air, no fireworks tonight to muffle the sound, or disguise it.

He tried to make out a shape in front of him. Could not. He thought he was catching up to the sound of the footsteps but couldn't be sure. If whomever it was knew the area, they wouldn't head toward the field, they'd run to the left now, to more woods running parallel to the water.

There was already the sound of a siren in the distance.

Somebody had already called in a gun being fired. *Cavalry to the rescue,* Jesse thought.

*Mine.*

He came into the small clearing and stopped. There was some light now. He looked up and saw the moon no longer covered by clouds, just too late to do him any good.

It was their guy, he was sure of it. Maybe Jesse was the one who'd dropped his guard tonight. He had to have been followed to Marshport, then to Lily's, then the lake. But he hadn't noticed a thing.

Was the guy getting ready to take another shot before he'd made enough noise to get Jesse's attention?

Whatever.

He was back.

Jesse saw the flashing lights from the softball field then, walked over there, saw Gabe Weathers stepping away from his car, own gun drawn until he saw it was Jesse walking from the outfield in his direction.

"Oh, good," Gabe said. "I don't have to shoot my boss."

"Well, not tonight," Jesse said.

Gabe nodded at him.

"You discharge your weapon, sir?" Gabe said.

"Warning shot," Jesse said.

Gabe grinned.

"Those don't even work on cop shows," he said.

# Twenty-Five

Jesse thought about swinging by Molly's, but decided to go home instead. He'd been checking for tails for the past couple days, but had seen nothing on the way to Marshport, or Lily's, or the lake. The only way somebody could have known Jesse was at the lake was if he was somehow able to track him.

Jesse had put a spy app on his phone a long time ago, which left one more possibility. When he got to the condominium, he parked the souped-up new Explorer in his designated space on the side of the building, got a flashlight out of the back, checked the wheels, and slid underneath and found nothing. Made a thorough search of the inside. Found nothing there, either.

He'd been lucky twice.

Strike two.

When he got upstairs he realized he hadn't eaten, and

fixed himself a bologna-and-cheese sandwich, garlic pickles and chips on the side.

And immediately thought how good a cold beer would have gone with that. They talked about triggers—people, places, things—in all the AA literature. Maybe somebody had talked about it tonight at the First Episcopal Church. Sometimes the thing was as simple as a bologna sandwich.

But almost everything made him think about drinking.

It was like the old joke about the psychiatrist doing a word-association exercise with a patient, and no matter what word he uses, the patient always responds with "sex." When the psychiatrist wants to know why, the guy says, "You keep using all those sexy words."

Jesse got himself a Coca-Cola instead. Caffeine-free. He'd long since decided he liked the world better when everything wasn't something-free.

# Twenty-Six

When Molly and Sunny arrived at the office, they informed him that they'd already been to the gym. Jesse told them he was happy for both of them.

"I thought you were coming over for dessert?" Sunny said.

"Why does every other thing you two say to each other sound dirty?" Molly said, shaking her head.

"You have a dirty mind?" Jesse said.

Molly put up her arms, as if in surrender. "Well," she said, "you got me there."

Then he told them what had happened at the lake.

"You think he had you lined up again?" Molly said.

"If he did, I caught another break," Jesse said.

"Are you sure," Sunny said to him, "that I'm *not* shadowing the wrong member of this department?"

"Wishful thinking," Jesse said.

"Again with the talk," Molly said.

She and Sunny headed for the conference room, which

had been turned into a war room. Jesse sat back down at his desk, finished the corn muffin he'd bought at Dunkin', and called Lily Cain.

"Got a few more questions about my dead guy," Jesse said.

"For me?" Lily said.

"I was actually hoping I might talk to the nurse about the night Paul Hutton got dropped off there," Jesse said.

"I asked her again," Lily said. "She said no one called from the gate before she went to bed."

"I'd just like to hear for myself," Jesse said. "Why would the guy go to the trouble of going there and then not try to get into the house?"

"Maybe it was the wrong address," Lily said.

"Or not."

"Dog with a bone," Lily said.

"Canine police," Jesse said.

# Twenty-Seven

Jesse and Lily and Karina Torres sat in Lily's living room, the terrace doors opened wide. A small army of landscapers were at work on the back lawn, tending to trees and privet and Lily Cain's own botanical gardens, and grass that looked to be in better shape than the field at Fenway Park.

Jesse hadn't known what to expect from a woman who was effectively Whit Cain's nanny at this point, for whatever time he had left. He hadn't expected someone as attractive as Karina Torres. A knockout. Were you still allowed to think of women as knockouts? Probably, just as long as you didn't say it to her face.

She had long, thick black hair, pale skin, and eyes as blue and bright as Lily Cain's. Jesse wondered if Torres might be a married name. She wore a lemon-colored summer dress and sat next to Lily on a long leather couch, knees pressed together, hands clasped in her lap.

Whit Cain, she'd told Jesse, was napping.

"He sleeps quite a lot these days," she said.

"Even though he isn't much more alert when he's awake," Lily said.

Karina didn't move her head, but seemed to give Lily a brief, sidelong look with her eyes.

"He has good days and bad days," Karina said.

"Don't we all," Jesse said.

He smiled at her. She did not smile back.

Karina said, "I hate that you wasted time coming over here, Chief Stone. But I already told Mrs. Cain that I had no contact with this man on the night he died."

"You don't know him?" Jesse said.

"No, sir," she said. "I do not."

"And you would have heard the phone if he'd tried to call from the gate?" Jesse said.

"Not after I turned it off that night," she said.

"What time would that have been?" Jesse said.

"Perhaps sometime around ten?" she said. "Or perhaps before that."

"Don't you think it odd," Jesse said, "that he'd come out here and then not try to contact somebody inside the house? He was picked up in Marshport around eight forty-five. He would have been here twenty minutes later. Half-hour, tops."

"We might have gone to bed at nine that night," Karina said. "I wish I could be more specific, Chief Stone. But it varies from night to night."

"He could have been coming to see somebody else who works here," Jesse said.

"But Mr. Cain and I were the only ones here," Karina said. "Mrs. Cain gave everybody else the night off."

"Paul Hutton would have had no way of knowing that," Jesse said.

"But who would he have been coming to see on a Saturday night?" Lily said.

"Trying like hell to figure that out," Jesse said.

Lily was wearing a long robe, her silver-blond hair slicked back, as if she'd just finished a swim before Jesse arrived. Or showered after a run. Another knockout, he thought, even at her age, thirty years older at least than the woman sitting next to her.

But calling Lily a knockout to her face would probably make her whole damn day.

Jesse smiled again. Lily smiled. Karina acted as if she'd much rather be upstairs listening to a dying man snore.

"You're sure you don't know this man?" Jesse said.

"Mrs. Cain showed me the picture," Karina said. "I have never met him in my life. Since I came to work here and before that."

"How did you come to work for the Cains?" Jesse said.

"How is that possibly relevant to the murder?" Lily said.

"Just curious," he said.

Lily put a hand on Karina's knee and took charge here. Lady of the manor.

"It was after Whit's first mild stroke, last spring," she said. "He'd planned on spending the whole winter in Palm Beach, anyway, and decided that would be a much better place for him to rehab. I needed to be back here. So I reached out to a quite reputable visiting nurse service, recommended by some friends. Karina was the one they sent for the interview."

Lily turned and smiled at her. "It obviously didn't hurt, once Whit met her, that she's obviously quite stunning."

Sure.

*She* could say it.

"He was in better shape then, even after the stroke?" Jesse said.

"The decline over the past several months," Lily said, "has been rather precipitous."

"But has turned him into a sweet man," Karina said.

"About fucking time," Lily said.

The f-word seemed to jolt Karina Torres slightly.

"He keeps saying that he doesn't know how long he's supposed to live," Karina said. "I tell him to not worry about such things. And there are still the days when he is very much himself."

"Is it possible that Paul Hutton may have had some personal business with Whit, Lily?" Jesse said.

"What could that possibly have been?" Lily said.

"Maybe I could ask him sometime," Jesse said. "On a good day."

"I'd have to ask my husband," Lily said.

Jesse turned back to Karina and said, "Was it difficult, up and leaving Florida to move up here?"

"There was nothing to keep me there," she said.

"Married, if you don't mind me asking?"

"I don't," she said. "And I was, a long time ago. I was quite young."

"You're still quite a young woman," Jesse said.

"I was a girl," she said.

They all heard a buzzing sound. Karina reached into the pocket of her dress and came out with a phone.

"He's awake," she said, and stood.

She looked at Jesse.

"Is there anything else?"

"Not right now," Jesse said.

She walked past Jesse and toward the stairs in the foyer. The foyer alone was bigger than Jesse's condominium. There had never been a single time when he'd visited this house when he didn't want to ask Lily where the gift shop was.

"Satisfied?" Lily said.

"Rhetorical question?"

"What were you hoping to find out here today, really?" she said.

"Among other things, I'm trying to get Paul Hutton from here to the lake, where somebody shot him dead, Lily," he said. "There's some kind of connection to somebody here, whether you know what it is or not." He grinned at her. "To put it in language you'll understand, nothing else makes any fucking sense at all."

"You're right," she said. "And when you do make sense of it, I'm certain you'll let me know. But for now, I'm going to send you on your way because my granddaughter is on her way over here. She's taking one college course this summer, and wants help on the inglorious history of our inglorious family."

Jesse stood. "Inside or outside the statute of limitations?" he said.

She laughed. "God," she said, "I hope outside."

She stood. They were about the same height.

"One more question," Jesse said.

"I would have expected nothing less."

"The guy was working and living down in Wellington, Florida, earlier this year," Jesse said. "It's only about a half-hour from Palm Beach, if that. Is there any chance at all that his path might have crossed with Whit's somehow?"

Lily Cain sighed.

"Only if he looked the way Karina does in a summer dress," she said.

"Have fun with your granddaughter," Jesse said as she walked him to the front door.

"Despite who her father is," Lily said, "she's turned into a great kid."

"Must get it from you," Jesse said.

She sighed again.

"The endless mysteries of DNA," she said.

# Twenty-Eight

He was in Dix's office, four in the afternoon, sunlight slashing through the blinds behind the desk. Dix's bald head was gleaming, as always, as if he'd not only just shaved it, but buffed it. His long-sleeved white shirt looked as if it had just come out of a dry cleaner's box. Jesse knew without having to look under the desk that the black shoes Dix liked to wear with his pressed jeans were as shiny as the top of his head. All in all, Dix made Vinnie Morris look as sloppy as Pigpen in the old *Peanuts* cartoons.

He was tan, clear-eyed, curious, and attentive, the look on his face, no matter how serious the topic, making it seem as if everything in the world amused him, but only somewhat. From the start, Jesse had found it impossible to see him as the falling-down drunk he'd been when he'd been a cop.

Dix had told himself that when it came to world-class drinking, he had retired with all the championship belts you could win. *Belts*, he said, being the operative word.

There was only a blotter on the desk in front of him, and a brass lamp in the corner. No pens, no notebook, no landline. Just Dix's hands in front of him, palms down. There was even a shine to his fingernails.

They had spent some time today talking about Sunny, even though there had never been a single afternoon like this from when they started working together that Jesse had felt as comfortable talking about the women in his life as he did about copland, or drinking.

Dix had asked him if he was happy being with her.

"Very," Jesse said.

"She with you?"

"All indications are that she is."

"Then don't be a dick," Dix said.

"They teach you that language in Freud school?" Jesse said.

"Variations."

He had told him about the assault on his department and the precautions he had taken, but how he'd rejected help from Lundquist.

"You would, wouldn't you?" Dix said.

Finally Jesse got around to the Hutton investigation, all the way through his meeting with Lily Cain that morning.

Dix asked if Jesse felt she was telling him the truth, and that the nurse was.

"I did," Jesse said.

"And you're usually such a suspicious-type person," Dix said. "But let me ask you something, cop to cop: You ever find out that somebody you believed in the past was lying their ass off?"

Jesse grinned.

"Once or twice," he said.

"The old man spent time in Florida," Dix said. "The nurse came from Florida. The dead guy lived in Florida. Until you find out there's no connection, you have to assume there is one."

"Maybe we should switch seats," Jesse said.

They sat in silence, as if retreating briefly into their own interior selves. Jesse had once told Dix that, more than anybody he'd ever met, he knew who Jesse was, who he wasn't. And who he was trying to be. On the other hand, Jesse only knew things about the man seated across from him that Dix wanted him to know, and things really only relevant to Jesse's wellness, his sobriety.

Jesse always knew when they were coming to the end of his fifty minutes, without checking his watch. They were there now. He hadn't solved any of his own mysteries since he'd sat down across from Dix, but he felt better for having been here. Maybe Dix was right. Maybe he was becoming more assimilated.

"I feel like I owe this guy," Jesse said, "even though I met him just the one time."

"Because you both ended up in that room," Dix said.

"And because I know how hard it is to get there," he said.

"He got sober and then somebody killed him," Dix said. "Doesn't seem right."

Dix patted his hands gently on the blotter. Time was up.

"Next week?"

"I'll let you know."

Jesse turned and walked toward the door.

"Hey?" Dix said.

Jesse turned.

"If it was me," he said, "I'd like to know a little bit about how the old man spent his time in Florida."

"Does that count toward next week's session?" Jesse said.

"On the house," Dix said.

He smiled, teeth as white as his shirt.

When he got home and put his key in the front door, Jesse saw that it was already unlocked. He never left without locking the door behind him.

He quietly turned the knob, gun already in his hand, and stepped into the room.

Sunny had just come out of the bathroom, wearing only one of his big white bath towels.

She smiled and dropped the towel and put her hands up.

"I'm not armed," she said.

# Twenty-Nine

They were in his bed at twilight, windows open, shades partially drawn, the day having cooled as it became night, wind from the east making the ocean sound closer than it was. Sunny's hand was on Jesse's chest. She'd always said she liked to feel the beat of his heart after they made love. She had covered them with a sheet.

"When did you decide this would happen?" Jesse said.

"I could ask you the same thing," she said.

"You know how they talk about undecided voters during an election?" Jesse said. "I was never undecided."

She turned slightly, leaving her hand where it was, so she could get closer to him and put her head on his shoulder.

"I feel like we've been slow-walking in this direction since I came up here," Sunny said. "And I did talk to Richie today."

"He still in L.A.?"

"Yes."

"You tell him where you were?"

"I did."

"How'd that go?"

"It started out badly," she said. "Then devolved from there."

"He didn't take your current, ah, proximity to me well?"

"I'd spent a lot of time on the call listening to him tell me how happy his boy is out there," she said. "How happy he was that they were all together. I finally asked how long he planned to stay. He said he wasn't sure. Then he asked me how long I planned to stay here. I told him I was working a case, and that I wasn't sure. He said, 'Must feel like old times with you and Jesse.' Or words to that effect. That's when the devolving occurred."

"So this was revenge sex?" Jesse said.

She couldn't see him smiling. Maybe she heard it in his voice. She was smiling when she looked up at him and said, "What do you think, sailor?"

He was still smiling. "Fucking well is the best revenge?" he said.

"We're still good together," she said.

"Only good?"

"What is this," Sunny said, "one of those product reviews with stars? We both know the worst sex we ever had was great."

They lay there in silence. Sunny reached up with her hand and put it to Jesse's lips and he kissed it.

"How long do you think Molly and Suit will be at dinner?" Jesse said.

"I told her I'd call."

"They know this was a conjugal visit?"

"Oh my, yes," Sunny said.

Jesse laughed. He hadn't laughed much lately. Didn't laugh much, period. It felt good, she felt good, they felt good.

"I told Dix today that being with you made me happy," Jesse said. "Or as happy as I can be."

"Low bar," Sunny said.

"No shit."

"Anyway," he said, "he told me I should try not to be a dick about this."

Sunny giggled. "Dix talked about dicks?" she said. "You think he appreciated the irony of that?"

"Dix pretty much appreciates the irony of everything," Jesse said. "Life, mostly."

"Yours?"

"Everybody's," he said.

He leaned over and kissed her hair.

"Have I ever told you I find the smell of your hair intoxicating?"

"Pretty fancy notion there, Chief."

"I have my moments."

"Whatever turns you on," she said. "Intoxicatingly."

"Is that a word?"

"Is now."

They lay there in silence again. It seemed to Jesse that the sound of the waves had grown louder.

"I just want you to know that I'm up here as long as you need me," Sunny said.

"Want you or need you?"

"Either way."

Just like that, the sheet was off them and she was on top of him, their faces close, her hair falling into his eyes.

"Which one do you suppose it is right now?" Sunny said. "Want or need?"

"Either way," Jesse said.

Then neither of them spoke for a long time.

An hour later Jesse was cooking them up eggs and bacon when Lundquist called.

"We may have your bomber," he said.

# Thirty

The other two Paradise High boys involved with Bo Marino in the rape of Candace Pennington were named Troy Drake and Kevin Feeney. The three of them had raped her and photographed her and threatened to shame her.

One of Molly's daughters had run into one of Bo Marino's old football teammates at a party a few months ago, and said Bo was living in Maine now. Kevin Feeney was back in Paradise, running a small business called KF Audio Visual Services.

Troy Drake was now sitting in Jesse's office.

Jesse hadn't seen him since he'd played the three punks off against one another, before they'd all gotten off with community service because of good lawyering and because they were minors. Bo had gotten kicked off the Paradise High football team and lost any chance at a college scholarship. After the incident with Candace Pennington, Feeney had gone off to boarding school.

Drake, Jesse knew, had dropped out of school. His parents

had left Paradise, same as the Penningtons had. But now Drake was back, looking as if he'd aged thirty years since high school, and as if he'd been living under a bridge somewhere, maybe the one to Stiles Island.

He had long, stringy hair, and a complexion that was at least one of the shades of gray. Even from across the desk, he smelled of booze. There was a hole in the front of his polo shirt, near the shoulder.

Lundquist sat in the chair next to him.

"This is bullshit," Drake said.

"We've been checking hardware stores in the area," Lundquist said. "Just to feel as if we're keeping busy. Turns out that a couple of the ingredients used to make the bomb were purchased at Duryea's Hardware last week on our friend Troy's credit card."

"What ingredients?" Jesse said.

"BBs," Lundquist said. "And the same kind of nails. Purchased the same day. About a week before the bomb showed up at Detective Simpson's house."

"I told him already," Troy Drake said to Jesse, "and now I'll tell you. I didn't build a fucking bomb. I didn't send a bomb. Do I look to you like I could *make* a bomb?"

"There's not really a profile for guys who do shit like this," Lundquist said. "Other than 'fuckup.'"

"What are you doing back in Paradise, Troy?" Jesse said. "Heard you left a long time ago."

"Wanted to see if anything in this shithole had changed," he said.

"Some things haven't," Jesse said. He smiled. "I mean, here you and I are. Like old times."

"This is a setup," Drake said.

Lundquist said, "Next time you want to build a bomb at home, Sparky, don't buy your supplies at your local hardware store."

"I didn't say I didn't buy the stuff," he said.

"What'd you need the nails for?" Jesse said. "You don't strike me as the home-improvement type."

"My room needs some fixing up," he said. "I don't have the money to hire somebody."

"What about the BBs?" Jesse said.

"I've got a BB gun," Drake said. "I like to go out and shoot at squirrels. Like for sport. There a law against that?"

"Be more of a sport if the squirrels could shoot back," Jesse said.

"We didn't see any work being done at the house," Lundquist said.

"You went to my fucking house?" Drake said.

"Probable cause," Lundquist said. He smiled and shrugged. "I know. It's a bitch."

"This is a setup," Drake said.

"You said that already," Jesse said. "But who's setting you up, Troy, the guy who sold you the stuff at Duryea's? It was your card."

"This is bullshit," Drake said again.

Jesse thought that if he slid any farther down into his chair, he was going to end up under the desk.

"You said that already," Jesse said.

"What, I'm the only one who bought BBs and nails the last week?" Drake said.

"Nobody bought both at the same time," Jesse said. "And

you're the only one who did with a prior grudge against the Paradise Police Department."

He slid the piece of paper in front of him across the desk.

"Check it out," he said.

It was a letter Troy Drake sent a few months after the rape of Candace Pennington, addressed to Jesse, Molly, and Suit. It featured bad handwriting, worse spelling, indicating, at least to Jesse, that Troy had lost interest in English classes after he'd mastered personal pronouns.

It was all about what they'd done to ruin his life, that he and Kevin Feeney didn't even want to go along. Nothing about her, what had happened to her life. He wrote that they knew he wasn't the real bad guy, but they'd taken him down the same as they'd taken down Bo, shamed *him* in front of the whole town. He couldn't stay in Paradise, he couldn't stay in high school now. Fuck them. Goodbye.

"Maybe somebody will fuck you all over the way you fucked over me" was the way it ended.

"Remember this?" Jesse said.

"You brought me in after I sent it, in case you forgot," Drake said. "I'm not saying what we did was right. But you know what Bo was like. We were afraid not to go along."

"Tell me why we should believe you didn't make the bomb," Lundquist said.

*"Because I didn't goddamn make it!"*

"You own an AR-15?" Jesse said quietly.

"What's that got to do with anything?"

"Just curious. Somebody tried to shoot me with one the night of the big storm."

"I don't own any kind of gun," Drake said. He turned to

Lundquist. "I thought you searched my house. You find a gun?"

"We did not," Lundquist said. "And, not to make too fine a point of things, but it's your parents' old house. One you could think about cleaning up once in a while."

"Blow me," Drake said.

"Good one," Lundquist said.

Jesse asked where Drake had been the night of the marquee lighting.

"Drunk."

"Drunk where?"

"Home."

"Alone?"

"I like drinking alone," he said. "That way I don't have to waste time talking to people."

Jesse thought: *At least we have something in common. Not much. But that.*

Jesse asked him his whereabouts the night somebody had tried to rape Molly in her backyard.

"Home alone," Drake said. He laughed suddenly. Jesse really did wonder if he was drunk right now. "I loved that fucking movie."

"None of this is funny, Troy," Jesse said. "Hasn't been funny since you did what you did to Candace."

Drake didn't appear to have heard. He looked at Jesse instead. "Answer me this," he said. "If I wanted to come back and fuck you all up, why'd I wait so long?"

"You wanted to fuck up your own life first?" Jesse said.

"That didn't take long," he said. "Trust me."

"Which one are you?" Jesse said.

"Thelma," Sunny said. She shrugged. "Taller."

Molly said, "Louise was bigger up front."

"You can say that again," Jesse said.

Kevin Feeney was a balder, heavier version of the seventeen-year-old Molly remembered. Even though he knew they were coming, he seemed as happy to see them, Molly especially, as he would have a process server. They sat with him now in the reception area of KF Audio Visual Services. The door to what they assumed was his office was closed. Molly asked what he did at KF Audio Visual. He asked if they'd ever heard of TaskRabbit guys. Sunny said she had, that they were the guys you called to install things and fix them and assemble them. Kevin Feeney said he was like that, just with home entertainment systems.

"I have an installation scheduled on Stiles Island," he said. "I can't be late."

"We'll try not to keep you," Molly said.

She noticed a picture of an attractive dark-haired woman on the wall behind him.

"Are you with the Paradise police?" Feeney said to Sunny.

"Think of me as her bodyguard."

"I heard somewhere they made you deputy chief," Feeney said to Molly. "Wasn't aware that the position came with a bodyguard."

"Gets lonely at the top," Molly said.

"Why are you even here?" Feeney said. "What happened with me happened a long time ago. I'm a different person

He slid farther down into the chair. Jesse thought it was a matter of time before gravity took over and he did end up on the floor.

"I've hated your guts since I was seventeen years old," he said. "But not enough to try to kill you or anybody else. The only person I ever think about killing is myself." He looked at Jesse. "Trust me on that, too."

"What are you doing back here, really?" Jesse said.

"I had nowhere else to go."

"You plan to stick around?" Jesse said.

"Got a better question," Drake said. "You gonna charge me?"

"I am not," Jesse said.

Lundquist gave him a look but didn't say anything.

"You don't think I did it?"

"Making a bomb, even a shitty one, requires work," Jesse said. "And some discipline."

"What's that supposed to mean?" Drake said.

"It means you're free to go," Jesse said. "But before you go, I want you to do one thing for me."

"What?"

"Drop your pants."

"The fuck?"

"Somebody attacked Deputy Chief Crane," he said. "She got out from underneath him when she tried to stab him with a garden tool. Upper leg. I want to see yours."

Drake looked at Lundquist. "Can he make me do that?"

"I were you," Lundquist said, "I'd humor him."

Drake stood. When he did, Jesse saw the stains on the front of his baggy jeans. Tried not to think too hard on where they might have come from. Drake unbuttoned the pants and dropped them over chicken legs. Turned one way, then the other. No visible bruises.

"You done messing with me?" Drake said.

"For now," Jesse said. "But Troy? I find out you lied, about any of this? That's when I mess with you."

Drake turned and walked out of Jesse's office. He left the door open behind him. As he passed Jeff Alonso's desk, Jesse heard Drake say, "What *are you* looking at?"

Jesse got up and shut the door.

"You don't think it's him?" Lundquist said.

"He's a punk," Jesse said. "But I don't think he was lying. And I do think he's got about as much chance of building a bomb as he does getting into med school."

"I still think we should keep an eye on him," Lundquist said.

Jesse smiled again.

"Like a friend of mine says," he said. "We'd be fools not to."

# Thirty-One

We need to talk to Kevin Feeney," Molly said. "And Bo Marino, if we can locate him."

She and Jesse and Sunny were having breakfast the next morning at Daisy's. Molly and Sunny had both ordered oatmeal, in the afterglow of just having been to the gym. Jesse ordered eggs over easy, corned beef hash, and English muffins. A short stack of pancakes. If he died, he died.

"We have nothing to tie them to any of this," Jesse said.

"But they might carry the same old grudge," Molly said. "Right?"

"Right," Jesse said.

"We know where Feeney is," Molly said. "Finding Bo might take some doing."

"Not for Thelma and Louise," Sunny said.

"Didn't they die in the end?" Jesse said.

"I was thinking more along the lines of buddy movie," Sunny said.

now. I moved back because I didn't want to feel as if I were running anymore, even though my parents passed a few years ago."

Molly knew it had been a car accident, on the Mass Pike near Worcester, she remembered reading about it at the time.

"I'm sorry," she said.

"At least I couldn't humiliate them anymore," he said.

Molly let that go.

"I haven't seen you around town," Molly said.

"I keep to myself," he said. "And hope that my customers don't remember my name."

Molly said, "Did you know Troy Drake was back in Paradise as well?"

Feeney said, "I haven't heard from him since he quit school. But it's not as if I ever had the urge to stay in touch."

"Would you be able to answer some questions about your whereabouts over the past week?" Molly said.

"Why?" he said.

"There have been some incidents involving me and other members of our department," Molly said.

"Incidents," Feeney said.

"Someone seems to be targeting us."

"Well, it isn't me," Feeney said. He shrugged. "I'm a one-man shop, like I said. All I target is good word of mouth."

Molly gave him the nights in question anyway.

"I was home," he said.

"With your wife?" Molly said.

"Alone," he said. "She's visiting her family in Vermont. It's where I was living before I came back."

"Does she know what happened in high school?" Sunny said.

Feeney looked at her as if he'd forgotten she was there.

"She knows because I told her, because I knew she'd find out eventually," Feeney said. "She didn't judge me the way everybody else did, or think I should have gotten some kind of death sentence for being a stupid kid."

"We were all stupid kids," Molly said. "But hardly any of them ever do what you guys did."

"Troy made no secret that he used to think about getting even with the Paradise cops," Sunny said. "Did you have similar urges?"

Feeney leaned forward, his hands clenched tightly on the desk in front of him, his knuckles almost the color of his white shirt.

"I took responsibility," Feeney said. "I went away for a long time. Now I'm back. There was nothing that should have brought me back. Here I am anyway."

"What do you know about Bo's life since high school?" Molly said.

*"Don't know,"* he said. "And don't care."

He looked at his watch.

"Are we done?"

"For now," Molly said.

He stood. There was something sad about him, the kid who'd gone along with the others. But he'd stopped running. She had to give him that.

"Anything you'd like us to say to Bo if we talk to him?" Molly said.

"I never had anything to say to him," Feeney said. "I was just too dumb to know at the time."

When they were outside Sunny said, "Where to next?"

Molly grinned.

"We need to make a stop at the office of the second-biggest asshole in Paradise, Massachusetts," she said.

"Only second?"

"I'm just assuming there has to be a bigger one somewhere," Molly said.

# Thirty-Two

Joe Marino, Bo's father, had expanded his business over time into the largest highway and heavy construction company north of Boston. His new offices were in a corporate mall he'd built just over the line from Marshport. He'd put on a lot of weight since Molly had seen him last, his hair had gone completely white, and he had a big, veiny drinker's nose.

One thing, though, had remained unchanged with Joe Marino, and was evident to Molly within a few minutes after she and Sunny had taken seats across the desk from him: He was as mean and graceless as he had ever been, and still reminded her of a pit bull. Even his son had admitted to them, after the rape of Candace Pennington, that his father used to smack him around. Trying to make a man out of him.

"I got no time for this shit," he said.

Molly smiled. "Nevertheless," she said.

Joe Marino jerked his head in Sunny's direction. "Tell me why she's here again," he said.

"Think of her as kind of my partner," Molly said. "She's kind of a cop herself."

"How are you kind of a cop?" Marino said.

Molly smiled as if she'd just been elected homecoming queen.

"Unlike Molly," Sunny said, "I can't simply arrest people, no matter how much I feel the urge to do so."

"Is that supposed to be funny?" Marino said.

"Apparently not," Sunny said.

He directed his attention back to Molly.

"You said you wanted to talk about my kid," he said. "Apple of my fucking eye."

Molly told him as succinctly as she could about the events of the past week, the attacks on her and directed at Jesse and Suit. She told him they were currently investigating a possible link between those attacks and the rape of Candace Pennington, and that they'd already spoken with Troy Drake and Kevin Feeney.

"Those pissants," Marino said.

"Nevertheless," Molly said again, and told him they were now seeking an interview with Bo.

"So you people can do him all over again?" Marino said.

He wore a short-sleeved white shirt straining against his belly, a paisley tie. His face was red. His thick hands were clasped in front of him, hands that looked, Molly thought, as if he'd built his business with them, busting as many heads as he had to along the way.

"What Bo did, he did to himself," Molly said. "He raped a teenaged girl while his friends watched and then he watched them do it and then he tried to threaten her into silence with naked pictures they took."

"Yeah," Marino said. "They got themselves into that Him Too shit ahead of their time."

"Me Too," Sunny said.

"Whatever," Marino said. "Now you spend too much time checking out a woman's ass you're looking at a lawsuit."

"Woke," Sunny said to Molly. "Definitely woke."

"Huh?" Marino said.

"Do you know where we could find Bo, Mr. Marino?" Molly said.

"Maine, last I knew."

"Could you be a bit more specific?"

"Living in Biddeford," he said. "Working some construction over in Kennebunkport. I offered him work with me. He turned me down."

*Imagine,* Molly thought.

"Did he ever marry?" Molly said.

"If he did, I didn't get the invitation."

"Would he get married without telling you?" Molly said.

"He was pissed off at me the way he was pissed off at the world," Marino said. "Because of the thing with the girl. I'd lose track of him for a couple years at a time."

"No college?" Molly said.

"In the end he didn't even finish freaking high school," he said. He closed his eyes, shook his head. "My only kid."

"When you two were in contact after he left Paradise," Molly said, "did he ever express a desire for revenge against Chief Stone or the rest of us?"

Marino barked out a laugh. The sound was as unlikely as if it had come from a pit bull.

"When it first happened? With the girl? All day and every day. Especially with Stone. Said if *he'd* been wearing a gun and not Stone when he was doing his community service, he would've shot him right there. Talked a lot about that. Maybe being the one with the gun someday."

"And now somebody does take a shot at Chief Stone," Molly said.

"And you think that after all these years, my kid has come back here looking to settle things with Stone and the rest of you?" Marino said.

"As Molly said," Sunny said, "we'd just like to talk to him."

She was wearing a short black skirt today, one that showed off her legs nicely. Sunny crossed them now. Molly watched Marino watch her do it. Maybe he wasn't that worried about the Him Too movement after all.

"Fuck it," he said.

He reached into the top drawer of his desk, came out with his cell phone, jabbed at it with stubby fingers. "What's your number?" he said to Molly.

She gave it to him. Marino jabbed at the phone again and said he'd just texted her Bo's address in Biddeford, and his cell phone number.

"When was the last time you were in contact with him?" Molly said.

"Christmas," he said. "He called to tell me he'd stopped drinking."

"Drinking a problem with him?" Molly said.

"One of several."

Molly stood then. Sunny stood. Joe Marino stayed in his chair. He looked up at Molly.

"I don't think he'd start a regular job and stop drinking and then do shit that would put him in jail for real this time," Marino said.

"Then he has nothing to worry about," Molly said. "Does he?"

She and Sunny turned to leave.

"Hey," Marino said when they got to the door.

They turned back to him. He was addressing Molly again.

"Can you give your boss a message for me?" he said.

"Certainly," Molly said.

"Tell him to go fuck himself," Marino said.

"First thing," Molly said.

When they were outside, Sunny said, "You were only wrong about one thing."

"What?"

"There can't possibly be a bigger asshole in this town than him," she said.

# Thirty-Three

While Molly and Sunny were with Joe Marino, Jesse was at the Massachusetts Correctional Institution in Concord, seated across from Hasty Hathaway in the middle of the afternoon.

Hasty: former top guy on the Board of Selectmen in Paradise. Head of the Rotary Club. A pillar of the community who was also a tinhorn general in a cockeyed militia group called Freedom's Horsemen. Currently serving twenty-five-to-life for the first murders Jesse had investigated in Paradise, before charging the guy who had hired him. He had been in the courtroom the day Hasty was convicted.

His first parole hearing had been the one at which Jesse testified. Hasty had been denied. Now here they were. Jesse had been surprised at the hearing that the geek he remembered seemed to be in much better shape on the inside than he ever had been on the outside. The warden had told him that Hasty ran his prison block the way Jesse had read that

Bernie Madoff used to run his in North Carolina. Like he was still chairman of a board.

Jesse had told the guard he could uncuff him, that he'd never felt threatened by Mr. Hathaway when he could see him, but the guard said rules were rules, and he'd be right outside.

When the guard had shut the door Hathaway said, "The stones on you, coming to see me." He smiled. "See what I did there? Stones?"

"Still a silver-tongued devil," Jesse said.

"You must want something," Hathaway said.

"You've got nothing I want, Hasty," Jesse said. "But I would like you to answer a couple questions for me."

"So you do want something," Hathaway said. "I get a lot of that here. It's more like Paradise than you'd think. Very transactional. Just with a better class of people."

"Hope you're not trading sexual favors for more phone time," Jesse said.

"Fuck you, Stone."

"Silver-tongued devil."

"So what do you want?"

"You trying to have me killed again?" Jesse said. "At first you don't succeed?"

"Been there. Done that. Didn't work out as well as I'd hoped." He swiveled his head around, as if taking in their surroundings.

"Thought you might have worked up a brand-new grudge because of the parole hearing," Jesse said. "Almost like I put you away all over again."

Hasty started to lift his hands, realized they were cuffed, put them back on the table.

"You know, I was thinking that day that you were the two biggest mistakes I ever made," Hathaway said. "The first was hiring a drunk like you. The second was that I didn't have you killed when I did have the chance."

"Have to say getting me was a lot easier for you than getting rid of me."

Hathaway shook his head. "Who knew I was hiring the last fucking boy scout? At least when you'd crawl out of the bottle and do your job."

He smiled again. "Heard you got sober. That true?"

"Where'd you hear?"

"I hear a lot of things. You'd be surprised."

"Hear that somebody tried to shoot me?"

"Heard they missed," Hathaway said. "Good help's hard to find these days. Even with the Horsemen."

"Some of them still hanging on, Hasty?"

"You'd be surprised at that, too."

"You send somebody after me and my cops?" Jesse said. "Looking to square the books once and for all?"

"From here?" Hathaway said. "I'm just here living my life, and doing my time. Thanks to you."

He smiled again.

"I ever tell you about the bomb guys we recruited for the Horsemen, back in the day? Man, those were some gnarly fuckers."

"You'd know."

Hathaway was enjoying this.

"And I gotta say," he said, "that even though that Molly of yours has some miles on her by now, she's probably still one good-looking piece of ass."

"I can check the visitors log and phone records," Jesse said. "See who you've been talking to."

"Kiss *my* ass," Hathaway said. "You think if I did send somebody after you I'd leave bread crumbs? I'm getting older in here, Stone. Not dumber."

"Surrounded by all the other geniuses who ended up in here."

Hasty Hathaway leaned forward, liver-spotted hands in the cuffs. Jesse could see tattoos on both forearms.

"Why'd you really come here today?" he said. "Think I was going to confess to something you think I had done?"

"Just wanted to look you in the eyes when I asked."

"Now you have," he said. "So get the fuck out."

"You know if you did have it done, I'll find out."

Hathaway laughed.

"And do what? Have me arrested and thrown in jail?"

They were done. They both knew it. Jesse got up, walked to the door, gave it a single rap with his knuckle. The door opened and the guard stepped back into the room.

"Hey, Stone," Hathaway said.

Jesse turned around.

"You watch your back, you hear?" Hathaway said.

# Thirty-Four

**M**olly and Sunny had dinner together at Molly's house. Jesse had been invited to join them, and asked Sunny who was cooking. She asked what difference it made.

"A lot," he said.

"Is that a reflection on my kitchen skills?"

"It is," he said.

"Molly's cooking, if that influences your thinking," she said.

Jesse told her that while it did, he wanted to stay home and do some work on the Paul Hutton case.

"Got my book to keep me company," he said.

They both knew he meant his murder book. He never made a big deal of it, but Molly and Suit and Gabe and Peter all knew he kept one. So, too, did Sunny. He kept the same kind of book he had when he'd worked Robbery Homicide. The only difference was that he used a Moleskine notebook now. Upscale.

"I know you," Sunny said on the phone.

"Oh, boy," he said.

"I mean, you think you're missing something," she said. "Even though you hardly ever miss anything."

"Missing you right now."

"I could call later and talk dirty to you on the phone," Sunny said.

"Maybe we should pin down a time right now," Jesse said.

Sunny said, "You think this Hathaway guy might be the one behind everything?"

"He's a vindictive son of a bitch," Jesse said. "And probably still thinks of himself as some kind of king rat, even from prison. But I got the sense that he just wanted me to think it was him, once he knew why I was there."

She had put them on speaker.

"But we are going to check the visitors logs and his phone calls, right?" Molly said.

"Yes, sir."

He had food delivered from a new fusion place a couple blocks from the station. He always ordered the Drunken Noodles. Another private joke.

Now he ate at the kitchen table and slowly went through the notes he had been taking on the unlined pages since Christina had found Paul Hutton's body, all the way through his last meeting with Lily Cain.

Next to his notebook was a yellow legal pad.

In big letters he had once again written:

WHO WAS HE THERE TO SEE?

Underlined it.

If he knew that, it didn't mean he'd know who shot Hutton in the back of the head on the other side of town. Wouldn't mean he had the murder weapon, or motive. But he would know a hell of a lot more than he knew now.

He went back and started at the beginning. He read his notes on his meeting with Ellen Chagnon and Karen Boles, from Stony Hill Stables, struck again by how much of this seemed to run through Florida. Whit Cain had been there a lot. Karina had come from there. Hutton had worked there when he was still a drunk, but showed up in Paradise sober. Searching for someone or something. Talking about amends.

From whom?

For what?

Jesse also ended up back there, spinning his wheels.

He cleaned the table. Saved the leftovers. Thought about firing up the Keurig he kept near the coffeepot for a single cup. He'd finally given in and bought one for himself, though part of him was resistant to the whole idea. The Keurig made a perfect cup of coffee, every time, but Jesse had always thought that took the sport out of it.

What he really wanted to do was open the cabinet where the bottle had always been and begin fixing himself a good strong drink in a tall glass with just the right combination of scotch and ice and soda. Level himself off. What he used to tell himself. The word he used. Like booze was one of those levels that carpenters used to make sure planes and angles were straight.

Jesse knew he was kidding himself—it was the ultimate drinker's game, bullshitting yourself, even after you were sober—by not keeping liquor in the house. Not even for Sunny.

He knew by heart how late the stores stayed open in Paradise. Franco's, the best liquor store in town. The chains. He knew he didn't even need the stores, he could drive over to the Gull and ask whichever bartender was on the stick tonight to sell him a bottle of scotch.

It was always there if you wanted it.

He'd explained that once to Marcy Campbell, one of the times when he was sober again before rehab, when they were still hooking up for casual sex, just for the sheer uncomplicated fun of it.

"The way I'm always there when you want me," Marcy had said.

He'd quit Marcy, too, even though she made it abundantly clear every time they ran into each other that she was still abundantly available to him.

He made himself a cup of coffee and took it into the living room. He'd been with Sunny drunk and sober. He'd been with a lot of women both drunk and sober. The ones he'd left, the ones who'd left him. It was different with Sunny. More than any of them, including Jenn, Sunny had always accepted who he was. Didn't mean the others hadn't. He'd tried to explain it to Dix once, badly, finally telling him that he'd always found his relationship with Sunny nontransactional, without expectations or boundaries.

Or commitment.

Maybe until now.

She was here now because she wanted to be with him, not her ex-husband. He knew she still loved Richie. Probably always would. Maybe he'd been her drug of choice. Maybe she was the one in recovery, from him. There had been a part of

Jesse that'd never completely understood the connection she felt with Richie, the romanticized version of him she'd carried around inside her since she'd first fallen for him. Saloon owner. Son of the Irish Mob. Now full-time father to his son.

Whatever the connection, Jesse had always thought the best version of Sunny was when she was here. With him. Working with him, again.

He walked over and turned on the Red Sox game and felt himself smiling. Better to be thinking about her than about drinking. Bullshitting himself into thinking that a drink in his hand, a night like this, used to help him think better. More clearly. But then he'd have one and he'd be off, making himself the next one. And he'd wake up in the morning and look at the notes he'd been taking and feel as if he were trying to read Sanskrit.

He drank coffee, picked up the book, went back to the beginning, again, read it all the way through. Wondering all over again why Paul Hutton would make the effort to go to the Cain house and then not make any attempt to get in.

Maybe he went to see Lily, not knowing what was happening at the theater. Or the old man. Or Karina. Maybe there was a prior relationship with her in Florida, and she was the one lying her ass off. Maybe Troy Drake had been lying. Maybe Kevin Feeney had been lying to Molly and Sunny. And Joe Marino, Bo's father, always made Jesse think of a line he'd read once about a guy looking like a bouncer who'd come into some money.

The shit you thought about, alone in the night.

He closed the notebook and fell asleep in front of baseball again, despite the perfect cup of coffee next to him.

Didn't have to be drunk to still be able to do that. Had plenty of practice.

Tomorrow he would go back to the Cains' and bother Lily again and talk to Karina again. Karina and the old man, if it was one of the old man's good days.

When he woke just past two in the morning, they were replaying the game on the Red Sox network. He shut off the television and went to bed.

Another big night for the chief.

# Thirty-Five

By the time Jesse and Suit were in Jesse's office having coffee and donuts, Molly and Sunny were in Sunny's car and on their way to Maine. Jesse had already spoken to Lily and arranged to come by the house at eleven.

"Maybe you should have your own room here," Lily had said.

"Only with a view."

"They *all* have views," she said, before hanging up.

Now Suit said to Jesse, "Why does Sunny get to drive?"

"She wants to be Louise," Jesse said.

"From that movie *Thelma and Louise*," Suit said.

"Look at you," Jesse said.

Jesse drank some Dunkin' coffee. He'd already eaten two jelly-filled donuts. He wasn't worried about donuts. He could quit them anytime he wanted.

He just didn't want to.

"But Thelma and Louise were criminals," Suit said.

"Badass," Jesse said.

"Molly and Sunny think they're badass."

"Because they are," Jesse said.

When he got to the Cains', a house man Jesse didn't recognize showed him in. Lily was waiting for him in the precinct of the big front room she called the sunroom. Her granddaughter, Samantha, was with her. Jesse vaguely remembered her as a high school soccer player. She was as tall as Lily, not quite as blond.

"I know you've previously met Samantha Cain," Lily said.

"Granny knows everything," Samantha said.

She turned the kind of sarcastic smile on Lily that Jesse noticed kids were mastering at earlier and earlier ages.

"Samantha," Lily said.

Jesse sensed he'd come in on the end of something unpleasant between them.

"Center middie, as I recall," he said. "Number ten, right?"

Samantha smiled at him now and seemed to mean it. He could only imagine the effect of that smile on college boys.

"Good memory, Chief Stone," she said. "You a soccer fan?"

"Not even a little bit," he said.

"Samantha is on her way to Harvard Business in the fall," Lily said. "Her plan is to be running Cain Enterprises eventually."

The kid snorted. "I could do it better than dear old Daddy even without a Business degree."

Lily said, "She's off to Europe for hiking through the Alps. They call it the Tour du Mont Blanc. Or it's just an excuse to meet European boys."

"I promise to stay out of trouble, Granny," she said.

More sarcasm.

"You cause quite enough around here," Lily said.

"You forget I'm twenty-one now," Samantha said.

"And proud of it," Lily said.

Jesse was thinking that somebody should ring a bell and end the round.

Samantha sighed. "I didn't come over here to have a fight, just say goodbye," she said. "But whatever. See you in a week or so."

Now Lily was the one who sounded sarcastic. "I look forward to that, dear," she said, and then her granddaughter gave a quick wave to her and Jesse and was gone.

"I see a lot of you in her," Jesse said.

"Is that supposed to be a compliment?" she said.

"You were young once, too," Jesse said.

"Please don't remind me." Now she sighed. "But you're not here to talk about me, or Samantha."

"I'll try not to take up too much of Whit's time," Jesse said. "I'd just like to know if there's any possibility that his life might have intersected at some point with Paul Hutton's."

"He says no," Lily said.

"Just like to hear it for myself."

He followed her back to the foyer, up a curving staircase, and down a long hallway. He heard Whit Cain before he saw him in the wheelchair in front of another view of the Atlantic. It was a terrible sound that started with sneezing and then became something that sounded like a one-man lung ward.

"He starts like that sometimes," Lily said. "And it's as if he's never going to stop."

She turned and left the room. Karina was standing next to the wheelchair and waved Jesse over, pushing the chair out onto the terrace as she did. She gestured to a chair out there, where Jesse sat. Karina stood next to Whit Cain, a hand on his shoulder.

When Jesse had first met Whit Cain, not long after arriving in Paradise, it was as if every room organized itself around him once he was in it. He was tall, taller than Jesse, with a thick head of what was gray hair at the time, always with a tan, no matter the season, a voice and presence bigger than he actually was. Jesse wasn't sure how old he was now. Maybe Lily's age, maybe a few years older. But it seemed irrelevant as Jesse looked at what was left of him, blanket over his legs, wearing a cardigan sweater despite the heat of the day, his body seeming to have collapsed into itself, like one of those buildings you saw implode on television. His hands were in his lap, almost as if he'd forgotten they were there.

But when Jesse sat down, the old man surprised him, extended his right hand and said, "Jesse. Goddamn it's good to see you."

Jesse gently shook his hand, as if afraid it might break if he gripped it too firmly.

The old man smiled.

"Goddamn," he said again. "That's no way to shake a man's hand. Even one older than dirt."

He started coughing again. There was nothing to do but wait for it to run its course. Karina patted his back the way you would a baby's. Then she handed him the glass of water from the tray in front of him.

"Allergies, can you believe it?" Whit Cain said. "After every goddamn thing that's happened to me, I've got to deal with these allergies."

He stared out at the water. Jesse did the same. He went back and forth on whether he believed in an afterlife. But Jesse knew he didn't want this one to end for him like Whit Cain's, vultures already circling.

"Whit," Jesse said finally. "You know why I'm here, right?"

"Because you missed me?" the old man said and laughed, which touched off another coughing fit.

When he stopped this time he said, "You never liked me all that much, admit it."

"Not true," Jesse said.

"Don't lie to a dying man," he said. "You just thought I was the dickhead in Paradise with the most money."

Jesse grinned. Maybe there was still some fight in the old man. Even some fun.

"Am I under oath?" Jesse said.

"Never bullshit a bullshitter," Whit Cain said.

"So," Jesse said, "I assume you know about the murder I'm investigating."

"The Florida man," he said. "My wife and Karina told me."

"Then you must also have been told he came here the night he died," Jesse said.

The old man nodded. "They told me that, too."

"What I'm just wondering is if he might have come here to see you," Jesse said. "He worked in the horse business, and I know you spent time around it."

Whit Cain smiled.

"Goddamn, Jesse, there were some good-looking girls in that world. Talk about ass. Those riding pants? I'd go down there for the season and my dick would be hard the whole time."

A raspy sigh came out of him, no coughing spell behind it this time.

"Those were the days," he said. "I used to wish there were pills to stop my dick from *getting* hard."

Jesse looked up at Karina. Hand still on his shoulder. They sat in silence until Whit Cain said, "You got secrets, Jesse?"

"Pretty sure everybody does," Jesse said.

"Well, I've got some beauts," he said. "But it was never a secret that I wasn't somebody you fucked with. I protected myself. Protected what I had. Whatever it took." He nodded again. "You know where I learned it? Some very bad guys in Boston I did business with from time to time. Joe Broz. Gino Fish. Desmond Burke. Guys like that, ones who got it done, whatever it took." He smiled. "I always got it done."

Whit Cain pointed a shaky finger at Jesse. "You ever hear of them?"

"Desmond Burke used to be father-in-law to a friend of mine," he said.

"Ask how he handled things back in the day," Cain said. "Probably still does."

He needed to bring him back from wherever it was he'd just been. Jesse took out the picture of Paul Hutton he'd brought with him and handed it to Whit Cain. He told Jesse that Lily had already shown him the same picture. Jesse asked if he'd take another look at it.

Cain held it close to his face. Handed it back to Jesse.

"Nope," he said.

Jesse handed the photo to Karina now.

"What about you?" he said.

"I told you before, Chief Stone," she said. "I do not know this man."

"Sure it's not one of your old boyfriends, Kat?" the old man said.

"No, Mr. Cain."

"You can only imagine what this one was like when she was young," Whit Cain said. "Am I right?"

"Mr. *Cain*," Karina said.

Talking to him the way she would to a child.

The old man leaned his head back suddenly, closed his eyes. For a moment, Jesse was afraid he'd fallen asleep. But when he opened his eyes, he reached down and angled the wheelchair toward Jesse.

"You know what all this is?" he said. "Me being in this chair like this? *Dues*. For all the fun I had. All the parties and all the booze and all the ass I grabbed, with both hands."

"Those were the days," Jesse said.

The old man closed his eyes again. This time they were closed so long Jesse briefly wondered if he'd died.

"All that's left to do is make amends," he said in a voice so soft Jesse had to strain to hear it. "Settle up."

Then he was asleep. Karina put a finger to her lips. Jesse left them there. Karina's hand still on Whit Cain's shoulder.

Jesse walked down the stairs. Lily was no longer in the sunroom. Jesse showed himself out. The last thing he heard as he opened the front door was more coughing from upstairs.

The old man had talked about dues. But he'd talked about making amends.

So had Paul Hutton.

Whose secrets had he died knowing?

# Thirty-Six

I'm telling you," Molly said to Sunny from the passenger seat. "Geena Davis was in the passenger seat when they drove off the cliff."

Sunny grinned. "Is this just a way to start talking again about Susan Sarandon's breasts being bigger than Geena's and yours being bigger than mine?"

"Four kids," Molly said. "I earned these babies."

They had driven along the water as long as they could. Then they were on I-95 in Amesbury, before crossing the New Hampshire line. Waze had said the whole trip would take ninety minutes unless they encountered unexpected traffic. Molly had called Bo's number before they left Paradise, left a message when he didn't pick up, and followed that up with a text. No response to that, either. But they had the address in Biddeford. Molly had called Joe Marino back after they'd left his office and gotten a contact with the construction foreman for whom Bo had been working. She'd called there and been told that Bo had taken some time they owed him after the Fourth, because he'd worked through the holiday weekend.

Molly asked the foreman if he could remember the last time he'd seen Bo.

"Last week sometime," he said. "Is he in some kind of trouble? He told me one time he'd put all the trouble in his life behind him."

"No trouble," Molly said. "Just want to ask him a few questions about a case I'm working."

Now they were less than an hour out from Biddeford and back to talking about Jesse. Like he was a case they'd both been working for a long time.

"Tell me this," Sunny said. "There was never a chance of something happening with the two of you?"

"Never."

"So you're telling me that you never thought about him that way?"

Molly considered. "That's a different question. Maybe when we first met, but it was the way you imagine being with an actor on TV or in the movies, an impossibility."

She reached over to the console, picked up her to-go cup of iced coffee, took a sip, put it back. A sign said they were coming up on Hampton, New Hampshire.

"I know this sounds lame," Molly said. "But for a long time I've thought of him as a brother."

"Oh, brother," Sunny said in a throaty voice, and they both laughed. They were listening to one of Sunny's jazz CDs. John Coltrane and Thelonious Monk at Carnegie Hall.

"You wouldn't be here if things were good with Richie," Molly said. "You're not the type to juggle two men at the same time."

"Are you kidding?" Sunny said. "I can barely handle one." She reached over for her own iced coffee.

"I can't be what Richie wants us to be," she said.

"One big happy family."

"Yup," Sunny said. "Did you ever feel that Michael saw your relationship differently than you did?"

"Amazingly, no," Molly said. "That doesn't mean everything is perfect with us. It's not. We've had our problems. I think everybody except Barack and Michelle do."

Sunny smiled. "Oh, I don't know," she said. "I was with Spike at a bar one time and a guy we both thought was hot came walking in. And Spike said, 'Somewhere somebody's tired of him.'"

"But no matter what," Molly said, "Michael always knew who he is, who I am. Who we are."

"I feel that way with Jesse most of the time."

"I can tell."

"Doesn't mean he doesn't remain a hot mess."

Molly smiled. "Hot and a mess. Yes."

"But in a weird way, even though he's still dealing with not drinking," Sunny said, "I feel as if I'm seeing him at his best at a time like this."

"Under pressure."

"Yeah."

"The old ballplayer in him," Molly said. "He wants the ball hit to him when the game is on the line."

"I really don't like baseball."

"He told me," Molly said. "I think there's couple's counseling that can help out with that."

"You think he's glad I'm here?" Sunny said.

"Extremely."

"What do I do when Michael comes back?"

"Stay with him," Molly said. "Bring Rosie. He's a dog lover."

"I can't leave Boston," she said. "And he can't leave Paradise."

"You're both smart people," Molly said. "You'll figure it out."

There were signs for Portsmouth.

"You looking for permanence, Sunny?"

"Beats the hell out of me," she said. "All I know is this, if it makes any sense: Sometimes I feel like my best self is when I'm with him."

"He told me the same thing."

"He did?"

"He's like you. Trained investigator."

Sunny said, "I don't want to hurt him."

"Don't worry, Louise," Molly said. "I won't let that happen."

They drove the rest of the way to Biddeford, Maine, hoping to talk to Molly's old friend Bo Marino.

# Thirty-Seven

Sunny said they should stop at a place called Mabel's Lobster Claw in Kennebunkport for lunch. Molly said they could do it on their way back after they'd talked to Bo, if they talked to Bo.

"You really Maced him on the school bus?" Sunny said.

"I did," Molly said.

"Where was Mace when I needed it in high school?" Sunny said.

"Oh, please," Molly said. "You probably needed to be armed as much in those days as I did."

The house looked exactly as it had on Google Maps, a run-down white ranch set back about fifty yards from the road, past an apartment complex called The Lofts at Saco Falls.

The first thing they noticed when they were out of the car was what looked like a week's worth of newspapers on the small front porch. No car in the driveway. The lawn needed mowing, badly. No one would have looked at Bo Marino's circumstances and thought he had much of a life at all to turn around.

"Young Bo appears to be away," Molly said.

They made their way up the front walk, overgrown with weeds, knelt down, and looked at eight days of the *Journal Tribune*, which Molly assumed was the Biddeford daily paper.

"I'm impressed he was even subscribing to a newspaper," Molly said.

"Or still having it delivered," Sunny said. "I thought that wasn't even a thing anymore."

Molly walked back to the mailbox. It was filled with bills and flyers. All were addressed to Bo. Nothing in there resembled personal correspondence. If he'd gone on vacation, he'd done so without alerting the post office to hold his mail.

Sunny had walked over to the garage and was staring through a dirty window.

"No car in there, either," she said.

"Maybe he drove it down to Paradise to take a shot at Jesse and build a bomb for Suit," Molly said.

"And put you on the ground in your own backyard," Sunny said.

"He could have accomplished a lot in the eight days he's been gone from here," Molly said.

"Or," Sunny said, "he did just take a vacation and neglected to inform his newspaper delivery service or the people delivering his mail."

"Be nice to know which," Molly said.

"We could walk the neighborhood and knock on doors and ask if anybody has seen Bo lately," Molly said.

Sunny smiled. "Or," she said, dragging the word out as if pulling on taffy.

"I don't like that look," she said.

"What look?" Sunny said.

"The look that suggests to me that *you* are about to suggest something inappropriate to the deputy chief of police from Paradise, Massachusetts. Or flat-out illegal."

"I'm really, *really* good at picking locks," Sunny said. "I know this guy back in Boston."

"I was afraid of that," Molly said.

"Tell you what," Sunny said. "Why don't I call Jesse and ask him?"

"You mean have the conversation about breaking and entering that we're not even having right now?"

"Exactly!" Sunny said.

Sunny walked back to where her car was parked on the street. Molly watched her walk around the car, phone to her ear, smiling and nodding and talking. When she was finished, she stuck her phone in the back pocket of jeans Molly knew were way more expensive than hers. By now she was used to being outbranded by Sunny.

"What did he say?" Molly said.

"I think his exact words were 'Don't fucking get caught.'"

"Front door or back, Louise?" Molly said.

# Thirty-Eight

Jesse had just gotten off the phone with Sunny when Bryce Cain called to tell him that his father had died.

"My mom wanted you to know," Bryce said. "He passed about an hour ago."

"I was just with him yesterday," Jesse said, not sure what else to say, other than he was sorry. Or that it was a blessing. All the phony rhetoric of death.

Bryce said, "My mom was with him. He just stopped breathing."

There was a silence. "Where's the body?"

"What does it matter?"

"Just want to make sure that everybody's following the proper protocols."

"Hospital," Bryce said. "I guess they take blood. Once they finish with him, we're having him cremated."

"That soon?"

"Why wait?"

Jesse didn't have a good answer to that.

"Funeral?" he said.

"Mom wants to have a memorial service down the road," Cain said. "For now, she just wants us all to get on with things."

"I assume his affairs are in order, as they say."

"I'm not just his partner," Bryce Cain said. "I'm his lawyer. I don't fuck around when it comes to business any more than he did."

A beauty to the end.

"I'll bet," Jesse said.

"What the hell is that supposed to mean?" Cain said.

"Nothing," Jesse said, thanked him for calling, and told him he'd call or stop by later to see Lily. After they ended the call, he walked out into the bullpen area and told Suit he was on his way to the hospital.

Suit grinned. "Somebody die?"

"As a matter of fact," Jesse said, and told him.

Suit let out a low whistle. "No shit," he said. "You want me to come along?"

Jesse told him sure. They walked to his car. Now two people who'd been at the Cains' on the Saturday night of Fourth of July weekend were dead. Both right after talking about making amends.

What were the odds?


When they got to the hospital Suit went inside to check on whether or not the doctors were finished with Whit Cain's body.

Jesse stayed outside because when they'd pulled up to the

Emergency Room entrance, he'd spotted Lily Cain in a small alley, smoking a cigarette.

"Odd day to start smoking," Jesse said.

She did not seem startled to see him. Just took another drag and blew smoke toward the sky.

"You going to report me to the principal?" she said.

"I'm sorry, Lily," he said.

He leaned against the wall next to her.

"I honestly wish I could say the same, Jesse," she said. "I don't frankly know what I am. Relieved, maybe?"

"You two were together a long time."

He saw a small smile work its way across her face.

"Define 'together,'" she said.

She took another drag of her cigarette, blew out the smoke, dropped the butt to the ground, and snuffed it with her black running shoes.

"Don't report me to the authorities for that, either," she said.

"I know it's easy to forget sometimes," he said. "But I *am* the authorities." He turned to face her fully. "Why are you here?" he said. "Been my experience that most people are relieved when the body is taken."

"I know it's easy for *you* to forget sometimes," she said. "But the Cains, bless our hearts, have never been most people. I mean, that's always been the object of the game, right, Jesse?"

He knew she was right. As much as he liked her, and he liked her a lot better than most of the rich in Paradise, he never forgot that there was a gulf between her world and his—even in a town this small—that was as wide as the ocean.

"Other than Karina," Lily said, "you were probably the last person to have a real conversation with him."

Jesse said, "Surprised me, to tell you the truth. How present he was."

She was wearing a pale blue cotton hoodie with the yacht club emblem on it.

"Karina said he was full of piss and vinegar when you were with him." She smiled another thin smile. "Do people still say that?"

Jesse smiled. "Most people? Probably not."

"How come you haven't told me it's a blessing that his suffering is over?" she said.

" 'Cause I usually think that's a load of crap," he said. "And you probably do, too."

"This is going to sound terrible," she said, "but, fuck it, I'm going to say it anyway: You know the one for whom this is a blessing? *Me*."

"Honest," he said.

"Getting to where I am in the world," Lily Cain said, "and in this town, isn't for the faint of heart."

She showed no urge to leave this spot, go back inside, go home. She apparently just wanted to talk. He'd always known how tough she was. He'd seen it when she wanted something done in Paradise, whether the theater marquee or something else. She didn't back up. Even from this.

"You know what he told me one time, the first time I ever caught him cheating on me?" Lily said. "He told me that it didn't matter to him, and shouldn't matter to me. That I was the only woman he'd ever loved." She shook her head. "But then you know what he told me, practically in the next breath? That he sure liked a lot of them."

"What did you say to that?"

"I slapped him," she said. "He laughed and told me he deserved it, but to remember one thing. They'd all want to put flowers on the top of the casket. And so would I."

"From what Bryce told me, there isn't going to be a casket," Jesse said.

"Imagine that," Lily Cain said. "Whit would have been so disappointed, to lose one last show of their affection."

Jesse said, "When I talked to him yesterday, he talked about making amends. Any idea what he meant by that?"

"None," she said. "But it might have been just the ramblings of a dying man. A figure of speech. Because making amends would mean he was thinking about somebody other than himself, which he never really did."

"Ask you something?" Jesse said.

She turned to face him.

"Why did you stay with him?" he said.

Now she smiled fully. "I thought I'd told you this once before," he said. "I still loved being a Cain long after I'd stopped loving him."

"Ties that bind," Jesse said.

"Something like that," she said.

She turned to face him. He remembered Jenn one time trying to find the perfect shade of blue to paint the walls in one of her apartments. She finally settled on what she called "ice blue." It was the color of Lily Cain's eyes in that moment.

"I used to love to go to New York for shows," she said, "from the time we got married. By myself, or with a friend sometimes. Whit wasn't much for the theater. But my favorite was *Follies*. You're probably too young to know it, but there was a song in it that I've never forgotten. You know how it ends, Jesse? 'Look who's here. *I'm* still here.'"

He watched her walk around the corner. People talked all the time about grieving widows. Jesse wondered how many actually grieved, when you got right down to it.

# Thirty-Nine

**M**olly and Sunny went in through the back door, after Sunny had retrieved her lock-picking pouch from the glove compartment of her car.

"Can you get something like that at Best Buy?" Molly said.

"It was a gift," Sunny said. "Friend of mine named Ghost Garrity."

"Thief?"

"He prefers *performance artist*," Sunny said.

Molly watched with admiration as Sunny worked her magic with a wrench and pick on the deadbolt. Short end of the wrench into the bottom of the keyhole. Pick into the top part of the lock. It took her less than five minutes. Molly knew because before Sunny had started she said, "Time me."

"When I get home, I'm changing all the locks at my house," Molly said.

Molly wasn't sure what to expect once they were inside,

just knowing the kind of general slob Bo Marino had been as a teenage boy. Slob in his thinking, worse slob in his behavior. At the time, he'd made his father look like a prince of the city in comparison.

But the place was surprisingly neat. It was a small house consisting of a living room, two bedrooms, a kitchen, a dining area with a table. The first thing they looked for was a laptop, but they couldn't find one. A pair of Timberland boots, caked with dirt, rested near the back door. There were a couple pairs of faded carpenter jeans and short- and long-sleeved shirts hanging in the closet of the bedroom. There was one piece of luggage that they could find, the kind of small one on wheels you could fit into the overhead compartment.

There was milk and bread in the refrigerator, the milk past its sell-by date, the bread starting to mold. There were two bottles, unopened, of Mountain Dew. They went through all the kitchen cabinets and could find no liquor of any kind. *Like Jesse's condo,* Molly thought.

There was a pack of condoms in the top drawer of the bedside table. Not a single book or magazine anywhere. The living room was dominated by a mounted Samsung television that Molly guessed was a fifty-incher. Maybe bigger than that.

All of his toiletries seemed to be in place on the counter in the bathroom: razor, shaving cream, a small jar of Old Spice pomade. Deodorant. Tylenol and Zantac in the cabinet above the sink. Shampoo in the shower.

"This look to you like the home of someone who packed for a vacation?" Molly said.

There were wall air conditioners for the living room and

bedroom, both turned off. The temperature outside was in the low 80s. The heat seemed more oppressive inside, the air thick and hot and heavy and stale. Molly walked over and threw the switch on the living room air conditioner, and it groaned to life.

"We won't be here long enough for me to stop feeling as if I'm standing in a pool of my own sweat," Sunny said.

"We're assuming he owns a car, right?" Molly said.

"Hard to believe he was the type to be Ubering back and forth to work," Sunny said. "Unless he lost his license somewhere along the way."

"Easy enough to check," Molly said.

"Just because there's a suitcase in the bedroom doesn't mean it's his only one," Sunny said. "And he could have shopped for the basic bathroom stuff when he got to his destination."

"Paradise?"

She looked at Sunny, who shrugged.

Molly said, "He's been gone over a week. Maybe he's on his way back."

"Or still there."

"Or on the run," Molly said.

Molly went into the kitchen and went through a couple drawers before finding a plastic sandwich bag. She took it to the bathroom and put Bo Marino's toothbrush inside.

"You can never have enough DNA, that's my motto," Molly said.

"You think he's the one?" Sunny said.

"Put it this way," Molly said. "I don't think he's not."

They went through the house a second time. Molly

pointed out that there wasn't just an absence of reading material of any kind. There wasn't a single photograph anywhere.

"Airbnb's are more personal than this," Molly said.

While Molly kept opening drawers, Sunny pulled out her phone and tried to find any sort of presence for Bo on social media. Molly had already looked for any trace of Bo Marino in the system from the time he'd left Paradise, but had found none. The only time he had been arrested was because of what he and Troy Drake and Kevin Feeney did to Candace Pennington.

"This could be a wild-goose chase," Sunny said. "So far all we've really got to go on is the other loser that Jesse hauled in . . ."

"Troy Drake," Molly said.

"Just because he had the fixings for a bomb doesn't mean he or Marino is the one," Sunny said.

"Call it a gut feeling that one of them is involved," Molly said. "Even though there are a lot of other people probably holding grudges against Jesse and Suit and me."

"But now Bo Marino is missing, even if he's technically not a missing person."

"He's not anything," Molly said. "He's not even a suspect. Maybe I am trying to talk myself into something. Maybe my gut is wrong this time."

"That happen much before?"

Molly grinned. "Rarely."

"That's my girl," Sunny said.

They left the house through the back door. Molly asked if Sunny could lock a deadbolt from the outside.

"Watch me," Sunny said.

Then they walked back to the car. Molly took one last look at Bo Marino's house.

"But what if it *is* him?" she said.

"Then he's still out there," Sunny said.

"I had a feeling you were going to say that," Molly said.

# Forty

Sunny dropped Molly in Paradise and kept going to Boston, on her way to pick up her dog, Rosie. Molly said she could spend the night in Boston if she wanted, and come back up in the morning. Sunny said she hadn't been dismissed by the boss, and would be back sometime after dinner.

"Since you're now referring to Jesse as your boss," Molly said, "wouldn't this fall into the category of workplace romance?"

"Turns me on just thinking about it," Sunny said.

"What doesn't these days?" Molly said.

Now Molly and Jesse were in his office, in the late afternoon.

"So where's Bo?" Jesse said. "From what you guys saw, it's like he left and has no immediate plans of coming back."

"Does that make him more of a suspect?" she said.

"Doesn't make him less of one."

"It certainly does not," she said.

"You checked out Hasty?" Jesse said.

"If he was orchestrating all this from Concord," Molly said, "he was doing it on a phone somebody smuggled in for him."

"Email?"

"He's not on CorrLinks," Molly said. "It's a way for federal prisoners—"

"I know what it is, Mols."

She gave him a thumbs-up. And a look.

"And I should know you'd know," she said. "If he's emailing people on the outside, he's found a way to game the system."

"Once a slippery bastard, always a slippery bastard," Jesse said. "What about the missus? She been to visit recently?"

"According to the logs," Molly said, "the only time she went to see him was to bring him their divorce papers, about five years into his stretch."

"Stretch?" Jesse said. "You watch too much TV."

"Do not."

"You went that far back?"

"You know me," she said. "I went all the way back." She put her head back, closed her eyes, sighed. Loudly. "God, I need a drink."

As soon as she said it she came forward in her chair, hands up, as if surrendering.

"Sorry," she said.

"Don't be," he said. "I need one, too."

"So what do we do now?"

Jesse said, "I call the chief up in Biddeford and tell him that you went up there, and why. Maybe have him keep an eye on the house."

"I assume you'll be leaving out the part about me and your girlfriend breaking and entering."

"She's not my girlfriend."

"Sure," Molly said. "Go with that."

After Molly left he closed the door, reached into the top drawer of his desk, and took out the file he'd been keeping on Paul Hutton, spread everything out on the desk in front of him. Went all the way back, the way Molly had on Hasty. Reread the notes he'd taken in Florida after his meeting with Karen Boles, who'd told Jesse about Paul Hutton having been an orphan.

In the quiet of his office, with the last of the afternoon sun knifing through the blinds behind him, he stared down at the page in front of him and underlined *orphan* now.

Twice.

He was guessing Paul Hutton was around forty when he died. Maybe more, maybe less. He'd told Karen Boles that he'd grown up in that area. Jesse wondered now how many orphanages there were in that part of Florida that would have been in business around the time Paul Hutton was born.

Maybe he hadn't gone back far enough trying to figure out who the guy was.

Jesse got up now and opened the door. Suit was still at his desk. Jesse waved him over.

"Got another job for you," he said, then told Suit what he needed. In the morning Jesse was on the first flight from Boston back to Palm Beach, thinking he was the only guy up here who'd turned into a snowbird in the middle of summer.

# Forty-One

Nora Hayes wasn't thrilled signing off on another Florida trip, but Jesse assured her there was plenty left in the PPD piggy bank.

"Piggy bank, Jesse?" she said. "How old are you?"

Suit had done good, fast work trying to find an orphanage where Paul Hutton might have been left sometime in the late '70s or early '80s. There turned out to be several in the state that had been around that long. He made some calls despite it being late in the day, and finally got a hit at a place called the Palm Beach County Catholic Youth Home. The woman Suit had spoken to said that yes, they'd taken in a baby whom they'd given the name Paul Hutton in the fall of 1979. Suit asked if there was anybody at the orphanage now who'd been around then, and learned that Sister Beth, who ran the place, had worked there at the time. He told Jesse, who decided to go down there and talk to Sister Beth himself.

"Once a flatfoot, always a flatfoot," Jesse had told Molly at dinner. "Cole tells me that all the time."

"Look 'em in the eye," she said.

"I really have taught you so well."

"You wish," she said. "Surprised you didn't ask Sunny to go with you."

Jesse said, "By the time I get back, I expect the two of you will have located Bo Marino."

"You wish," she said.

The Palm Beach County Catholic Youth Home had been established in 1968. It was a mile east of 441, maybe two miles from an entrance to the Florida Turnpike, the building looking more like an old red-brick Catholic school that Jesse had briefly attended the year he and his parents had lived in Santa Clarita.

A young woman at the front desk introduced herself as Sister Theresa. She had short dark hair, big brown eyes. Jesse was long past thinking that nuns were supposed to be dressed in black robes. Sister Theresa wore a short-sleeved polo shirt, cargo shorts, and had a nose ring. Jesse had no way of knowing where Jesus came down on those.

Jesse showed her his badge and his ID card. She said she had spoken to one of his detectives the night before. "Suitcase Simpson," Jesse said.

"Suitcase?" she said.

Jesse said the nickname came from an old-time ballplayer. Sister Theresa seemed about as interested in that as if Jesse had tried to tell her how the Asian markets had opened.

"You want to see the Boss Sis," she said. "She's been around here almost since the place opened."

"Boss Sis," Jesse said. "How far is that below Pope?"

Sister Theresa lowered her voice and leaned forward.

"After you meet her," she said, "you might wonder where His Holiness ranks below *her*."

She walked down a short hallway and came back a couple minutes later with a small, white-haired woman wearing blue jeans and pink running shoes and a rose-colored sweatshirt rolled to her elbows. If she'd been around as long as Sister Theresa said, she had to be somewhere between seventy-five and eighty. But she seemed to be bouncing toward Jesse as much as walking, as if the best part of her day was starting right now. Somehow he imagined a gymnast who'd just stuck a landing and wanted you to know she was damn proud of it.

"Beth," she said, sticking out her hand.

"Jesse," he said.

"Guess you already know I'm allegedly in charge around here," she said.

"Allegedly?" Jesse said. "As soon as I saw you coming up the hall, I stood up a little straighter, Sister."

"Don't blow smoke up my butt, young man." She smiled, white teeth set off against her tan. "I'm told you want to know about Paul Hutton." He could see green eyes narrowing behind her round, wire-rimmed glasses. "Something has happened to him, hasn't it?"

"He died," Jesse said.

"How?"

"Shot to death in my town in Massachusetts."

She gestured in the direction of a small sitting room just off the lobby. The furniture reminded Jesse of her. Old.

Sturdy. But she already reminded him of a line he'd heard once in a bar from an old actor friend: I can play younger.

She sat down on the sofa. Jesse took the armchair to her right.

"Shot to death," she said.

"Afraid so."

He watched as she made a quick sign of the cross, then said, "What do you want to know about him?"

"He told a friend of mine he was abandoned," Jesse said. "I guess the best place to start is with his birth parents."

"Good luck with that," she said.

"Who brought him here?"

She snorted.

*"Brought him here?"* she said. "He got left in a dumpster."

So that's what he'd meant when he told Karen Boles it was no accident his life had turned into a dumpster fire, Jesse thought.

Sister Beth said, "That poor boy got put in a dumpster by somebody who didn't care whether he lived or died. It was a big story around here for a couple days. The dumpster baby. Please help us find who left the dumpster baby. Then the papers and the police moved on. Doesn't work that way around here. He was ours. Him and his troubled damn soul."

She asked if Jesse wanted something to drink. Jesse said he was fine. He asked if anybody ever adopted the boy.

"There was one couple finally," she said. "From up in Stuart, who couldn't have children of their own. I think that lasted a year. He was around thirteen or fourteen at the time."

"Already more than just a troubled soul?"

"Just trouble," she said. "He started stealing from them.

Was already drinking. Getting into fights at school. Never got arrested, as far as I knew. But the diocese wouldn't let us take him back after the Stuart couple surrendered him. That's when he started bouncing from one group home to another." She sighed. "Then I lost track of him."

"Never heard from him again?"

"No, that's the thing," she said. "I was getting to that. He stopped by out of the blue a few months ago. Sometime in March, I think it was. Said he wanted me to know that he was back on what he called *the straight and narrow*. I remember asking if that meant regular attendance at Sunday Mass. He said no. Told me he'd been a bad drunk, but that he'd stopped. Seen the light, he said."

Sister Beth said, "The boy, I still thought of him as a boy, said it had taken him his whole life, but he was finally feeling good about himself. Said he might even be ready to know who he really was."

"Metaphysically?" Jesse said.

"You talk pretty for a cop."

"Somebody told me once that the key to life was hanging around with people smarter than you," Jesse said. He grinned. "Doing a little of that right now."

"More smoke up my butt," Sister Beth said.

"What did he mean about finding himself?"

"I asked him that myself," she said.

"What did he say?"

"Just hugged me and told me that he'd be in touch," she said. "Where's his body?"

"In the morgue," he said.

"How long does it stay there?" she said. "I'd like you to

have it shipped down here so I could give that boy a proper Catholic burial."

"I'm gonna need to hold on to it for a while longer," Jesse said.

"You let me know when you're done with it," she said. "Or else."

"If I ever mess with you, Sister," Jesse said, "it will mean my life has taken a wrong turn."

"More smoke," she said.

"How'd you come up with the name Paul Hutton?" Jesse said. "Just curious."

"Paul because of my late brother," she said. "Died in that damn war in Vietnam. Hutton? I never told him this and he never asked. But it was the brand name on the dumpster."

Jesse stood. So did she. She wasn't more than five feet tall, if that. Jesse still wasn't sure he could take her in a fair fight.

As she walked him to his car, she said that this seemed more than just another case for him. Jesse told her about meeting Paul Hutton at the AA meeting, that he was a recovering alcoholic himself. But that he was trying to stay the straight and narrow now.

"I'll pray for you, too," she said.

He grinned again. "Dirty job," he said.

"I don't like to make snap judgments about people, Chief Jesse Stone," she said. "But you seem like you might have a bit of a troubled soul yourself."

"Sister," he said, "you have no idea."

He was on his way back to the airport when Suit called.

"Well, I might've spoke too soon at the lake that day," he said.

"What's that mean?"

"It means we've got ourselves another floater."

Jesse reached over and turned down the volume on the car radio.

"You know who it is?"

"Troy Drake," Suit said.

# Forty-Two

Molly, Sunny, and Suit were waiting for him at the station when he got back to Paradise at around eight o'clock.

By now Suit had filled him in on the discovery of Troy Drake's body at a small dock maybe half a mile from the Stiles Island Bridge. It was all done by the book after that: The ME wagon had arrived not long after Suit did. Then he ID'ed the body before it was tarped and loaded onto a gurney and wheeled up into the wagon for the ride to the morgue, where Dev went to work immediately.

Suit said, "You were right the first time I ever saw one of those. One floater is too many."

"How long did Dev think the body had been in the water?" Jesse said.

"He guessed a day, at least," Suit said. "Maybe two. The crabs had already done a pretty good job on the poor bastard."

"You know if Dev has talked to the evidence specialist from the staties?" Jesse said.

"I did," Molly said. "He was with Dev when I called."

"I don't suppose he was shot with a .22," Jesse said.

"No gunshot wound," Molly said. "No initial sign of blunt-force trauma. You know Dev. He's not much of a bear for speculation. But he's thinking Troy might have taken a flyer off the bridge."

The guy who had sat in Jesse's office and said the only person he ever thought about killing was himself.

Sunny had just made more coffee. Jesse had tasted his and said it was strong enough to fuel a small plane. She said, "You're welcome." Jesse told them that when he was still playing ball, there was one coffee urn for the players and one for everybody else. He said the player urn made Red Bull seem like a sedative.

Jesse reminded Sunny what Drake had said to him about suicide.

"Did he seem depressed to you?" she said.

"Who the hell knows?" Jesse said. "When he left here I thought he was probably headed for the nearest bar."

"We could check around town to see if anybody's seen him the last couple days," Molly said.

"Let's say he *was* a jumper," Sunny said. "Do we intuit that guilt may finally have caught up with him?"

"I do like the way my new partner talks," Molly said.

"Few don't," Jesse said.

"Or did somebody throw his ass off the bridge?" Suit said.

They sat and drank coffee. If Jesse had any more, he wasn't going to get to sleep until Labor Day.

"Where's Rosie the dog?" he said to Sunny.

"Anxiously awaiting Molly's and my return, I expect."

Molly said, "Bo Marino is still out there somewhere."

"Isn't he," Jesse said.

He knew he should be tired. Flying always made him tired, but he wasn't, and he knew it wasn't just Sunny Randall's coffee. It was another body. The added mystery of it. The responsibility.

"We liked Bo for the attacks on us because of how much we *dis*liked him when he was a mean kid," Molly said. "But now one of the other three mean kids involved in the rape of Candace Pennington is dead, and Bo is missing."

"Something at that house didn't feel right," Sunny said. "Could Bo be a victim and not a suspect?"

"Or maybe he killed Troy Drake after he missed on Jesse and me and tried to rape Molly," Suit said.

Molly sipped her new cup of coffee and winced.

"Maybe Troy knew something," she said.

"And maybe," Sunny said, "we need to tell Kevin Feeney that he might be in danger."

"Not if Drake was a jumper," Jesse said.

"Or," Suit said, "maybe Drake's death, whether he killed himself or not, had nothing to do with what happened to us."

"Let's see what Dev comes up with," Jesse said.

He had waited to tell them about his day. Now he did. Everything he'd learned from Sister Beth about Paul Hutton being the baby left in a dumpster forty years ago.

"Who does that?" Molly said.

"Maybe that's what he spent his whole life wanting to know," Sunny said.

"Something brought him here," Molly said.

"Or somebody," Jesse said.

"From everything you know," Sunny said, "there were two people at the Cain house that night. The old man and the nurse."

"You think Karina might know more than she's telling?" Jesse said.

Sunny winked at him.

"Just about all women do," she said.

# Forty-Three

The next morning Jesse and Bryce Cain were in Cain's office on the top floor of the old Paradise Bank building, a block up from the movie theater. Jesse idly wondered, but decided not to ask, if Bryce Cain had missed a day's work since his father had died.

"I don't have a lot of time for you" was his greeting as Jesse sat down.

"You rarely do," Jesse said.

"Why do you suppose?"

This was a trip down a rabbit hole for which Jesse didn't have the time or energy.

"How's your mom doing?" he said. "I haven't spoken to her since I saw her at the hospital the day your dad died."

"She's fine," Bryce said. "Like the divorce they've been in the process of having, just without any papers, is final."

"How about you?" Jesse said.

"What about me?"

Jesse took a closer look at him. He had a can of ginger ale on the desk in front of him, and a glass next to it filled with ice. He'd either skipped shaving that day or was unshaven by design, to have that stubbled look. There was puffiness under his eyes. The long hair looked like it needed washing. It was when he reached for the glass that Jesse saw the noticeable tremor in his hand. Maybe you had to have been a boozer to pick up the signs that Bryce Cain was hungover. If Jesse came around the desk, he was sure he'd be able to pick up the faint stink of last night.

"How are you dealing with his death?" Jesse said.

"All due respect?" Cain said. "None of your fucking business."

"Thanks for the pro tip."

"Why are you really here, Stone?" he said. "Because we both know it's not for grief counseling."

"Something's been bothering me," Jesse said. "The time I came to the house and Lily wasn't there, you used Paul Hutton's last name. Only, at that point, I'd never mentioned his last name to anybody outside my department."

"I don't remember saying that."

"I do."

"Who the hell knows how I knew his last name?" Cain said. "Maybe one of your cops mentioned it to somebody who mentioned it to me."

"Who?"

"Who what?"

"Who mentioned it to you?" Jesse said. "I could go talk to that person and ask which one of my cops gave out Hutton's last name."

Cain put his palms up in a helpless gesture.

"You want to know the truth?"

"Always a good option," Jesse said.

"I have no idea why I would have known his last name."

"Unless maybe you knew it before he got here."

"I told you already," he said. "My mother told you. We have no idea who this guy was. And if I did, why would I lie to a cop about it?"

"Good question," Jesse said.

Bryce Cain shook his head suddenly, the way horses do with flies. Jesse wasn't sure whether the question had startled him. Or if he was just buying time, through the fog of what was clearly a hangover. Jesse knew the look.

"Maybe you mentioned the guy's name and don't remember," Cain said. "They say that drinking kills brain cells. Maybe you lost more than you think when you were on the sauce."

" 'On the sauce,' " Jesse said. "You don't hear that a lot anymore."

"Even I know people don't have to talk to cops if they don't want to," Cain said. "Even when they've got nothing to hide. So we're done here."

"*Do* you have something to hide?"

Cain blew out a lot of air, slapped his palms on his desk, stood up.

"Done," he said.

Jesse stood up himself, knowing they were done, at least for now.

"Bryce, you need to know something," he said. "If there was a connection between Paul Hutton and your family, eventually I'm going to find it."

He knew it wasn't much of an exit line, but would have to do for now. He walked through the outer office, giving Cain's secretary his best public servant's smile on his way past her.

He thought of something Dix had told him one time about narcissists, and their lying to maintain the image they held of themselves. And how getting called out as liars made them angry.

"They know that one of these days their bullshit is going to be exposed," Dix had said.

*Just not today,* Jesse thought.

# Forty-Four

I stopped being afraid of Bo Marino a long time ago," Kevin Feeney said.

He had been out on a job when Molly had called him. Now he was back at his office. Molly and Sunny were there with him. He'd acted surprised that Troy Drake was dead, but not shocked. Or disappointed.

"Do you think he killed himself?" Feeney said.

"Unless somebody put him in the water," Molly said. "Maybe from the bridge."

"Wouldn't somebody have seen two people walking on the bridge?" Feeney said.

"Not necessarily," Molly said. "Depending on the time of night."

"What about security cameras?" Feeney said.

"On the bridge? In the process of being replaced, unfortunately," Molly said.

"You think Bo might have had something to do with it?" Feeney said.

"At this point, we're not ruling anything out," Molly said. "We went up to Maine hoping to talk to him. But he hadn't been in his house for at least a week."

"Here's what I don't understand," Feeney said. "Say it is Bo. Why would he blame me or Troy for what happened with Candace Pennington? He's the one who got us involved. You could make a case that he's the one who tried to ruin our lives, right?"

"We just want you to be aware of the potential threat," Molly said, "to both you and your wife. Is she back yet from Vermont?"

"She goes for three weeks every summer," he said. "Her dad passed away last year. It's a chance for her to get some quality time with her mom."

They could hear his phone buzzing. He took it out of his pocket, looked at it, shook his head. "Shit," he said. "I gotta go back. Somebody unplugged something at the job I just left."

"Just a couple more questions," Molly said. "Did Troy Drake attempt to reach out to you after Chief Stone brought him in for questioning?"

"He called, actually."

"Do you remember when the call was?" Sunny said.

Feeney frowned. "The day before yesterday," he said. "Said he wanted to talk, to clear the air once and for all. Said that he'd always felt as bad that he didn't stop me from going along as he was for going along himself."

"What did you say to that?" Molly said.

"I wanted to tell him that he was full of shit, but what would have been the point in that?" Feeney said. "But he *was* full of shit. Troy *liked* watching Bo do it as much as he liked doing it himself. He liked being there. And Bo told both of us that if we didn't go along, he'd tell everybody that neither one of us could get it up."

Molly thought: *For high school boys with raging hormones, a fate worse than death.*

"So you went along," she said.

"You know what they say: Go along to get along."

Neither Molly nor Sunny said anything to that.

Feeney said, "And Troy and I have been paying for it ever since. And maybe Bo, too, if he somehow became capable of taking any responsibility. Now here we all are, still talking about it all this time later." He blew out some air. "You pay and pay and pay," he said.

Molly started to speak. Feeney put up a hand to stop her.

"You think I don't see it on your face?" he said.

Talking to Molly now.

"You think I don't hear the contempt you still feel for me?" he said. "For all of us? You don't think I see it from people who were around then, every day of my life?"

"But you chose to come back," Molly said.

"Wherever I went, somebody would have found out eventually," he said.

Molly could hear his phone buzzing. He took it out of his pocket and said, "On my way."

"I can't lie to either one of you," Kevin Feeney said when his phone was back in his pocket. "If one of us had to be fished out of the water, I wish it had been Bo."

"You could be in danger, Kevin," Molly said. "If he came for Troy, he might come for you next."

"Don't worry about me," he said. "If I have to, I can go somewhere Bo would never be able to find me."

When they were in the parking lot Molly said to Sunny, "I've been bitching at Jesse for more than ten years that none of those kids did real time. But maybe, in the end, they all did."

# Forty-Five

Jesse and Vinnie Morris sat with Cokes in front of them at the Gull in the middle of the afternoon. Candace Pennington would be at Jesse's office in an hour, having told him that she'd make the trip up from Newton, that he didn't have to come to her. Suit was the one who had tracked her down. When he'd gotten her on the phone and told her that he was calling about Bo Marino and friends she said, "I hope something terrible has happened to all of them."

Vinnie said, "You still think this guy Marino is a threat to youse?"

Jesse smiled. Vinnie still sprinkled just enough of the old neighborhood into his conversation to remind you where he came from and who he was. But Jesse never needed reminding, even when their interests were aligned, the way they were now.

"He is until I establish he's not," Jesse said. "But I told you

221

when you came up that you should leave whenever you needed to."

"Still looking at this shit as a working vacation," Vinnie said.

Vinnie wore a summer blazer the color of eggshells, a white polo shirt underneath buttoned to the neck. His mannerisms, as always, were as neat and precise as a neurosurgeon's. He sipped some of his Coke, put the glass down on its coaster. Jesse was about to ask him if he'd recently had a manicure but was worried Vinnie might shoot him in broad daylight.

"Marino is missing," Jesse said. "The other one who was a part of the rape of that girl just went into the water."

"World's a random place," Vinnie said. "But my experience is that it ain't *that* random."

It was Vinnie who had dealt with Mr. Peepers, the man who'd killed Jesse's fiancée, Diana. Jesse had allowed it, if not sanctioned it. There had been times in Jesse's life, in his career as a cop, when he knew that the legal system would fall short of true justice. That was one. Vinnie had asked Jesse once about that, if he had any regrets. Jesse told him only that he wasn't able to do it himself. Vinnie had said they were probably more alike than Jesse liked to think. Jesse told him not to let that get around. Somehow their similarities had never gotten in the way of their differences, at least so far.

They sat quietly now and looked out the front window.

"I was thinking today," Vinnie said, "that looking at the water is like looking at ass. You think you'd never get tired of it, but you do."

Jesse smiled.

Vinnie said, "Who you think will leave town first, Sunny or me?"

Jesse smiled again.

"You asking me to choose?"

"Just curious."

"Unclear," Jesse said.

Now Vinnie almost smiled.

"You think about it," he said, "what the fuck isn't?"

Jesse said, "Who watches Elena when you're not?"

"Don't worry about it," Vinnie said.

"I'm the chief of police," Jesse said. "Makes me a worrier by nature."

"No shit," Vinnie said. "Why I'm here."


**C**andace Pennington was no longer the scared, wounded teenager that Jesse remembered. She was a beautiful and confident young woman, entering Jesse's office as if she wanted to sell him something, or buy the whole place. She was very blond now, wearing a rose-colored summer dress. The strap of her Apple Watch seemed to try to match the color of the dress. Maybe she had a collection of them. He noticed a simple gold band on the ring finger of her left hand.

She sat across from Jesse's desk, in one of the two visitor's chairs. Molly sat next to her.

"I appreciate you making the ride up here," Jesse said.

"My first time here in years," she said. "What's the old line? Happiness for me was Paradise in my rearview mirror."

Molly said, "How are your parents?"

"Divorced," Candace said. "My dad's still an architect, working in New York City now. My mother is full-time on Nantucket." She sighed. "Trying to live her best life."

There were things that stayed with you. Jesse could still remember Margaret Pennington slapping the back of Candace's head from the chair in which Molly sat now.

"I liked your dad," Jesse said.

"I do, too," she said.

"Still remember him slugging Bo and *his* dad," Jesse said.

"He's still grateful that you let him."

"Better him than me," Jesse said.

Candace Pennington folded her hands in her lap.

"I heard about Troy," she said. "Did he kill himself?"

"To be determined," Molly said.

"And you think Bo might have had something to do with it?" Candace said.

"Also to be determined," Jesse said.

"I'm not afraid of him," Candace Pennington said.

"We're not saying you should be," Molly said. "We just wanted you to be aware." Then told her about the attacks against Jesse and her and Suit, about Bo's house seeming to have been abandoned, now Troy's death.

"Have you noticed anything in your own life lately out of the ordinary?" Molly said.

"My life since high school has been out of the ordinary," Candace said.

"Are you married?" Jesse said.

"Not that it's relevant, Chief Stone," she said, "but I am."

"Has your husband noticed anything out of the ordinary?" Jesse said.

"Wife," Candace Pennington said. "And no."

Jesse saw Molly smiling at Candace Pennington. "Chief Stone," she said, "sometimes isn't nearly as modern as he likes to think he is."

"We're not trying to alarm you," Jesse said. "Just wanted you to be aware of our circumstances. And how they might impact your own."

"So you're still looking out for me," she said.

"In a way," Jesse said, "I guess I am."

"What about the other one, Kevin Feeney?" Candace said. "Whatever happened to him."

Molly told her.

"So he left and came back," Candace said. "Maybe he finally grew a pair. He always seemed to be the weakest of the three."

"He said what you said," Molly said. "He's no longer afraid of Bo Marino."

Candace smoothed out the front of her dress.

"I let all of them control my life for a long time," she said. "For far too long after I left town. I have no plans to ever let them do it again." She looked at Jesse. "There was a time when I wanted to kill all of them. Would it shock you to know I learned how to shoot a gun?"

Jesse smiled.

"Forewarned is forearmed," he said.

"I wish I'd had a gun back in those days," she said.

She leaned back in her chair and closed her eyes for a moment.

"Not one of them ever sought me out to apologize," she said. "I'm not sure I would have accepted it. But none of them even tried. Not even Kevin, the one the other two made fun of because he didn't want his turn." Her eyes were still closed. It was as if she were talking to herself. "You know the only boy in the whole school who apologized? A friend of theirs who didn't go along with them that night. Jerry Brock."

Molly said, "He's still in town. I think he's in real estate now."

"He swore he had no idea that it would go that far," Candace said. "But that he should have said something to me."

Then she asked Molly if she could have a private moment with Jesse before she left. Molly shook her hand and left. Then it was just Jesse and Candace, in the same office where they'd met when she was a girl scared of everything and everybody: Bo and Kevin Feeney and Troy Drake and her classmates. And her bitch of a mother.

"You were there when I needed you," she said. "I'll never forget that."

"Part of the job."

"But you don't have to worry about me anymore," she said. "You know what they say. What doesn't kill you makes you stronger."

"Glad to hear it," he said.

"And I'll tell you a little secret," she said. "When I fire my weapon, I hit what I'm aiming at."

She gave him a quick hug before she left. As she did she said, "You better find him before I do."

"Wasn't aware you were looking for him," Jesse said.

"Figure of speech," Candace Pennington said, then was gone.

# Forty-Six

They had skipped dinner and gone straight to bed.

"I feel like a babysitter fooling around with my boyfriend," Sunny said, "while I'm on the clock."

"Should I have tried to finish before Mom and Dad got home?" Jesse said.

Sunny grinned.

"I'm sorry," she said. "*Did* you finish?"

"We could be getting better at this."

"*This* meaning sex," she said, "or us?"

"Thinking both."

"Michael Crane isn't going to be away at sea forever," Sunny said. "And when he's back, I'm back to Boston. And real life."

"This isn't real?"

"You know what I mean."

He did. She knew he did, as they lay in the big bed, Jesse just having gotten up to open a window. He'd kept it closed before because he said he didn't want to frighten the neigh-bors.

"Do we need to talk about this now?" he said.

"*This* meaning us?" she said.

"And feelings?"

She grinned again. "You can do it, soldier."

Jesse said, "They tell us in my club not to project."

"The club does seem to be working for you."

"Day at a time."

"Like us," she said.

"Long as we don't project."

"In the old days," Sunny said, "we'd be having a drink right now."

"Those were the days," Jesse said. "Until they weren't."

"You still miss it?"

"Every damn day," he said.

"And night?" Sunny said.

"More at night," he said.

He heard a boat horn in the distance, then another. He turned to look through the window at the splash of pale color in the sky, as if daylight were hanging on as long as it could. *Another day sober,* he thought. But way too early to spike the ball. He hadn't been to a meeting since his last one at Marshport. Maybe tomorrow. It was one of his dirty secrets about drinking. One of many. Sometimes talking about it made him miss it more. Went against all the talking they did in the rooms. There it was, anyway.

Sunny turned to face him, chin cupped in her hand, blond hair covering half her face.

"You think you'll ever drink again?" she said.

"Cole always asks me that," he said.

"What's the answer?"

"Yes."

"Really."

"Really," he said.

"When?"

"When I'm old," he said. "Just don't know how old. But you'll be the first to know, if you're still around."

"Just not today."

"So far."

They turned into each other, at almost the exact same moment.

"We need to change the subject," he said.

"And talk shop?" she said.

"No," he said.

He kissed her. She kissed him back.

"Oh, that," Sunny said.

# Forty-Seven

It turned out Jesse didn't have to go looking for Karina Torres, she came to him.

She was waiting in front of Jesse's building when he came out the next morning, a little after eight o'clock, Sunny already on her way to the gym. Karina was wearing a T-shirt and jeans, sneakers, and a baseball cap with the yacht club emblem on the front.

She told him they needed to talk.

"Agreed," Jesse said. "But we could have talked at the station."

"I did not want people to know."

"The Cains, you mean."

She shrugged. Jesse said, "Let's take a walk."

They headed for the beach, the same route Jesse had taken the night he'd gone after the shooter in the rain. But when they got to the water today, he saw how calm it was, and quiet, the waves hitting the sand as softly as a pillow hitting a bed.

Karina had been silent on the walk over, occasionally looking over her shoulder, as if someone might be watching them.

"So what's on your mind," Jesse said.

"Mr. Bryce Cain," she said. "He is a bad man."

"Not exactly breaking news," he said.

"He was terrible to his father until the end," she said.

"Evidenced in what way?"

"The fighting," she said.

"About what?"

"Money," she said. "What else do the rich fight about?"

They walked in the direction of the Stiles Island Bridge. Jesse saw some fishing nets in the distance, assuming that the nets had been hauled and they were on their way back in. Jesse liked fishermen as well as anybody in Paradise. They were hardworking, no-bullshit people. Like him. He envied them sometimes, their workday ending as his was usually beginning. And he liked looking at the boats. Vinnie Morris might be tired of looking at the ocean, but he was not. For all the Higher Power talk in AA, the ocean was one of the things that actually made Jesse believe there was one.

She retreated again into silence. Jesse saw a long, thick piece of driftwood ahead of them. He gestured at it. They sat.

"What about money?" Jesse said. "Is Bryce afraid they're going to run out sometime before the world ends?"

"He had gotten very upset about his father's will a month or so ago," she said, "though I do not know why. Mr. Bryce would always make me leave the room when they'd start to argue. One time I was in the hall and heard Mr. Cain say that it was still his money. And Mr. Bryce said, 'Not for long.'"

"One big happy family," Jesse said.

"Never," she said.

He reached down, picked up a small, smooth stone, side-armed it from a sitting position into the water. And felt the same pull he always did behind his shoulder when he tried to make any kind of throw, like being pulled back into the past.

"They could not wait for him to be dead," Karina said. "And for the money to be all theirs."

"You say *them*," Jesse said. "That include Lily?"

"They would fight, too," she said.

"About the money?"

"Not the money," she said. "Sometimes I thought they fought like people just trying to stay in practice. The worst was about six months ago. She went to Florida and came back and said she was selling the Florida house, it was just sitting there empty now. He said it was the only place where he had happy memories, and she'd have to do it over his dead body. I was in the room this time. And she smiled at him, not in a nice way, and said, 'Have it your way.'"

Jesse threw another stone into the waves. The pain wasn't as bad this time. Maybe he was just getting warmed up.

"There are secrets in that house," she said. "Maybe you can find out what they are. I will not be around long enough."

"You're leaving?"

"Mr. Cain the son told me I could stay until the end of the month," Karina said. "He fired me like I was one of the land-scapers."

Jesse stood now, reached down with his hand to help her up. The sound of the waves had picked up force and volume.

"Why'd you really come to me today?" Jesse said.

"Are you a spiritual person, Chief Stone?" she said.

He told her that he supposed he felt the presence of God when he was this close to the water as much as he did anywhere else.

"But do you believe in the spirit world?" she said.

"You mean ghosts?" Jesse said.

She nodded. "There are ghosts in that family," she said.

Jesse said, "I thought we were just talking about secrets. Whit talked to me about secrets the last time I saw him."

"Sometimes they're the same," Karina said. "Secrets and ghosts."

He asked if she wanted him to drop her somewhere. She said she wanted to walk. He told her it was a long walk back to the Cains'. She said she didn't care.

"Good luck," he said, shaking her hand when they were back in front of his building.

"Maybe you're the one who needs luck," she said.

"You can say that again," Jesse said.

# Forty-Eight

Ellen Chagnon, Jesse's bartender friend from Florida, called in the late afternoon and asked if Jesse had forgotten her. Never, he said. She called him a liar and said that they hadn't forgotten him down there, and that her manager had found a credit card receipt with Paul's name on it.

He asked her to send a screenshot, and within seconds his cell phone pinged and there it was. He thanked her. She said that maybe someday he could thank her in person. He told her he was kind of involved with somebody these days.

Ellen Chagnon said, "I'm not jealous."

"Good to know," Jesse said.

"You think this will help?" she said.

"Like they say," Jesse said. "Couldn't hurt."

Jesse told Suit to call Dan Malmon at the DA's office, send him the screenshot, and tell him they needed to subpoena Hutton's credit card history from Capital One.

"On it," Suit said at his desk. Then he grinned and said to Jesse, "What's in your wallet?"

"What?"

"The Capital One commercials," Suit said. "With Samuel L. Jackson and Jennifer Garner?"

"Who's Jennifer Garner?"

"Seriously?" Suit said. "She was married to Ben Affleck."

"The actor who's the Red Sox fan," Jesse said.

"Luther," Molly said from behind them, "I don't know why you even try."

"Dan knows the drill," Jesse said, ignoring them. "He's just got to find the rep from Capital One. They all have one. Tell them it's exigent circumstances."

"Life and death," Suit said.

Molly said, "You have learned well, grasshopper."

"What grasshopper?" Suit said.

Sunny was at Molly's house, walking Rosie the dog. Jesse told Molly and Suit he was going out for a drive.

"Anywhere in particular?" Molly said.

"Securing the perimeter," he said.

"You want to get away and think and you don't want us bothering you," she said.

"Sounds so impersonal when you put it that way," he said.

"Dinner later with the women in your life?"

"Sounds good."

He thought about calling Dix, seeing if Dix had time this afternoon. Sometimes his brain just worked better when he was in the same room with Dix. Hanging around with someone smarter.

He drove aimlessly for a while, past Indian Hill overlooking the harbor, where they'd once found the body of a radio guy named Walton Weeks. Then he was going over the bridge and into Stiles Island, thinking back to the time when the bridge had blown and the island had essentially been taken hostage by Jimmy Macklin and Wilson Cromartie, known as Crow. Then to Paradise Neck on the causeway and back.

Karina Torres had talked about ghosts and the Cains. They weren't the only ones who had them. But you thought too hard on them, Jesse knew from experience, and they could drive you to drink. He drove to Marshport for the six o'clock meeting at the First Episcopal Church.

Couldn't hurt.

# Forty-Nine

**W**hy would Bryce and Whit have been arguing about money?" Jesse said to Lily.

"I forget sometimes," Lily said, "Are you investigating us, or your murder?"

"I can't do both?" Jesse said.

They were at a window table at the yacht club the next morning. Lily had told Jesse she preferred meeting there, wanted to get out of the house. Karina, she told him, was packing up Whit Cain's clothes, and she didn't need a front-row seat to that. Jesse had asked if it was all right to wear jeans to the yacht club, it had been so long since he'd been there he'd forgotten the dress code. Lily reminded him that he'd be there with her, and could wear whatever the fuck he wanted to.

"In answer to your question," she said, "my son and my husband argued about everything."

She wore what looked to be business clothes. A pale green

linen blazer over a white shirt. Black pants. When Jesse had told her she looked nice before sitting down she told him to get over it, she was on her way to a board meeting.

"Should be spelled B-O-R-E-D," she said.

Now she tilted her head slightly. "Only Karina could have told you they were arguing about money," she said. Lily smiled. "But then she never thought of herself as working for me, not from the start. Always him. I always wondered if she'd been one of his girls down in Florida, as much as they both denied it."

Jesse tucked that observation away and returned to the topic of Bryce and Whit. "Seems odd, though," Jesse said. "Wouldn't their wars about money have been fought a long time ago?"

"Odd for everybody else," she said, "or for the Cains?"

"Was it about the will?"

"My," Lily said, "how truly chatty Miss Karina has become. At this rate, she's going to be lucky to make it to the end of the month."

"She's leaving?"

"Bryce's decision," Lily said. "But I didn't do much to stop him."

Jesse said, "I think she still sees herself as taking care of him."

"What, his ashes?"

Jesse sipped coffee, Lily her tea. For the moment Jesse felt as if they'd gone to neutral corners.

Lily said, "I still don't see what this has to do with this man Paul Hutton's death."

"Still trying to figure out why he was here."

Lily smiled again. "The existential question," she said. "Why are any of us here?"

"I heard there were also arguments between Whit and you," Jesse said.

No point in trying to protect Karina now. They were past that. Jesse imagined her packing up her own belongings before the day was out.

"Karina," Lily said.

"Don't blame her," Jesse said.

"She will be well compensated with parting gifts," Lily said. "Or maybe she thinks of it as combat pay at this point."

"Don't mess with Lily Cain," Jesse said.

"We've known each other a long time, Jesse," she said. "By now you should know as well as anyone that I'm a good sport until I'm not."

"Were you always this tough?"

"Let me ask you a question," she said. "Don't you think I had to be?"

"*Was* there an issue with the will?"

"No."

"No recent changes that might have upset Bryce?"

"Bryce was about to get everything he wanted," she said. "The money and the power."

"Didn't he have enough of both already?"

Lily sighed. "The only way my son was ever going to get out of his father's shadow," she said, "was when there was no shadow."

Jesse imagined Karina now, in the big bedroom on the

second floor, packing up secrets along with the old man's clothes. Maybe ones she hadn't shared with Jesse.

"Could Paul Hutton have had something on Whit?" Jesse said. "Something he thought he could use to shake him down, like shaking a money tree?"

"Many tried that with my husband," Lily said. "Hardly any ever succeeded."

"What happened to them?"

She smiled. "They went away and never came back."

"I thought that's the way Whit's father was supposed to have done business," Jesse said.

"My husband," she said, "never completely abandoned those methods. Especially if he thought someone was after his money."

"Paul Hutton was abandoned as a baby in Florida," Jesse said, "not far from Palm Beach. Left in a dumpster."

"Good Lord," she said. "Who would do such a thing?"

"Someone."

"And you think it's somehow part of the story?" Lily said.

"His story, anyway."

"You don't give up."

"If it was a member of your family who got shot in the back of the head, would you want me to?" Jesse said.

Lily smiled a thin smile. "Which member?"

She sighed again. "Jesse, I would help you if I could," she said. "You know I would. But I can't."

"There was a reason he came here."

"You're convinced he wanted something from us."

Jesse shrugged.

"If he'd lived," Lily said, "he would have had to take a fuck-ing number."

She said "fucking" loud enough that the nearest waiter turned his head.

"Man, you are tough," Jesse said.

He smiled at her now.

"You know the old line about how getting old isn't for sis-sies?" Lily said.

"Lot of people gave Paul Newman credit," Jesse said. "But an old actor I knew back in L.A. said it was actually Bette Davis."

"Either way," Lily said. "Being a Cain isn't for sissies, ei-ther."

"You must have wanted it," Jesse said. "And Whit."

"Not as much as he wanted me," Lily said.

# Fifty

**C**andace Pennington's wife was waiting for Jesse when he got back to the office.

She introduced herself as Anderson Pennington, told Jesse she went by Andy, and that she had taken Pennington as her married name. All in the first thirty seconds, before she got to it.

"Candace is missing," she said.

They were in the front lobby. She was short and dark-haired, looked older than Candace. There was so much nervous energy to her Jesse imagined a sprinter about to come out of the blocks.

"Let's go into my office," he said.

He saw Suit at his desk. No sign of Molly or Sunny. Jesse motioned her into his office, and into a chair across from his desk.

"I think she's been taken," Andy Pennington said. "And that's my best-case scenario."

"Tell me about it," Jesse said.

She clasped her hands in front of her.

"I haven't heard from her since she left here yesterday," she said. "I was in Los Angeles, about to get on a flight. Delayed, of course. Originally supposed to get in about midnight. Didn't end up landing until two."

You had to let them tell it their way.

"She called when I was going through security," Andy Pennington said. "Said she was going to see an old friend. It was a bad connection. Kept breaking up. One of those stupid 'Can you hear me?' calls. I told her I'd call her when I was at the gate. When I tried, it went straight to voicemail. I texted her from the plane. No response."

"Might she have had a couple drinks at dinner and decided to spend the night?" Jesse said. "Rather than leave her car?"

"I've already checked every hotel and inn around here," she said.

She hugged herself now, as if to keep herself from flying apart.

"Do you have that friend-finding app on your phone?"

"We both do," Andy Pennington said. "But it's either died or been turned off. Or somebody smashed it to bits. The last location was Paradise." She shook her head. "What a fucking name for this place, by the way," she said.

Jesse verified Candace Pennington's number with her, wrote it down. Told her that if the phone was still intact, they had ways to ping it, through her carrier.

"Could she have lost the phone somehow?" he said.

"Impossible," she said. "She's one of those people who

takes her phone with her into the bathroom." She was rocking back and forth now in her chair. "Something terrible has happened," she said. "You know how you know things? I *know*."

Then she muttered, more to herself than to him, "I never should have let her come back here."

"If she's still here," Jesse said, "we'll find her."

It was just bullshit small talk. He wasn't sure if she was even listening to him. She was helpless and angry and scared. Growing more frantic by the moment. He imagined the inside of her head being filled with voices, all her own.

"We may find out there's a simple explanation," Jesse said.

"Stop saying 'we'!" she said. "There is no *we*. There's just Candace out there somewhere. All because she came back to this godforsaken place."

"Her text didn't say who the old friend was?"

She shook her head.

"*Did* she still have friends up here?"

"A few girls who didn't abandon her back then," Andy Pennington said. "She said most of the girls treated her like she was wearing some sort of scarlet letter, the bitches."

"Do you remember any names?"

She shook her head again.

"It has to be Bo Marino," she said. "Candace told me what was going on up here. That he'd come back for you and your friends. But maybe it was her he wanted all along."

Jesse asked her if Candace had an E-ZPass on her car. She said she did. Jesse asked if she could get the number.

She pulled it up on her phone and gave it to him. "I pay the bills," she said.

He told her he would check to see if there had been any activity on the pass, and that they would recanvas all the hotels and inns. He asked if Candace had ever been in contact with Kevin Feeney.

"The other member of the Paradise Three?" she said. "Never."

"Candace said she had a gun," Jesse said, "and that she knows how to use it."

"Damn right," she said. "Concealed carry permit and everything. Just like a big girl."

"Would she have it with her?"

Candace hadn't had a purse with her when she'd come to the office. Maybe she hadn't wanted to bring a gun into a police station.

"I'm sure she had it with her," Andy Pennington said. "She doesn't go to Whole Foods without it."

Jesse said to her, "Without offending you, I need to ask one more question."

"Everything is offending me this morning," she said.

"If she somehow saw Bo Marino in Paradise," he said, "is there any chance that she was the one after him, and not the other way around?"

# Fifty-One

J esse told her he would be in touch as soon as he heard something. She said she was driving back to Newton, just because she didn't want to be in Paradise, Massachusetts, five minutes longer.

When she was gone, Suit knocked on Jesse's door and told him he'd just received Paul Hutton's credit card records from the DA's office.

"How far back do they go?" Jesse said.

"Ten years," Suit said.

"Fuck," Jesse said.

"Took the bad word right out of my mouth," Suit said. "Anything in particular we're looking for here?"

"Anything interesting and everything."

"Fuck," Suit said.

"We just need to get a sense of where he spent whatever money he had," Jesse said. "Where he ate and drank. Amazon charges. Plane tickets. Car rentals. Flag what you think needs to be flagged and we'll go over it together when you're done."

"Ten years," Suit said.

"You want me to get Gabe or Peter to help?" Jesse said.

"I got this," Suit said.

"Pretend you're following the guy," Jesse said.

"Through a goddamn spreadsheet?" Suit said. "Not exactly a high-speed chase."

Jesse called Molly, who was on her way in with Sunny. He told her about Andy Pennington, and told her they should take a detour to Kevin Feeney's office. If Bo had somehow surfaced with Candace, maybe Feeney was in danger, too.

They called back fifteen minutes later and said there was no one at the office. No answer when they tried Feeney's phone. No sign on the door that he'd be back in fifteen minutes. They said they were on their way to his house next. Called back again and said nobody was home and no car in the driveway. Yesterday's *Globe* on the doorstep.

He looked down at the yellow legal pad in front of him. He'd written PARADISE THREE when Andy Pennington had used the expression. But there was an unwilling fourth person there that night: Candace. Her life about to be changed forever. Like all of them. Only she was the one who'd had no choice in the matter.

"Four people there that night in high school," Jesse said to Molly. "Right now they're all gone."

"All?" she said.

"Bo, Kevin, Troy, Candace."

He was on speaker. He heard Sunny say, "Kevin said if he had to, he could go someplace where Bo couldn't find him."

"Maybe he did," Jesse said.

"Or maybe he's missing along with Candace," Molly said.

"Or he's the reason Candace is missing," Jesse said.

Molly said, "Maybe we need to track down Kevin's wife and talk to her."

"Remind me where she is," Jesse said.

"He said she was visiting family in Vermont," Molly said.

"We know what her name is?" Jesse said. "Or maiden name?"

"Never asked," Molly said. "She only came up in passing."

"Maybe we need to find out," Jesse said.

He sat there at his desk and stared back down at his pad. PARADISE THREE. He picked up his pen and scratched out *three* and wrote a 5 over it.

"What are you going to do?" Sunny said.

"Go talk to somebody who wasn't there that night in high school," Jesse said.

# Fifty-Two

J esse hadn't mentioned it to Molly or Sunny, but he had seen Jerry Brock at a few AA meetings, in a basement room at the Paradise YMCA. Jesse heard him speak one time, mostly about his drinking days at Boston University, where he said he tried to set binge-drinking records that might never be broken, at least not by anybody wanting to live past the age of thirty.

But he had never once mentioned a friendship with Bo or Troy Drake or Kevin Feeney. He hadn't come forward to volunteer information when they were all at Paradise High together. At the time, Jesse and Molly and Suit had spoken to a lot of students at Paradise High, both boys and girls. Just not all, and not him. The first time Jesse had ever heard his name associated with the rape had been from Candace Pennington the day before.

Jerry was currently a vice president of Cain Real Estate. His father, Ned, was a member of the Board of Selectmen, and had been when Jerry was in high school. Maybe he was the one who had advised his son to keep his mouth shut and head down. Now he was clean and sober, or had been the last time Jesse had seen him at a meeting, with a wife and young son.

When Jesse had called, Jerry Brock had told him to come right over. Things were quiet these days in the real estate business; it was a buyer's market in Paradise.

"What does that really mean, I've always wondered?" Jesse had said.

"It generally means no market," Brock had said. "The council is thinking about passing a town ordinance making everybody take down their *For Sale* signs. They think it's a bad optic."

The night Jerry'd spoken at AA, he'd said he replaced going to bars with going to the gym. It showed. His upper body strained against a tight black polo shirt. The tattoos on his upper arms looked as if they'd been chiseled onto him and not inked there. Jesse wondered if the tatts were a product of his drinking days, idly wondering, not for the first time, when tattoos had started taking over the world.

"Is this about Troy?" Jerry Brock said.

He'd made them both coffee from his own Keurig.

"Peripherally," Jesse said. "It's actually about all of them."

"What a group," he said.

"Candace told me that it nearly included you," Jesse said.

His cup was nearly to his mouth. He stopped it, put it back down.

"She told you that?"

"And that you apologized later."

He put a big hand to his forehead and rubbed it hard.

"I should have said something to her," he said. "But I was a coward, afraid of Bo the way everybody in school was." He blew out some air. "It's amazing now when I think back, and I think back on that a lot, that I didn't drink about half a bottle of vodka and go along."

"Candace was here yesterday to talk to me," Jesse said. "Later that evening she told her partner that she'd run into a friend. Wasn't you by any chance, was it?"

He shook his head.

"I'd actually like to have seen her," he said. "But it's funny. I'd already taken care of step eight with her before I was ever in the program, when I apologized. The one about making things right with people you'd wronged."

"Know the drill," Jesse said.

Brock frowned at Jesse now. "Wait, what was she doing here?"

Jesse told him about the attacks on the department, the death of Troy Drake. And about Bo and Candace having gone missing, and perhaps Kevin Feeney, too.

"Had you seen Troy Drake around town?" Jesse said.

Brock shook his head.

"What about Bo?" Jesse said. "Any contact with him since high school?"

Another shake of the head.

"Kevin I ran into one time," he said. "It was the night of the ceremony at the movie theater. Saw him on the street after. Everybody else was going out. I was going home. Almost didn't recognize him with the beard."

Molly and Sunny hadn't mentioned a beard.

"So you two talked?"

"He told me he'd opened some kind of techy business," Brock said. "Gave me a business card, asked if I could throw him some business. He must have rented his space from some other agency, and I just missed it."

"Was he with his wife that night?" Jesse said. "We're trying to locate her."

Brock smiled now.

"His *wife*?" he said.

"He told Molly Crane she was away visiting his in-laws," Jesse said.

"Chief," Jerry Brock said. "Kevin's not married."

"He told Molly he was."

Brock shook his head. "That night, he asked me if I was married, and just to be polite I asked him the same. I'd always felt bad for Kevin, at least before what happened to Candace. He was the weak one of the three. Some of the guys used to call him Bo's bitch. The rumor about him, after what they did to Candace, was that he couldn't even get it up."

Jesse took a deep breath, let it out slowly. A Dix drill for relaxation. Feel it coming in, feel it going out.

"But he told you he wasn't married."

"Said he'd just gotten dumped," Brock said. "Tried to make a joke out of it, actually. 'Same old Feens,' he said. 'Even when he can get a girl, can't hold on to her.' Then he said he had to bounce, he had to go meet somebody."

"So nothing about Vermont?" Jesse said.

Brock gave Jesse a "What the fuck?" look.

"Why would he have been talking about Vermont?" he said.

# Fifty-Three

J esse and Suit and Molly and Sunny were back in the conference room. Jesse had already put Candace's name and information into the National Crime Information Center. He'd called Lundquist and told him she was a possible abduction, gave him all of her information. They both knew that the longer you waited when someone was missing, the chances of finding the person safe diminished by the hour.

"We're going to find her," Jesse said.

"If she's alive," Sunny said.

"She's alive," Jesse said.

"Because?" Suit said.

"Because she has to be," Jesse said.

They had put her license plate number into the system, along with Kevin Feeney's. And Bo Marino's. Gabe Weathers was in charge of trying to get a hit on either Feeney's phone or Candace's. Jesse had asked Molly and Sunny if Kevin Feeney had a beard. They said he did not. He knew it meant nothing, he could have shaved it off the next morning. But Annie Fallon said the man who'd tried to rape her had a beard.

"Why would Feeney tell us he was married when he's not?" Molly said.

"It was even more elaborate than that," Sunny said. "He said he'd told her about what had happened in high school."

"Sometimes one lie falls apart, the whole thing falls apart," Jesse said.

"Do we really think it's him and not Bo?" Molly said.

Jesse said, "Candace and Jerry Brock both said he was the weak one. Brock said they called him Bo's bitch in high school. Maybe it ate him up a long time, until he got tired of being the weak one."

"Unless we're making too much out of a stupid lie from this guy," Molly said.

"Or stupid fantasy," Sunny said.

"My experience?" Jesse said. "You start lying, you don't stop. Like a drunk telling himself he's just going to have one."

"So now we think that everything we thought Bo was doing, Feeney might have been doing?" Suit said. "Does that mean he might have gone after Bo, too?"

Molly was turning her pen over in her fingers.

"Or it's still Bo and both Candace and Feeney are in trouble whether Feeney lied or not," she said.

They sat there in silence. They all had their phones on the table in front of them, not one making a sound. *Figured,* Jesse thought. They never rang when you wanted them to.

He looked at Sunny.

"You up for breaking into another house?" he said.

"Feeney's?" she said.

He nodded.

"You want to aid and abet this time?" Sunny said.

"I'm going to his office," Jesse said.

"And break in there?" Molly said.

"If the alarm sounds," he said, "what are they going to do, call the cops?"

He stood.

"I hate being lied to," he said.

"Technically it was me he lied to," Molly said.

Jesse told her it was a distinction without a difference.

# Fifty-Four

**B**efore he left the station Jesse told Gabe to stay on Feeney's phone. They both knew how many dead zones there were in Paradise. He could still be in town and holed up, with Candace and the phone, in one of those zones. Feeney was a tech guy, though they had no way of knowing how good he was. Maybe he knew the possibilities of enhanced GPS, whether a phone was turned on or not. Maybe not. Or maybe he was already in some remote area nowhere near Paradise and had ditched his phone and hers.

Maybe when he said he was going somewhere where Bo couldn't find him, he meant somewhere *they* couldn't find him.

If it was him, though, he'd make a mistake. These mutts always did. Then they'd find him.

*Check that,* Jesse told himself.

I'll *find him.*

"Lot going on in our sleepy little town," Gabe Weathers said.

"Have I ever mentioned that I don't like being lied to?" Jesse said.

He still didn't know where Bo fit. Maybe he'd never been in it. Maybe he was dead like Troy Drake. Or maybe Feeney was still Bo's bitch and they'd been in on it together. Maybe they'd missed on Jesse, Molly, and Suit and were raising their game as they went along. In the end, Jesse told himself, it didn't matter. Even Paul Hutton didn't matter right now.

All that mattered right now was that Candace Pennington needed saving again.

There was a dumpster in the small parking lot behind Feeney's office. No other cars. Jesse got out and tried the door handle. Locked. He took his gun out and used the butt end to break the window, reached through, unlocked it. Maybe there was a silent alarm, maybe not, didn't matter. Jesse didn't care either way. If it wasn't Feeney, he'd pay for the window later. If Feeney *did* have Candace, this was no time to dick around.

It was just two small, stuffy rooms. No AC. There was an empty desk in what looked like a reception area. Molly and Sunny said there had been no sign of an assistant when they'd been there, no reference to one. They hadn't seen Feeney's office. Jesse walked into it now, went through the drawers of his desk. There were some pens and index cards in the top left. In the middle drawer were a couple credit card receipts, both from the Gull. He took them, folded them neatly, and stuck them in the breast pocket of his shirt. More credit card records for Suit to check out. Jesse imagined his excitement.

Jesse knew Feeney had been in this office as recently as a few days ago, but it still felt abandoned to him. No landline, no laptop, no computer, no iPad. Molly said he'd taken a call while they'd been with him, saying he had to get to a job. But where? With whom? Business did not appear to be booming at KF Audio Visual Services.

If there was any business at all.

The picture that Molly had mentioned, of the woman Feeney said was his wife, was on the wall in the reception area. Jesse walked back to study it more closely. Young blond woman, smiling at the camera, standing in front of a tree, more trees behind her. She could have been anywhere.

Where was she?

*Who* was she?

Maybe someone Kevin Feeney had just photoshopped into his fantasy life.

Had he cleared out because he was afraid Bo was coming for him? Or had he been hiding in plain sight all along? Maybe it had been Candace Pennington he wanted, and Jesse had done everything except deliver her to him, gift-wrapped?

Jesse checked the file cabinet next to the window.

Empty.

He sat down behind Feeney's desk. Thinking about lies now, and the way people told them, even when talking to a cop. Knowing from experience how often they folded truth into their lies, making them easier to manage. Almost like they were using truth to prop up the lies.

Drake was dead. They couldn't find Bo. Or Candace. For now all they had was Feeney.

Jesse slammed his right hand hard on the desk, the sound like the crack of a bat in the empty office.

*Think,* he told himself.

You were supposed to think more clearly now that you were clean and sober. That's what they told you in the books and the meetings. You started to get better as soon as you put down the drink.

Just maybe not smarter.

He sat there now and remembered how he'd feel when he'd wake up hungover. One of those mornings when he wasn't sure if he was waking up or coming to. Knowing that the cop—the *chief*—who loved being in control had been out of control again. Feeling weak, scared, as afraid of today as he was of last night. Helpless sometimes.

He felt that way now.

*Think, goddamn it.*

He leaned back in the swivel chair and closed his eyes.

Feency's imaginary wife could have lived anywhere, but he'd said Vermont. Maybe that was where he'd slipped up. Maybe thinking they'd never check.

Truth in a lie.

He went out the back door and got behind the wheel of the Explorer. He called Suit and read him the number on the credit card receipt.

"Another credit card check?" Suit said. "You're shitting me."

"Do I sound like I am?"

"No, sir," Suit said. "Looking for anything in particular?"

He told him, and told him to ask Molly to call the tax people in Vermont, or whoever up there could get her access to property records, and see if Kevin Feeney owned any property in the state.

"And tell them it's exigent circumstances, am I right?" Suit said.

"Look at you," Jesse said.

Then Jesse called Dix.

# Fifty-Five

As usual he was pressed and clean, bald head gleaming, nails looking as if they'd been manicured that morning. Dix looked as if he'd just come out of the box.

"This is a drive-through," Jesse said.

"I can tell."

"Thanks for seeing me on short notice."

"When you said it was important," he said, "I moved some things around, because it generally means you're not screwing around."

"Fuckin' ay."

"Tell me."

Jesse did. When he finished, Dix said, "So you're convinced it's him and not the Marino kid."

"Not convinced," Jesse said. "But leaning hard that way. What I need to know, just off what *I* know, is if you think Feeney could fit some kind of squirrely profile."

"Squirrely," Dix said. "I don't remember that from William James."

"Rage, revenge, guilt," Jesse said. "Could all of it have finally exploded the way his bomb didn't?"

"I'd like to know a lot more about his life between high school and now," Dix said, "but, sure. And don't forget humiliation. This guy got humiliated in front of the school, the town, everybody. That might be the emotion driving the bus."

"Could have internalized it for a long time."

"Now externalizing," Dix said.

"And he could have acted out in all these different ways? Even killed the Drake kid?"

"You're convinced he put him in the water?"

"Same deal," Jesse said. "Not convinced, but leaning."

"What about the Marino kid?"

"If he killed Drake," Jesse said, "maybe he killed him, too. Maybe first."

"You think it's Feeney who tried to rape Molly?" Dix said. "Didn't you say it was Marino that Molly sprayed with Mace and cuffed in the bus that day?"

"It was," Jesse said. "And another woman nearly got raped the night of the marquee lighting. By a guy with a beard. Feeney still had a beard then." Jesse put out his hands, surrendering. "Maybe it doesn't all fit neatly into the box."

"Sometimes not everything does."

"I'm not asking for a full workup," Jesse said. "But could Feeney be this fucked-up?"

Dix almost smiled. "More William James," he said. "But, yeah."

"Blaming anyone and everyone for ruining his life because he doesn't want to blame himself," Jesse said.

"You're pretty observant," Dix said, "for a small-town cop."

"Years of practice finally paid off."

"Could be a lot going on with this guy, if he is your guy," Dix said. "I'm guessing he might never have been able to have a relationship with a woman. Or keep a job for very long. Maybe the marriage and the photograph and all the rest of what he told Molly are a way for him to create the life he once imagined for himself."

"And in the modern world," Jesse said, "any woman he did meet would be able to check out his name online pretty easily."

"And find out who he is, and what he did," Dix said. "You said that they kept him off the sex offender list, correct?"

"Rita Fiore ended up lawyering all of them on that one," Jesse said. "She's very good."

Dix said, "But even if he wasn't on the list, if a woman he was interested in found out . . ."

"She'd run like hell the other way," Jesse said.

"And maybe every time that happened," Dix said, "the wolf would get a little closer to the door."

"Maybe," Jesse said, "he's always been obsessed with Candace."

"And saved her for last," Dix said. He leaned forward slightly, chin resting on his hands, focus as intense as it always was.

"Maybe he loved her," Dix said.

"And then stood by while the others had her," Jesse said.

"The guilt would be as powerful as the rage," Dix said. "Until you wouldn't be able to tell one from the other."

He nodded at Jesse.

"You got a lead?"

"Maybe," Jesse said.

"You need to find them," Dix said.

"Fuckin' ay," Jesse said.

He went outside and called Candace Pennington's phone, hoping for a miracle, that she'd pick up and tell him why she'd been missing, and that she was safe.

Went straight to voicemail.

"It's Jesse Stone," he said. "We think it's Feeney."

# Fifty-Six

Suit was able to fast-track the credit card from Feeney this time, with Wells Fargo. Didn't bother with anything except charges from Vermont. It turned out there were plenty, last year alone, from the Manchester area. Too many for him to just have been passing through. Molly came up with a property listing for a Mr. K. Feeney, in a town a half-hour from Manchester called Danby.

Jesse knew the chief in Manchester, a guy he'd met at a couple New England law enforcement seminars. Captain Pete Ciccone. Jesse knew that procedure dictated that he ought to call Ciccone, who had jurisdiction in his state. But if Feeney was there, he might be ready to blow. Jesse was sure Ciccone was a good cop, operating an even smaller department than the one in Paradise, and trusted him.

Jesse trusted himself more.

Before he left the office, Molly asked if he had a plan. He told her he was going up there in the morning, and she said she was going with him, and was sure Sunny would want to go, too.

"We missed the signs," she said.

"If it's him, we all missed them," Jesse said.

"It's still on us as much as anybody," she said.

"All of us," Jesse said.

"We still don't know for sure that it is him, or that he's up there," Molly said. "Or that he's got Candace with him."

Jesse told her that at this point, the list of things they didn't know about this case could stretch from here to the Green Mountains.

"We should maybe think about going up there tonight," Molly said.

"Let me think about it," he said. "But be ready to move."

Kevin Feeney wasn't the only one who could lie.

When Jesse got home, he called Pete Ciccone, told him he had a possible missing person, technically true, asked if he could get close to the address in Danby without being seen.

"You think this guy might be a runner?" Ciccone said.

"Hope that's all he is for now," Jesse said.

"You want me to wait until dark?" Ciccone said.

"No," Jesse said.

Ciccone called back forty-five minutes later, said he'd gotten to within a couple hundred yards of the house. No lights on inside, no cars. Said there were some tire tracks on the dirt road, but that didn't mean anything, as there were a couple hunting cabins farther up the mountain.

"I got pretty close," Ciccone he said. "Place looks deserted. Could the person you're looking for be out getting food or something?"

"Or I'm dead wrong about this," Jesse said.

"Hard to put a guy there without him being seen," Ciccone said. "Just the way the property is. But I could circle back in a couple hours."

"You coming up to check it out yourself?"

"Thinking about it," Jesse said.

Lying his ass off now.

He ended the call with Ciccone, grabbed a couple bottles of water, couple energy bars, locked up behind him, and got ready to drive to Danby, Vermont.

He was just outside Paradise when his phone chirped. The screen on the dashboard said "Biddeford PD."

The voice at the other end came through the Explorer's stereo system. The caller identified himself as Sergeant Nason, and said his captain had given him Jesse's number. Said they might have a lead on the case Deputy Chief Crane had been up there working on.

"Is this about Bo Marino?" Jesse said.

"Maybe, maybe not," Nason said. "A couple rabbit hunters found a body a few hours ago, out past Clifford Point. What's left of it, anyway. Face is pretty much gone. I just got back from there." He cleared his throat and said, "Can't say for sure, but it looks like somebody tried to blow the guy's head off with a shotgun. Or some kind of hunting rifle."

Jesse said, "So no ID."

"Thinking dental records aren't gonna be in play, sir," Nason said. "Other'n that, not sure the Lord himself could identify him at this point. We'll run his prints through the system, see if we get a hit."

"But white male?"

"Yes, sir."

"Average size?"

Nason said it appeared so. Then he said, "Aw, goddamn it all to hell and back," he might never unsee what he'd just seen. Not just because of what the gun had done. Animals, too. Bear country, he said.

"You had any missing persons up there lately?" Jesse said.

"Other than a homeless guy from Kennebunkport couple months back we never located, no, sir," Nason said.

It was quiet in the car.

"You still there?" Nason said.

It came out "they-ah."

Jesse told them that he was still there, and was on his way north, part of the same investigation that had sent his deputy chief up to Biddeford. He told Nason that if they somehow identified the body, to call back. If necessary, he could spend the night in Vermont and be there in the morning.

"You believe in coincidence, Sergeant Nason?" Jesse said.

"Beg pardon?"

"Coincidence," Jesse said. "Cops in Maine believe in it?"

"Not as a general rule, sir, no," he said.

"Me, neither," Jesse said.

He ended the call. The inside of the car was quiet as Jesse drove north, toward the night. Thinking there was at least a chance that the ghost, from the start, might have been Bo Marino.

"And then there was one," Jesse said.

# Fifty-Seven

Jesse picked up 91 north of Greenfield, crossed into Vermont with New Hampshire to the east, got on Route 11 heading toward Londonderry, finally on Route 7, driving fast when he had two lanes, slowing down when it was back to one lane heading into Dorset. The mountains were all around him. Maybe Candace Pennington really was up here somewhere.

Maybe he wasn't too late.

He was just getting on 7 when he saw the incoming call, this time from Molly Crane.

"Fucking bastard," she said.

In the background he heard Sunny say, "What she said."

"When I didn't hear from you, I decided to check your location on my phone, just out of curiosity," Molly said. "Lo and behold, I found out that my lying boss was on the move."

"Some things I still need to do alone," he said.

"It's my case, too."

"I know that, Mols," he said. "And I'm sorry."

"No, you're not," she said, and hung up.

Jesse thought more about what Dix had said about Feeney and his possible pathology, all the feelings he might have repressed since the night of the rape until he couldn't. Including feelings for Candace. If he was right, Jesse had practically handed her over to the son of a bitch.

Jesse didn't know how far up Bear Mountain Road the Feeney house was. He parked at the bottom of it. It was completely dark by now. Woods dark and deep. Who'd written that? Molly would know. He'd ask her later, when she was talking to him again.

He saw one light in the distance.

Now somebody was home.

He checked his phone and saw that he had two bars. He knew he should call Ciccone for backup, but if they were in there, no time for that now. Jesse shut off the phone, put on the duty belt he wore with his jeans, no Taser or flashlight, just cuffs hooked to the back, in case. He made his way up the hill toward the house, staying at the edge of the tree line.

One foot in front of another, they said at AA.

He finally reached the house, a two-story cabin with a porch in front. In the back, he thought he could make out a tree house.

The light was coming from the front of the first floor. Not much of a light at that. Like one lamp was lit.

Going somewhere Bo can't find me, Feeney had said.

Truth and lies.

Jesse took his gun out of its holster, came in a low scrabble out of the woods, footsteps on his old gray New Balances lost under all the night sounds around him, briefly wondering what kind of animals you could encounter in the mountains of Vermont.

He was at a side window now, shade halfway drawn, slowly raising himself up so that the window was nearly at eye level. Wanting to see if Feeney was in there.

Praying they both were there.

He was still in his crouch, gun in his right hand, when he felt the barrel of the gun in his back and heard a voice he somehow recognized, after all these years.

"Don't make me shoot you, asshole," he said.

Bo Marino barked out a laugh.

"Least not yet."

# Fifty-Eight

**M**arino had established a safe zone between him and Jesse, protecting himself from a sudden move.

"Gun on the ground, gently," Marino said. "Then hands up."

Jesse dropped the gun to his side, put his arms in the air.

"Now kick the gun back to me," Marino said.

"Not a soccer player."

"You used to say a lot of smart-mouthed shit when you were the one with the gun," Marino said. "When you were the one in charge. But I am now. You do what I say. Kick the fucking gun back to me."

Jesse did.

"Where's your phone?"

"Front pocket."

"Take it out and toss it back here."

Jesse did that, too.

Thinking: *I came up here because I wanted to take control of the situation.*

"Where is she?"

"That what you came up here to find out?"

"Among other things."

"Well, I don't give a shit what you want," Marino said. "I'm the chief now."

"Maybe I didn't come alone," Jesse said.

"Yeah, asshole, you did. Know how I know? Because my boy Feens has a surveillance camera on a tree at the end of the drive. He used to get fraidy scared when he was alone up here at night."

"Where's he, by the way?"

Marino hit Jesse hard on the back of his head with either Jesse's gun or his own, the force of the blow surprising him and nearly putting him on the ground.

"Now do something else," Bo Marino said. "Reach behind you and take those cuffs off your belt and put them on."

Jesse unhooked his cuffs, but fumbled trying to put them on behind his back.

"You're going to have to help me," he said over his shoulder.

"So I have to get close to you?" Marino said. "How dumb do you think I am?"

*How much time do you have?*

Jesse kept fumbling with the cuffs and finally Marino said, "Fuck it. Front will do. You're not going to have them on for very long."

Jesse put on the cuffs, over the fat part of his hands, bitching as he did that they were too tight. But at least his hands were in front of him now. *Wasn't much,* he thought. *But wasn't nothing.*

"Where's Candace?" he said.

"Inside," Marino said. "Waiting for the show to start."

"What show?"

"You'll see."

"What about Feeney?"

"Up the mountain where I stashed my van," Marino said. "I don't need him yet."

"For what?" Jesse said.

Marino barked out another laugh.

"To look like he killed both of you, the poor bastard, before he killed himself," Bo Marino said, shoving Jesse toward the door.

# Fifty-Nine

Marino had moved a queen-sized bed into the living room area. Candace Pennington was tied to its posts, hands and feet. Wearing the same clothes she'd worn to Jesse's office. Gray duct tape over her mouth, eyes frantic, makeup around the eyes a raccoon mess. A bruise was darkening on her left cheekbone.

"Had to tape her mouth," Bo Marino said. "Some shit never changes. She still won't stop screaming."

He motioned Jesse into a chair maybe ten feet from the end of the bed, facing it. When Jesse was seated, Marino came up quickly behind him and threw what Jesse saw was the kind of rope harness that climbers wore over him, then pulled it tight.

"Fuck you," he said to Bo Marino, who swung the gun again and hit him in the back of the head. It felt like a baseball bat.

But thinking: *Second and a half.*

*Two, tops.*

Jesse sat there, cuffed hands in his lap. Took a better look at the man that Bo Marino had become. Heavier than he'd been in high school. Some kind of neck tat showing near the collar of a flannel shirt. Long hair, mountain-man beard. Carpenter jeans with big pockets on the sides. Work boots.

The gun in his hand appeared to be a .22. Jesse's .40 was stuck in his jeans, in front.

Jesse saw a semi-automatic rifle leaning against the wall near the bed, wondering if it might be the one Marino had used that night in the rain.

Marino sat down himself at the end of the bed, between Candace's splayed legs. Waving the gun in front of him as he began to talk. Some were like this. Not all. Some. Wanting to tell you all about it. Maybe Bo Marino had been waiting to tell somebody all about it his whole goddamn pathetic life.

"Want to know the best part?" he said. "You leaving that message for her telling her to watch out for Feeney. *Feeney?* Are you fucking *kidding?* You think he had the balls to pull off any of this? He couldn't find his balls with a fucking tracking device."

*Keep him talking.*

"Why'd you kill Drake?" Jesse said.

"Because he ratted me out same as Feeney did, is why," Bo Marino said. "Both of them blubbering to you like little babies to save their own asses. But when I called him, I told him I wanted to apologize for everything finally. Gave him a lot of bullshit about how sorry I was. How I'd changed. He was so happy I thought he might start blubbering all over again. Told him we needed to take a walk over the bridge like we used to. Sharing a bottle of Maker's Mark, just like the old days."

"You told your father you stopped," Jesse said.

"I tell that mean fuck a lot of things," Bo said. "One of these days I'm gonna come for him, too."

"So you got him drunk."

"Not much of a freaking challenge," Marino said. "Finally we stop and look at the water, up there at the highest point. He said he was feeling dizzy. Started to sway a little. Reached for me to help him." Marino shrugged. "Over he went," he said. "Pretty shitty dive, you ask me."

Jesse thought: *He sounds proud of himself.*

"How'd you end up here at Kevin's place?"

"The fuck you talking about, Kevin's place?" he said. "This place belonged to his old man. Kevin Feeney Senior. After we got our licenses we used to come up here to get wasted."

He looked around.

"Those were the days."

"I can see why you went after them," Jesse said. "Why me and my cops?"

"Because I *saw* you, that's why. All it took. There I am, the night they opened the movie theater back up, back in town for the first time in forever. I was maybe fifty feet behind you in the crowd. There you were, along with the bitch cop and the doofus you call Suit. You know what I was thinking that night? I wished I'd been the one to burn down that theater, and the whole freaking town along with it."

"You would have needed to be better at that than building a bomb," Jesse said.

"And you need to be a better cop," Marino said.

"Where'd you get the parts?"

"Stole them from my old man one night when he was the one passed out drunk. And then you thought Drake did it? No shit, that made me laugh my ass off. Yeah, he was a menace to society same as Feeney."

"You followed me to the lake that night?" Jesse said.

"Wondered where the hell you were going," Marino said. "But when you ended up there, nobody else around, I grabbed the rifle out of the trunk. It was going to be a much easier goddamn shot until you heard me. Pissed me off."

Jesse's eyes locked on Candace's. He nodded.

*I will get you out of this.*

For the moment, her own eyes seemed calm. Smaller. She nodded back, as if reading his mind, Marino's back to her.

Then she showed Jesse that she had freed her right hand. Marino turned slightly then, as if catching the hint of movement. But her hand was already back where it had been.

"But all of the shit in my life started with her," Marino said, jerking his head in Candace's direction. "Everywhere I went, and I went a lot of goddamn places, they'd look me up and find out what I did, and then I was the one getting it up the ass all over again. All because of her."

"All her fault," Jesse said. "And ours."

"Goddamn right."

"Was that you who tried to rape the other woman in the park that night?" Jesse said.

Marino laughed again.

"Why not tell you about that one?" he said. "I mean, what are you gonna do—bust me?"

He pointed the gun at Jesse, then dropped it to his side.

"Yeah," he said. "I saw her walking with the bitch cop, who was the one I wanted. Only the bitch got into the car with the doofus and his wife and drove off. But, see, I'd already gotten the urge. Something else that never changed. Getting the urge. So I waited and grabbed the other one. And there I am, grinding away, when I hear a goddamn gunshot sounding way too close. So I'm thinking, *Fuck it, I'll save it for the bitch cop,* and take off. Got run right into by some long-haired faggot in a baseball hat and one of those old-fashioned Patriots sweatshirts, running like a bat out of hell from the lake."

*Good to know,* Jesse thought.

But only if he and Candace got out of here alive.

It was as if Marino had been waiting for an audience.

"One goddamn night in high school when shit got a little out of hand," Bo Marino said. "And I spend the rest of my life paying for it." He leaned back, closed his eyes, tilted his head back. "My father had always beat the shit out of me. It got worse after that. Until I finally beat the shit out of *him* and left and never came back."

"He did hire the lawyer that kept you out of jail," Jesse said.

"Only good thing he ever did for me," Marino said.

"Maybe if you'd gone to jail back then," Jesse said, "you wouldn't be here now."

Marino got up and leaned down when he got to Jesse. This time he swung the gun and hit Jesse in the left knee. Jesse yelled out in pain, but only to distract him, because he could see Candace trying to get her left hand loose now.

"Now who sounds like a bitch?" Marino said.

Jesse rubbed his knee with his hands, making sure the cuffs didn't move.

"How'd you get them both up here?" Jesse said.

"You want Candace to tell you how I did it?" Marino said. "Oh, wait, I forgot. I finally got her to lay back and shut the fuck up." He was pacing now in front of Jesse.

He went back and sat down on the bed.

*Second and a half,* Jesse told himself.

*Two, tops.*

"You really think you can get away with killing us?" Jesse said.

"And making it look like Kevin finally snapped?" Marino said. "Well, yeah, Chief. I do."

He stood again, as if he couldn't keep himself still, as if he were on fire.

"I was thinking about making you watch me do her one more time," he said. "Like for old times' sake. But now I just think I'll let you watch me shoot her, make that the last thing you see."

He said, "Yeah, I'll go first with her, just like always."

He got up off the bed, turned toward Candace. Away from Jesse. Jesse started to slide the cuffs down off the fat part of his hands. He didn't try to get himself free from the ropes around his torso, no time for that.

He saw Marino's finger going to the trigger.

Things you never forgot. That were in your cop DNA. You had a second and a half, two tops, from perception to reaction if you could distract someone enough, and had this short a distance to cover. Ten feet. Maybe less.

*Now.*

Jesse rose up, the chair attached to his back, and charged Bo Marino, hitting him from the side, knocking him onto the bed, his momentum landing both of them on Candace Pennington.

Marino was as slow as Jesse hoped he'd be.

*"Fuck!"* Bo Marino shouted.

He tried to swing the gun at Jesse's head and missed. Jesse had enough movement in his arms to get his hands up and around Marino's throat as Candace tried to wriggle free of both of them.

Marino finally managed to get his gun hand free, rolled away on the bed, and pointed the gun at Jesse.

But he had gotten too close with it, and Jesse bit him, Marino yowling in pain as the gun fell out of his hand. Marino didn't try to grab it, reaching for Jesse instead. He got his arms around Jesse's upper body, still tied to the chair, and shoved Jesse off the bed, putting him on his back.

Marino looked down, chest heaving, face red, and suddenly seemed to remember that Jesse's Glock was still stuck in the front of his jeans.

Jesse was helpless now as he watched Marino smile and pull out the gun, finger on the trigger, raising it in a right hand Jesse could see was bloody from where he'd sunk his teeth into it.

Reaction time meant nothing to Jesse now. Out of time.

Marino's eyes were suddenly calm, even with the low growl, an animal sound, coming out of him.

"Hey, asshole," he said, "remember the time you told me nobody could protect everybody? Well, shit on a stick, you were right."

There was the sound of the first gunshot then.

Jesse saw Marino's gun hand freeze in front of him, then saw his body stiffening and straightening, just as the sound of the second shot filled the ground floor of the cabin.

Then Candace Pennington, on her side, but right hand steady, was firing again, and again, until she had emptied Bo Marino's gun into him and he was dead on the floor next to Jesse, everything that had started a long time ago between him and Candace finally over.

# Sixty

T hing is," Jesse was saying to Molly and Sunny the next morning at Daisy's, "Feeney *was* crazy. Just not as crazy as Bo was."

"Too close to call, if you ask me," Molly said.

Jesse had spent the night in Manchester after he and Candace Pennington had finished with Captain Pete Ciccone, gotten up at five in the morning, and driven back to Paradise. Andy Pennington had gotten to Vermont at around ten o'clock, announcing that she was turning right around and that she and Candace were going home.

Before they'd left, Candace had hugged Jesse and said, "Thank you for saving me."

"This time," he'd said.

Now Molly said, "How did Bo manage to grab them both?"

"He was getting ready to make a move on Feeney, then figure out a way to take him out the way he had Troy Drake," Jesse said. "He was across the street from Feeney's office, waiting for him to close up. At which point he can't believe what a lucky boy he is, because Candace shows up, too. He throws them both in the back of his van, and they were on their way to Vermont."

"Why was Candace there in the first place?" Sunny said.

"She told me it was a spur-of-the-moment thing," Jesse said. "Turned out she was being ironic when she told her wife she was meeting a friend. She knew Feeney was back in town. She just wanted to tell him to his face that she wasn't a victim, that in her mind she'd won and they'd lost because of their pathetic lives after high school."

"How'd Bo get them in the van?" Molly said.

"He told them that if either one of them made a noise he'd shoot them both," Jesse said. "Then he had Feeney tie her up with the same rope harness he used on me. When he was done, Marino sat him down and chloroformed him. Did the same to Candace. Took them out the back door, and off they went."

"He was able to get chloroform?" Sunny said.

"Online," Jesse said. "Like everything else."

Jesse ate some toast, drank some of his coffee.

"When did he kill Feeney?" Molly said.

"Not long before I showed up," Jesse said. "After he was finished with Candace and me, the plan was to bring Feeney's body back inside and put the gun back in his hand. Bo'd knocked Feeney out again when they got to the cabin, held the gun in his hand and shot him in the temple."

Sunny said, "Wasn't he worried about the chloroform showing up in a tox screen of whatever when the bodies were found?"

"Turns out modern chloroform leaves the system very quickly," Jesse said. "Guy had moments when he wasn't as dumb as he looked.

Molly looked at her. "He's the chief."

"I know," Sunny said. "He knows things."

"He almost got away with it," Jesse said. "Good that I left here when I did."

"You still should have taken us with you, cowboy," Molly said. "And I do mean *cowboy*."

"Next time," he said.

Molly looked at Sunny again and said, "Still lying."

Vinnie Morris was already back in Concord. Michael Crane was still out in the Pacific somewhere. There had been no discussion about Sunny going back to Boston. But they all knew it was going to happen. Maybe as soon as today, or tomorrow.

For now they were still talking about what had happened the night before in the woods.

"It took a long time," Molly said, "but in the end Candace finally got justice."

"Bo did all the prep work," Jesse said. "But she ended up with the gun."

Daisy came over and refilled their coffee cups. She was still rocking the purple hair. She nodded at Sunny and said to Jesse, "You two an item again?"

"I think the two of them like each other better than they like me," he said.

"Why wouldn't they?" Daisy said and left. She winked at Molly and Sunny and said, "Girl power."

Molly said, "How was Candace really, when it was over?"

"Relieved, I think," Jesse said. "He'd been threatening all the way up there to rape her again. She told me he would have had to kill her first."

"He nearly raped me," Molly said.

"You were stronger than him when he was in high school," Jesse said. "Still are."

"I was a part of this, though," Molly said. "Humiliating him on the bus that day."

"We all humiliated him, at least in his mind," Jesse said. "His father had been doing the same his whole life."

"Did I mention you should have taken us with you?" Molly said.

"You planning on dropping this anytime soon?" Jesse said.

"Like they said in *Thelma and Louise*," Sunny said. "You're in deep shit with her, Arkansas."

"What about you?" Jesse said.

"I have a more forgiving heart."

"Not what you said last night, blondie, when you found out he ditched us," Molly said.

Jesse told them then about what Marino had said about running into a long-haired guy in the park, right after he heard the gunshot, and that he was going to ask his friend Bryce Cain about that first chance he got.

Molly got up to go to the ladies' room. Just Jesse and Sunny now.

"My work here is done," she said.

"Don't want to help me solve my murder?"

"You don't need me," she said. "Not sure you ever really did."

"I liked having you on the team," he said.

"The PPD's," she said, "or yours?"

"Maybe I just wanted an excuse to have you around."

"Wanted or needed?"

"Both," he said.

There was a long silence now. At the end of the counter, Jesse could see Molly talking to Daisy.

"I need to get back," she said. "Back to my own house, back to my own work."

"Girl's gotta have it," he said.

"Or she's not worth having," Sunny said. "And you know you're the exact same way."

"How about you leave tomorrow," he said, "and we have dinner tonight?"

"I need to head out," she said. "Got a call from a potential client yesterday. And Rosie misses her daddy."

"Richie?"

Sunny smiled.

"Spike," she said.

Jesse smiled. "You can't leave when we're going good."

"Let's see how we both feel when I'm there and you're here."

She leaned across the table and kissed him.

"See you around, cowboy," she said.

He watched her get up from the booth, walk past the counter, hug Molly, and leave.

*Day at a time,* he told himself.

Some of them more interesting than others.

He was staring out the window when Molly sat back down.

"Yup," she said. "You are in deep shit. But not with me."

# Sixty-One

**B**ryce Cain looked at Jesse and said, "You look like you lost a fight."

Jesse had noticed the bruise on the left side of his face, from the last time Bo Marino had swung his gun at him, neither one of them knowing at the time that Marino had only a few minutes to live.

"Yeah," Jesse said, "but I still won on points."

"Aren't you supposed to say that I should see the other guy?"

"The other guy's dead," Jesse said.

"You want to tell me about it?"

"No," Jesse said.

They were at the juice bar at Bryce's gym, Paradise Fitness. Jesse had asked if he had a gym at home and Bryce said he did, but his trainer was jammed up and couldn't make a house call today. He made it sound sadder than the end of a dog movie.

Bryce looked even skinnier in gym clothes, as tight on him

as they were on the women Jesse had seen walking around. For the time being, he'd pulled his hair back into one of those man buns. Jesse wondered who'd told him it was a good look.

"I'm gonna hit the Peloton before I go back to the office," he said. "So can we make this short?"

"Sure," Jesse said. "I was wondering if you could tell me where you were after the marquee lighting that night?"

Bryce sipped something green through a straw.

"You came over here to ask me *that?*"

"Humor me. Somebody fitting your general description was seen running from the direction of the lake right after Paul Hutton was shot."

"General description?" Bryce said. "You mean ruggedly handsome and ripped?"

"Long-haired and skinny. Witness said the guy looked like a runner."

Not exactly what Bo Marino had said. Close enough.

"Wait, you're serious," Bryce said.

Jesse waited.

"Tell me something, Chief," Bryce said. "Are you going out of your way to piss me off? Because you can't believe that I'm the only person in Paradise who fits that description."

"No, you're not. But you're the one whose house the dead guy visited shortly before that."

"My parents' house," he said.

"So where were you?"

"At my own home. Alone on a Saturday night, sadly."

"What about your wife and daughter?"

Bryce drank more of his green drink. It was some kind of smoothie, the color of a pickle.

"My daughter was at a party," he said. "My wife and I are taking a break."

"*Were* you at the theater?" Jesse said. "I don't remember seeing you."

But he hadn't noticed Bo Marino there, either.

"I was there," he said. "I knew it was a big deal to Lily. First chance I got, I went home and curled up on the couch with a good scotch." He grinned at Jesse. "Probably a perfect Saturday night for you once, am I right?"

"I could have taught a master class," Jesse said. "So you could have been down by the lake."

"Fuck you," Bryce said. "You think I'm going to sit here and let you treat me like a suspect?"

"I thought we were just having a nice conversation."

"Like hell," Bryce said. "Let me explain something to you: My old man was the gun guy in the family, not me. They scare the shit out of me. Haven't handled one since he tried to teach me to shoot one when I was ten."

Jesse drank some sparkling water.

"Going to ask something again," he said. "Could Hutton have gone to the house that night because he had business with your father?"

"And I'm going to tell you again," Bryce said. "If he had, my father would have told me."

"I heard the two of you were fighting about money at the end," Jesse said.

Bryce said, "Only because he started to act like he really could take it with him."

"Is that an answer?"

"Did I miss a question?" Bryce said.

He put up his hands, as if in surrender.

"We're all being taken care of, handsomely," he said. "We haven't officially read the will yet, but I wrote the goddamn thing. Even Karina's going to get a nice check herself. There. You satisfied?"

"Almost," Jesse said. "Karina talked about secrets in your family. Can you think of any Whit died with that might help me out here?"

Bryce Cain smiled now, showing off a lot of white teeth. But to Jesse, it was as if he were baring them. He remembered a time, a case that took him up into the Hollywood Hills, when he'd come face-to-face with a coyote, who stared Jesse down and bared his teeth before running off. Only then did Jesse take his hand off his gun.

"You should have asked him that," Bryce said.

"What about you?"

"Secrets?" Bryce said. "A boatload. But none that would help you."

He reached behind him for whatever was holding his hair in place, let the hair fall nearly to his shoulders. Reached down into his gym bag and pulled out a baseball cap. Paradise Yacht Club.

"My Peloton awaits," he said, and headed back toward the gym, joining the beautiful people trying to make themselves even more beautiful.

Jesse felt a buzzing from his phone. Took it from the back pocket of his jeans, saw the text from Suit.

Got something.

# Sixty-Two

They were in Jesse's office. Suit had placed a small stack of paper in front of Jesse on his desk. The one on top was what he called the "money hit."

"I missed it the first time," Suit said. "I mean, I saw the one I've got circled there. 4Bears. But when I Googled it, it turned out to be a casino in frigging North Dakota. Thought maybe our guy had taken a trip to the great Northwest."

"Midwest, technically," Jesse said.

"Whatever," Suit said. "So I had nothing. I decided to start from scratch, go back through the list again. Lot of bars, all of them in pretty much the same area in Florida, around Palm Beach. A few in Miami, but not many. There were some of those middle-man accounts that cover porn sites."

"And you know about those accounts . . . how?" Jesse said, grinning at him.

"I wasn't always married," Suit said. He pointed at the top

paper. "But I got curious about how he'd end up in North Dakota. It didn't make sense. Geographically, you know. And it turns out that even though there is a 4 Bears casino, it's also the name of one of those DNA ancestry companies. That was where he got charged."

"The guy took a DNA test," Jesse said.

"Yup."

"How long ago?"

"Month or so before we found him at the lake," Suit said.

Jesse looked down at the paper. Suit had circled "4Bears .com" in red. Twice.

"That's why we thought he might have a shot at finding out who he was," Jesse said.

"Looking for relatives," Suit said.

"So he takes a DNA test and then he shows up here," Jesse said.

"I've been thinking about that," Suit said. "But you know who else lived at that house? That nurse who came up here from Florida."

"Or maybe the DNA test had nothing to do with him coming here, and he had another reason for going there that night," Jesse said.

"Buzz killer," Suit said.

"Just thinking out loud."

"You're the one who keeps talking about how much time Old Man Cain always spent down in Florida."

"And apparently kept it in his pants about as often as Epstein did," Jesse said.

"Or the movie guy," Suit said.

Jesse drank some of the coffee he'd made when he'd gotten back to the office. Then he reached for his pen and drew another circle around 4Bears.com.

"You think the old man might be our dead guy's father?" Suit said. "Or, holy shit, that Mrs. Cain could be his mother?"

Jesse said, "Be nice to know. I just don't know how."

"You gonna ask Lily about this?" Suit said.

"Not quite yet," Jesse said.

He tapped a finger on the papers in front of him.

"I'm hopeful the offices of *this* 4Bears isn't located in North Dakota," Jesse said.

Suit smiled.

"State Street, Boston, Massachusetts," Suit said.

"Boom."

"You really understand how all this DNA voodoo works?" Suit said.

"Nope," Jesse said. "But hoping to find out."

Suit grinned.

"You think there are any more little Jesse Stones out there running around?" he said.

Jesse told him to get out of his office.

# Sixty-Three

**C**ole had called from the road and told Jesse he was going to surprise him and take him out to dinner, but that when he'd thought about it, he didn't want to surprise him and Sunny. Jesse told him Sunny had gone back to Boston.

"Hoping that doesn't mean permanently," Cole said.

"Same," Jesse said.

Now they were seated at the kitchen table, eating truck-stop burgers, with fried potatoes and onions on the side and green beans lathered in Parmesan sauce. Jesse had said he could put together a salad. Cole had grinned and said, "What the hell for? Our health?"

Jesse had called on his way back from Vermont and given Cole the bumper-sticker version of what had happened the night before. Now his son wanted to hear all about it.

"You trusted you had time to get across the room," Cole said.

"Ever hopeful," Jesse said.

"So she emptied the gun," Cole said.

"If she could have reloaded somehow and kept shooting," Jesse said, "I believe she would have."

"So it's over."

"On to the next," Jesse said.

"Your vic at the lake."

Jesse told him about Paul Hutton and the DNA test.

"I took one of those," Cole said.

"Seriously?" Jesse said. "You never told me."

"It was after I got here," Cole said. "Got curious if there might be somebody else out there."

Jesse laughed.

"What's so funny?"

"Your friend Suit asked me a little while ago if I ever wondered if there might be other Jesses out there. Great minds," Cole said.

"Both of you wish."

Cole had cut his hair short, shaved off the beard he'd had the last time they were together. He was handsome and young and happy and tougher than an ultimate fighter. Not for the first time, Jesse thought about how well his mother had done with him. And wondered, also not for the first time, if the kid would have turned out this well if Jesse had been in his life from the start.

"Which site did you use?" Jesse said.

"Ancestry.com."

"Not that I'm worried," Jesse said. "But any hits?"

"Nope. You got unlucky just the one time."

"Lucky is more like it," he said, "even if it took as long as it did for me to find out."

Jesse said, "You understand how it works?"

"Kind of," Cole said, telling him what happened once you opened an account and sent them your money. They sent you a sample kit in the mail, you took a swab, sent it to them, and filled out what he described as an entrance exam worth of paperwork. Then you waited to see the results, and any relations in the system. Said that was the shorthand version.

"What if there had been one?" Jesse said.

"Then you have the option of using the company's messaging system," Cole said, "and trying to contact the person, or persons, you've matched up with. And then *they* have the option of responding or not."

"I need to find out if Paul Hutton got a match," Jesse said, "and if it might have been with Whit Cain."

"Can you get into Hutton's laptop?"

"Didn't have one."

"He had to use a laptop somewhere to access their site."

"Well, it beats the hell out of me where it was," Jesse says. "But it won't matter if I can get the company to hand over the results."

"Good luck with that," Cole said.

"If they're resistant to the notion," Jesse said, "I'll have to turn on the charm."

His son said, "You'd be better off threatening to shoot them."

# Sixty-Four

The headquarters for 4Bears.com was at 70 State Street, which Jesse knew wasn't all that far from where Sunny lived on River Street Place, over on the other side of the Common and the Public Garden. He hadn't been to Sunny's home since she'd moved there from Fort Point. Maybe after he finished on State Street he'd swing by. Or maybe he'd wait for her to make the first move.

Or maybe he could stop acting like a scared high school kid waiting for the girl he liked to pass him a note.

The offices of 4Bears were on the twenty-fifth and twenty-sixth floors. When he got out of the elevator and looked past the receptionist's desk at all the cubicles behind her, he could have been looking at an insurance company. Or a tech firm, which he supposed this place really was. Lots of young people tapping away at computer screens, or talking into their mics attached to their earpieces. Or both.

What he was really looking at, he thought, was the modern

world. People younger and more tech-savvy than him and able to find things out faster and solve problems quicker. Maybe he should walk in there and tap one of them on the shoulder and tell him or her everything Jesse knew and didn't know about Paul Hutton. Maybe they'd figure out what happened to him before somebody made the next coffee run.

The receptionist was more age-appropriate for him, streaked hair cut short, big black framed glasses. Pretty. SALLY CAMERON, her placard read.

"May I help you?" she said.

He identified himself, showed her his badge, said that he was here investigating the murder of a 4Bears client.

"Oh, my," she said. "I'm not even sure who you should be talking to about that."

Jesse smiled. Might as well start the charm offensive.

"I'm sure you'll make the right decision," he said.

She stood and said, "Excuse me for just one moment."

She walked into the large, sunny area where the cubicles were, toward actual offices Jesse could see in the back. She came back about five minutes later with a tall redheaded woman in a short summer dress. Long hair, long legs. She reminded Jesse of Rita Fiore, lawyer friend, once with benefits.

"Gwen Hadley," she said. Smiled. "Vice president in charge of something or other."

She put out her hand. Jesse shook it.

"Should I call you Chief?" she said.

"Not unless you want me to arrest you in front of Ms. Cameron."

She laughed.

"Follow me," she said.

She led him down to a corner office with a spectacular eastern view that stretched all the way to the waterfront.

"Does the president have a better view than this?" Jesse said.

"He does," she said. "Higher, too."

No wedding ring, Jesse noticed. Telling himself he *was* the chief and trained to be a visual person. She motioned him into a chair to the right of her door. She sat down on the small sofa next to it and crossed her legs.

*Sunny,* Jesse thought.

"Sally told me about the murder," Gwen Hadley said. "Maybe you can explain how I can help you."

Jesse told her about Paul Hutton: him being orphaned, about his last job, about him getting sober, about him showing up in Paradise not long after the charge from 4Bears appeared on his credit card.

"Why do you suppose he took the test now?" she said.

"No idea."

"But it doesn't really matter, does it?" she said.

"It matters to me," he said. "I believe that if I can find out if there was a match, it might help me find out who killed him."

She sighed.

"That doesn't sound good," he said.

"I'd love to help you out, Jesse," she said. Smiled at him again. "But I'm afraid I can't."

"Can't or won't?'

"If our customers don't trust our confidentiality policies," she said, "then before long we won't have any customers, because they're on their way to Ancestry or 23andMe or somebody else who *will* honor their confidentiality policies."

Jesse smiled now.

"All due respect?" he said.

"That *never* sounds good," she said.

"Bullshit," Jesse said.

"Excuse me?"

"Bull. Shit."

"We don't happen to think our privacy policies are."

"Maybe for people who are still alive," Jesse said.

"There's a place on the form for people to be contacted in the event of the customer's death," she said. "Almost always a family member. But you just told me he had no family."

"You could check," Jesse said.

"But if there's no contact listed," she said, "then we're back to where we started. If one person's information isn't safe, no one's is. Dead or alive, I'm afraid."

"Here's how I'd like this to go," Jesse said. "I'd like you to talk to whomever you need to talk to, all the way to the twenty-sixth floor if necessary. I'd like you to go into Paul Hutton's records and see if there's a contact. And if there's not? You do the right thing and turn over his information to me so I can get some justice for him. If not, I am going to call Wayne Cosgrove at the *Globe* and tell him Paul Hutton's sad story and how 4Bears isn't interested in justice for him, because they think the letter of the law is more important than the spirit of the law."

She sighed again.

"Well, then," she said.

He waited.

"I may have underestimated you, Jesse Stone."

"You're not the first," he said. "Pretty sure you won't be the last."

She stared at him with green eyes. They seemed to work for her the way just about everything else did.

"I'm not promising anything," she said. "If we didn't have protocols in place, I'd be doing a deep dive into the system right now."

"I believe you."

"I want to help," she said. "I really do."

"I believe that, too."

She got up, walked over to her desk, came back with her phone.

"Can you give me your number?" she said.

He did. She read it back to make sure she had it right.

"This may take some time," she said. "And some arm-twisting."

"My money's on you," Jesse said.

She stood. So did he. She shook his hand again, and said she'd be in touch. Probably his imagination that she held on a beat longer this time. Maybe more.

"Sunny," he said as he withdrew his hand from hers.

"Excuse me?"

"Nothing," Jesse said.

He was the one carrying the gun and badge, after all. No reason for her to know that he needed a safe word, too.

# Sixty-Five

Jesse had no idea how long it would take Gwen Hadley to get the information he wanted and, even if she did, how long it would take for her to get permission from the twenty-sixth floor to release it. But he had the sense that she didn't want to be on the wrong side of this. He had been a cop too long to expect everybody to always do the right thing. But he still thought most people wanted to, especially if it didn't cost them anything.

He decided to take a walk, even though he never felt completely at home in downtown Boston, not when Jenn had been working in local television and living here, not when he'd come down to visit Sunny. It wasn't about feeling out of place in a big city. He'd been a big-city cop in Los Angeles before he got to Paradise. He just always felt like a tourist here, no matter how many times he was downtown. Like no matter where he was, on Commonwealth Avenue walking toward Fenway Park or Back Bay or Government Center or over at the Seaport, there was just too much traffic for him now. Cars. People. The whole goddamn thing.

He had decided he didn't want to see Sunny today, that he wouldn't walk over to River Street Place and ring the doorbell. Why? Because he was afraid her ex-husband would be there? Jesse knew her well enough to know that she had as much problem disengaging from Richie Burke as he had from Jenn, at least until Jenn had finally remarried and moved away. It didn't mean that the feelings she still had for Richie were stronger than the ones she had for Jesse. They had history.

Jesse and Sunny had . . . what? He knew he loved her, even if he had not come out and told her that, at least not lately. It was good, whatever it was. They were happy when they were together. But maybe they were too much alike to ever sustain a full-time relationship with each other, one built to last.

He walked over to the Boston Common, then down Boylston to the Four Seasons, where he and Sunny had once sat on a winter night, during a Nor'easter, and sipped martinis and listened to the piano player and talked about getting a room.

He stood now and looked in the window at the Bristol Bar, saw a few afternoon drinkers in there, wondered if he might again be one of them someday. He thought about it every goddamn day, whether he had stopped for good. Whether he wanted to stop for good. Or if he was just taking a long break between drinks. Dix told him he should go to more meetings than he did. A way, Dix said, to keep the wolf away from the door, one day at a time.

Jesse had an AA app on his phone. He knew enough about Boston to know there was always a meeting going on somewhere in the Back Bay. He looked through the window now and saw a waiter making his way across the Bristol Bar, two martinis on a tray, placing them on a table in front of two guys in business suits. Were they starting a long, wet lunch? They toasted themselves.

One of them saw Jesse looking in the window and toasted him.

Jesse lifted an imaginary glass, turned his back on them, and headed back toward Boylston.

He felt his phone buzzing in the front pocket of his jeans, took it out, and heard Gwen Hadley say, "It's me."

"You got permission," he said.

"Not so's you'd notice," she said. "You just convinced me that finding out was the right thing to do."

"So did you?" Jesse said. "Find out?"

"I did."

"Paul Hutton found a match."

"He did," she said.

"Who with?"

"Well, the credit card on the matching account is in the name of Mr. Bryce Cain," she said. "He lives in . . ."

"Paradise, Massachusetts," Jesse said.

"You know him?"

"Better than I ever hoped to," Jesse said.

"But thing is, the match isn't with him," Gwen Hadley said. "At least he's not the one who sent in the sample."

Even over the sound of Boylston Street traffic, Jesse could hear his own breathing.

"Who did?"

"Someone named Samantha Cain."

"Bryce's daughter."

# Sixty-Six

Over the phone Gwen Hadley had given him a brief tutorial on matches. Jesse called it "DNA for Dummies." Matches and percentages and probabilities. Centimorgans. She spelled out *centimorgans*. Said the shorthand was "cM." Units of measure for how much DNA you shared with someone. The higher the percentage of centimorgans, the more closely you were related.

"Your guy and Samantha Cain were in the twenty-five percent range," she said. "I'd like to take a closer look at her form, but while we have a record that she had an account, the account itself has been deleted."

"'Deleted' meaning what?"

"That all the information is gone."

"Even you can't access it."

"Not sure God could," she said.

"Who deleted it?" Jesse said.

"I'm assuming either her or her father, since it was the father's credit card that was used," she said.

"So what was Hutton's relationship with the kid?"

"Not a hundred percent certain, but by the numbers, likely uncle and niece."

She then explained the various possibilities involving the girl's grandparents. Possibilities and probabilities. Some of which took Jesse to where he wanted to go, some of which didn't. When she was finished, he had her take him through it again.

"Thank you," he said.

"You still owe me a drink," she said.

"Rain check."

"Liar," she said. "You're in a relationship, aren't you?"

"Trying to be."

"Does she know?"

"I'm the cop," he said. "I'll ask the questions."

"I'm waiting."

"Her name is Sunny," Jesse said.

"So that's what that meant."

"My safe word when I'm in the presence of an attractive woman," he said.

"I scared you?"

"Hell yes."

She laughed again and said, "Hold the thought if you ever take me up on the rain check. And let me know how this all comes out."

He said he would, thanked her again, started walking back to where he'd parked the Explorer, near the Old South Meeting House.

When he was out of the downtown area, he called Bryce Cain and told him to be at the station in an hour.

"That sounded an awful lot like an order."

"You can come to me or I can come to you," Jesse said. "Your call."

"What's this about?"

Jesse said, "Family matter."

# Sixty-Seven

Jesse and Molly and Suit were in Jesse's office before Bryce Cain arrived.

"Well, at least we know why Paul Hutton was here," Molly said. "A reunion."

"Or a shakedown," Suit said.

"He didn't seem the type to me," Jesse said.

"Because you were at one AA meeting together?" Molly said.

Jesse took his glove and ball out of the bottom drawer of his desk, snapped the ball into the glove.

"I'd like to know how many Cains knew he was a relation," Jesse said.

"Can you ask the kid?" Suit said.

"Hiking with some of her friends through the Alps," Jesse said.

"You can't track her down?"

"To do that I'd have to ask her grandmother," Jesse said.

"You can't put off talking to her about all this forever," Molly said.

"Bryce first," Jesse said. "He's the one who paid."

"But it was the girl's sample," Molly said.

"You think her grandmother knows about this?" Suit said.

"I got the sense when I was with them that the two of them do more than their share of head-butting," Jesse said. "Lily gave the impression that Samantha's kind of wild."

"How old?" Molly asked.

"Twenty-one."

"She's pretty, she's young, she's rich as shit," Molly said. "I would've been wild, too."

"Wilder," Jesse said.

Molly put her thumb on the end of her nose and wiggled her fingers at him.

"Lily's a tough nut," Jesse said.

"Tough enough to leave a baby in a dumpster when she wasn't all that much older than her granddaughter is now?" Molly said.

Jesse said, "Nothing tough about that."


Cain was in casual work clothes: blazer, pink shirt, jeans, loafers, no socks. His hair was brushed back and landed nearly on the collar of the jacket. Jesse always wanted to ask him who told him he looked good with Fabio hair.

"I'm going to need to talk to Lily about what I'm going to tell you," Jesse said.

"She's in Palm Beach," she said, "packing up the old man's stuff, getting ready to sell the place."

"That didn't take long," Jesse said.

"When my mother wants to turn the page," Cain said, "she doesn't screw around."

Jesse told him what he knew.

"Bullshit," Cain said.

"Which part?"

"I don't know anything about a DNA test," he said. "Why in the hell would I need one? To see if I'm related to any other royal families?"

"You weren't listening," Jesse said. "But I'm assuming that happens a lot."

"Fuck off."

"Your daughter took the test," Jesse said. "You just paid for it. You're saying you didn't know?"

"Got any kids, Stone?"

"Son. Grown."

"And he doesn't know your credit card number and security code?"

"I'll have to ask him."

"Well, if he doesn't, you're one of the chosen few."

"You don't check your credit card bills?"

Cain made a snorting noise and shook his head. Like the steak he'd ordered wasn't rare enough.

"I have people to do that," he said.

"Well, she took a test," Jesse said. "And got a match with a guy who came to your parents' house the same night somebody shot him dead at the lake. It means he's related to your daughter and might be related to you."

Jesse could almost see wheels turning inside Cain's head as he put a hand to his face and pulled hard on his cheeks.

"Or he could be related to my dear, estranged wife," he said.

"Yeah," Jesse said. "He could be. Then why did he go to Lily and Whit's house and not go looking for your wife? But if it's you, he was your half-brother. Which also would have made him one of Whit's heirs."

"You don't know that," Cain said. "Unless you saw the will."

"Actually, I did," Jesse said.

"No fucking way?"

"I'm the chief," Jesse said. "I know shit." He smiled. "You're telling me you don't want to know if Lily might have been the guy's mother or Whit the father?"

Cain snorted.

"Are you drinking again?" Cain said. "It would have to be the old man. All the fucking around he did finally caught up with him."

"I assume you're going to ask Lily about this," Jesse said.

"First chance," Cain said.

"You think she might already know?"

"She's Lily Cain," Bryce said. "She knows shit."

Jesse sipped coffee gone cold. "Samantha didn't tell you about this?"

"We don't talk much these days," Cain said.

"Forget about your father for a moment," Jesse said. "You're convinced Paul Hutton wasn't Lily's son?"

"Leaving a kid in the trash?" Cain said. "Listen, she's always joked about growing up in White Trash, Florida. But come on, Stone. You know her. There's no way."

313

"But Hutton still could have been an heir," Jesse said.

"So you think I killed him over money?"

Jesse said, "Love and money."

"What?"

"Two things that people kill for."

"Unless your poor vic was related to my wife."

"Easy to find out."

"For Christ's sake," Cain said. "I didn't even know that guy was in town until you came to the house and told me somebody shot him. I didn't know about the goddamn test until you just told me. If you don't believe me, ask my kid when she gets back from Europe."

"For the last time," Jesse said. "You were home alone after the theater thing?"

"Phone off," he said. "Passed out after half a bottle of Dewar's. Living the dream."

Then he said, "Are we done?"

"For now."

Bryce Cain got up and walked to the door.

"Hey?" Jesse said.

Cain turned.

"Who do *you* think might have wanted Hutton dead?"

"Your problem. Not mine. Now fuck off."

When he was gone, Molly came into the office and said, "How'd that go?"

"The last thing he said was for me to fuck off."

"That well, huh?" Molly said.

"I need a break, Mols," he said.

The next day he got two.

# Sixty-Eight

Lily Cain returned to Paradise two days later and called Jesse, telling him they needed to talk. He said he'd been expecting her call. Asked where she wanted to meet.

"I'll come to you," she said. "I need to clear some things up, for both of us," then added, "as a friend."

Jesse asked if she'd find it inappropriate to come to his place. She said not at all, he should know by now she wasn't that much of a lady. She asked if he had anything to drink there. He said that if she meant liquor, no. She said she'd bring her own.

When she was in the living room, she took off her Paradise Yacht Club ball cap and shook her long hair loose. She was wearing jeans and sneakers, a windbreaker. Just folks.

"Do I get a tour?" she said.

"Trust me," Jesse said, "you don't want one."

"Then how about a glass with ice," she said, as she pulled a pint of Crown Royal out of the side pocket of the wind-breaker.

Jesse went into the kitchen and got the same kind of tall glass he once used when it was the cocktail hour here. When he came back, Lily was on his terrace. Probably thinking how much better her view was. Jesse handed her the glass and led her back into the living room and gestured at the small couch across from his television chair.

She poured whiskey into her glass and took a healthy swallow. Put the glass down on a coaster. Smiled at Jesse and said, "Bryce told me about your conversation."

"I expected that he would."

"Let me tell you a story," she said.

"I'm here."

"If one of us was Paul Hutton's parent, it had to be Whit," she said. "Because I sure as shit wasn't his mother."

She took a smaller sip of whiskey, closed her eyes, let it run through her and settle. He knew the feeling. Like you'd wrapped your insides in a warm blanket.

"Samantha didn't tell her father or me that she planned to take a goddamn DNA test," Lily said. "She's hardly ever around these days. They barely speak when she is. *We* barely speak. If we say up, she says down. Point is, I never got the chance to talk her out of it."

Jesse waited.

"But some of her friends were doing it, and so she did, too," Lily said. "She only came to me about it when she got a match. As you can imagine, I blew several fuses. And re-minded dear Samantha that she was a Cain. And that we didn't share our secrets with others, especially ones literally written in blood."

"Had Hutton reached out to her?"

"Not yet," Lily said. "I told her the implications of a stranger knowing he was related to us in some way, that it was practically an invitation for someone to come looking for money. I told her to turn the account over to me, it simply wasn't safe any other way."

"She went for that?"

Lily smiled. "You know me, Jesse," she said. "I can be quite persuasive when I need to be, even with a pigheaded young woman who reminds me far too much of myself at her age."

"Wasn't she even curious?" Jesse said.

"Mildly," Lily said. "But if it's not really about her, she loses interest pretty quickly. I explained to her that although I didn't want to burst her bubble about her grandfather, he might have a family tree apart from our own that looks like the Old Testament."

She sighed. "Then I reminded her again that I had given her a trip through France and Switzerland and Italy for her birthday and told her to let me handle it before people got hurt."

"Did you tell your husband about any of this?" Jesse said. "Or all of it?"

"I told him," she said. "I wasn't surprised, wasn't even angry, really. I asked who he thought the mother might be. He looked at me and said, 'It could have been anybody.'"

"Did he tell anybody else?" Jesse said. "He seemed to share a lot with Karina."

"He's the one who told *me* not to tell anybody," she said. "He always talked about keeping the circle tight. Said to let him take care of it, or have it taken care of. He winked at me and said, 'The way we used to take care of things in the old days.'" She shrugged. "When Paul Hutton turned up dead, I just assumed that he had taken care of things."

She drank. Jesse studied her face as she did, trying to imagine the girl she had been, the one who'd stolen the old bastard's heart when they were both young.

"You knew all this the first time I came to the house," he said, "the morning we found the body."

"I was a Cain," she said. "Keeping the circle tight."

"Didn't you want to know if your husband had it done?"

"More truth, Jesse? I didn't. I was just glad it was over."

She leaned forward, eyes on him, the full force of her focused on him. Who she was. Who she wanted to be.

"And now I very much want this to be over for you," she said.

"That your late husband may have been complicit in a murder?" he said. "Not your call, Lily."

"If he was or he wasn't," she said, "we'll never know. Just let it be enough that this is what I believe happened."

"And everybody lives happily ever after," Jesse said. "Except for Paul Hutton, of course."

"He's gone!" Lily said. "Whit is gone! I want you to leave what's left of my family alone."

"You think Hutton was coming after some of his money and Whit hired some old friend to take him out?"

"It makes sense to me, in an odd way," she said. "One last time, even in that chair, the life coming out of him, he got to feel like Whit Cain."

There was still some whiskey in her glass. He felt the urge to go across the room and finish it himself.

"Noble," he said.

"I'm sorry?"

"Noble of you to protect the good name of a man you say you stopped loving a long time ago."

"Not noble," she said. "Just practical. By now you should know we're very practical people."

Jesse stood up and walked to the terrace door and stared out at the night. When he turned around he said, "The only problem for me, just as a practical matter, is that you're full of shit."

"Excuse me?" she said.

"Whit wasn't the father," he said. "You were the mother. And Whit didn't hire somebody to kill Hutton. You killed him, Lily."

He sat back down in the armchair and said, "Now let me tell you a story."

# Sixty-Nine

amantha isn't the only one who reached out to Paul Hutton through the 4Bears messaging system," Jesse said.
"You messaged him, too, after you took over the account, and
before you closed it down."

Jesse had called Gwen Hadley the day before and asked if
anyone else in the Cain family had ever taken a DNA test,
telling her he was specifically interested in Bryce's wife, Tess.
She told him she would have checked for that before, except
she'd been on the clock that day. No, she said, Tess Cain had
never taken a test.

But Lily Cain had.

He stood with his back to the terrace door, the lights of
Paradise behind him, and the ocean behind them.

"You knew that Whit wasn't his father," he said.

"And how did I know that?"

"Because you panicked after there was a match with

Hutton and Samantha," Jesse said. "Because you knew a kid of yours was out there, one you'd left in a dumpster."

"And this you know . . . how?" Lily said.

"Because 4Bears told me."

"Those companies promise confidentiality," she said.

"This is a homicide investigation," Jesse said. "Shit happens."

She started to get up. "I'm not listening to any more of this."

"Sit," he said, with enough snap in his voice that she did.

"I don't know who you were back then, and how your life brought you to putting an infant in a fucking dumpster," he said. "Maybe I'll never know. It turns out that there's not much history anybody can find on you before you became Mrs. Whit Cain, because I've spent the last couple days trying my ass off. Maybe if I wanted to do a deeper dive, I could find out."

She raised her chin slightly. Almost imperiously. Still Lily.

"Good luck with that," she said.

But nothing more than that.

"But now you knew it had to be him," Jesse said. "And you reached out."

"I did no such thing," she said.

Jesse said, "We didn't find a cell phone on Hutton, and there was no service plan on his credit card bills. He'd probably bought a prepaid phone with cash. But once I got a warrant for *your* call records, I found a number for that. You called it, a couple times from Palm Beach. And he called you a lot after that, not that he ever got through."

"You never took my phone."

"I didn't need to. All I needed was the number to track your calls, and where you made them from. And who you made them to. The modern world, Lily. Sometimes it's a beautiful thing."

"Dog with a bone," she said.

"The last he called you was right about the time he got dropped at your gate. That one lasted a few minutes. You were still in town then. Not long after that, from the car, you called Bryce and Nora Hayes."

"Simply replaying a wonderful evening for our town," she said.

"But you were on your way to pick Hutton up and get him away from the house and to the lake," Jesse said.

He sat back down.

"What I can't figure is why you had to kill him," he said. "Why you couldn't just pay him off and tell him to go away."

"I didn't kill him," she said.

"I've actually got a witness saying somebody fitting your description was running from the lake after he heard the gunshot," he said. "Tall and skinny. Ball cap. Long blond hair. I thought it might be Bryce when I heard that. But it was you. The long-distance runner."

"It wasn't me," she said.

No need to tell her that his witness was dead. He was just trying to bait her into a mistake. All he had.

She didn't bite. Just smiled at him.

"Let's say *all* of this is true, Jesse," she said. "Or some of it is. If you had any real proof you would have arrested me, at which point the best lawyers money can buy would already be stuck to you like ticks. I don't know what you hoped to accomplish here, but I didn't shoot anybody." Still smiling, she said, "Are you sure you haven't started drinking again?"

He let that one go.

"Are we still speaking hypothetically?"

"Have at it," Jesse said.

*Keep them talking. Whether it was Bo Marino or Lily Cain. Just because you never knew.*

"You have no idea," she said.

"About what?" Jesse said. "Who you were?"

"No, goddamn you!" she said, spitting out the words. "What I had to do to *become* who I am. To become Lily Cain. And neither you nor anyone else is going to destroy that with your little story."

Now she stood.

"And now I have heard enough and said enough," she said.


Jesse got the call from Peter Perkins at about three in the morning that they'd found Lily Cain's body not far from where they'd found the body of Paul Hutton—her first child—near the lake.

Single shot to the head, Peter said.

Peter said he'd had to wake some people up and piss them off, but it turned out that the gun found next to the body, a .22, was registered to Whit Cain.

Jesse told him he was on his way. He got dressed and was walking through the living room when he saw the bottle of Crown Royal that Lily had left on the table. A third of it left, maybe less. He picked it up and stared at the amber liquid. Didn't have to smell it, because he knew the scent and the taste. He stood there for what felt like a long time and then walked into the kitchen and poured the rest of it into the sink and then headed for the lake, where it had all started, for the end of it.

# Seventy

There was no funeral for Lily Cain. Bryce Cain said there would be a memorial service later. At the theater. The cover story in Paradise was that Lily was more grief-stricken than anybody knew over the death of her husband. And as far as Jesse could tell, enough of the town seemed willing to buy that, or at least to pretend to in public. He didn't care, either way. He wasn't sure what he felt. He knew he couldn't make a case against Lily. She knew it, too. But there was a part of him feeling as if he'd somehow given her the death penalty anyway.

"You couldn't have known how it was going to turn out when you set everything in motion," Molly said.

"But I did set everything in motion."

"You were still the only one who knew," Molly said.

"It must have been one person too many," Jesse said.

They were at her desk out in the bullpen, drinking coffee.

Molly had just told him to get his feet off her desk. He'd refused. She seemed to accept that they were at an impasse.

"I feel sorry for her," Jesse said. "Even though I know I shouldn't. She'd carried around this secret for forty years. No indication that she ever tried to find out if the baby was dead or alive. Now here the guy was on her doorstep. It must have panicked her."

"Who the hell was she?" Molly said. "Really?"

"We're never gonna know," he said. "A lot we're never gonna know, though. Maybe just one more thing that gets buried."

"I can't feel badly about this," Molly said. "Not as a mother."

"You're a harder case than me."

"And don't ever forget it," she said.

They had made a plan to have dinner. Molly said he should see if Sunny wanted to come up. Jesse went back to his office and called her. She said she was having dinner with Richie.

"So he's back," Jesse said.

"So he is."

"*Back* meaning back in your life?" Jesse said.

"Never out of it," she said.

"You know what I mean."

"Not like that," Sunny said. "We just need to have a face-to-face. Then straight home to bed. Alone."

"So no sucking face," he said.

She laughed. The sound of it came out of the phone like a summer breeze.

"In this case, Chief Stone," she said. "My lips really are sealed."

Jesse told Molly he'd see her later at the Gull, that he was going home early, going for a long run to clear his head.

"You'd have to run all the way to L.A. and back to do that," she said.

He drove home and got into sweatpants and the running shoes he'd bought after rehab and an even older Dodgers sweatshirt, a cold front off the Atlantic having dropped the temperature into the low 50s the last couple days. He started out through town, on his way to the water. Passed that movie theater, ran under the marquee that now read: REST IN PEACE, LILY CAIN. Wondering if she finally was at peace, or if the chance of that had come off the books a long time ago.

He finally made the turn toward the bridge at Stiles Island and was on his way back over the bridge when he saw Bryce Cain coming in the other direction. He hadn't seen Cain since he'd identified his mother's body at the hospital.

"I'm sorry," Jesse had said that day.

"The hell you are," Cain said.

Cain stared briefly at Jesse now, looked like he might say something but didn't, just smiled and gave Jesse the finger. Then put his head down and kept going, picking up the pace as if suddenly being chased.

But Jesse stopped now, stared at his back until he disappeared, Brad Pitt hair blowing in the cold wind off the water. Then he was on his way home himself. Running a lot faster now than he had when he'd started. Like he was the one being chased.

# Seventy-One

Bryce Cain opened his front door a few minutes after six the next day, saw it was Jesse, and started to close it, saying, "I've said everything I need to say to you."

Jesse stopped the door with his right hand.

"Not quite," he said.

He handed Cain the envelope in his other hand.

"What's this?"

"A search warrant," Jesse said.

"Get lost," Cain said.

"Bryce," Jesse said, stepping past him. "We can do this the hard way, which is how I'm rooting. Or the easy way. Totally up to you."

They were standing very close to each other. Cain was holding an empty glass in his hand. Jesse could see him making a calculation about whether to stand down or not. He bought himself some time by opening the envelope and studying the warrant.

"I'll have Judge Victor's ass for this," he said.

"Nice to think so."

"What are you searching for, exactly?"

"Just one item of clothing," Jesse said. "Your Patriots hoodie. The one you were wearing yesterday when you flipped me off on the bridge."

"And why do you want that?"

"Because I believe it's the one you were wearing the night you shot Paul Hutton," Jesse said. "Your brother. Almost biblical, Bryce. Little like a Cain murdering Abel."

"Lily shot him."

"That's what I thought, too," Jesse said. "And what you were happy to have me think, especially now that, with her gone, all that fucking money goes to you."

"You're full of shit until the end," Cain said.

"Maybe so," Jesse said. "But let's go get the hoodie. See, here's the thing most civilians don't know, even smart lawyers like you. Gun residue stays on articles of clothing a long time. Lot of times it leaves a stain that won't come out even after a good washing. Kind of stain a lab can test."

Cain stared at him. His mother's icy blue eyes. Maybe trying to decide if Jesse was playing him.

"I'll go get it," he said.

"I'll go with you," Jesse said.

"Where do you think I'm going?"

"Hopefully jail," Jesse said.

Jesse took a Ziploc bag out of his back pocket now and opened it.

"What's *that* for?" Cain said.

"Drop the glass in here if you don't mind," Jesse said. "Most people also don't know how to properly wipe down a gun. Got a feeling the partial print on the gun we found next to Lily might just turn out to be yours."

They were still standing just inside the door. Bryce Cain finally shrugged and placed the glass in the plastic bag. Jesse set it on a small table in the foyer.

"Knock yourself out," he said, and led Jesse up the stairs to his bedroom. The walk-in closet was as big as Jesse's office. On top of one of the bureaus was the Patriots hoodie, the old-school one Bo Marino said he'd seen the runner wearing, minuteman in a tricorne hat getting ready to snap a football. Cain grabbed it and tossed it at Jesse.

"More circumstantial evidence for you to knock yourself out with," Cain said. "We both know if you had enough to charge me, I'd be in fucking cuffs already." He crossed his arms in front of him. "And if you ever *do* charge me on flimsy shit like this, all that means is I'll finally have your ass."

"Your mother called you that night and told you to go pick him up," Jesse said. "The timing lines up."

"She called," Cain said. "Not about that."

"But you were careful enough to leave your phone here."

"My phone was here because I was here after I came home from the theater," Cain said. "How would you even know that, by the way?"

He told her what he'd told his mother about the modern world.

"Whatever," Cain said.

He walked out of the closet and back down the stairs and through the foyer, opened the front door.

"Now get out," he said.

"What I'm curious about," Jesse said, "is what Lily told you before you did it. That he was here after your money? She tried to sell me that the old man might have had him killed. But it was you."

Cain smiled and shook his head slowly.

"Pass," he said.

"That's the ironic part, don't you think?" Jesse said. "The guy wasn't really after money. Just a family. Even one as fucked-up as yours."

"Let me explain something to you that my father explained to me one time," Cain said. "When they say it's not about the money, it's *always* about the money."

He walked over now to where Jesse was standing in the middle of the room. Not all the way into Jesse's space. But close enough that Jesse was hoping he was about to do something stupid.

"Do you have any idea how much shit I've had to eat in my life?" he said in a quiet voice. "Lily always talked about having to do that, because of the way the old man screwed around. Well, she had no idea what it was like being *me*. None. Do you know what it's like your whole life being told you'll never measure up, get out of the way and let the old man show you how it's done? But I took it, and I waited, and then I took over the business, knowing I was going to cash in when he finally did the world a favor and died."

Jesse noticed a slight sheen of sweat on his upper lip.

"Just for the sake of conversation?" Bryce said.

"Sure," Jesse said. "Just you and me here, couple of boys chopping it up."

Bryce said, "You think someone who had taken that kind

of shit his whole life was going to let some drunk show up and claim a share, whatever he was saying about family? Fuck him. And fuck you."

Jesse could feel himself smiling now.

"So you're finally Cain Enterprises, free and clear," he said.

"Bet your ass," he said. "President, chairman of the board, keeper of the flame."

"Well, for now," Jesse said.

"What's that supposed to mean?"

"Means that even though what I have on you might not stand up in court, there still might be enough to charge you," Jesse said. "And if I do that, it sure as shit will get the board's attention, don't you think?"

He reached over and patted Cain on the shoulder.

"There's all kinds of jail, Bryce," Jesse said on his way past him and out the door.

# Seventy-Two

L ook at me," Sunny said. "Two dates in one night."

"I am looking at you," Jesse said.

They were in the bed that had once belonged to the owner of her house at River Street Place, a writer named Melanie Joan Hall. Sunny had once described the bed as being big enough on which to land a jetliner.

He had dropped off the sweatshirt and the glass with Dev, knowing that Cain had been right, knowing that gunpowder residue wasn't weapon-specific, and that even if Cain had wiped the gun with a dry cloth before returning it to Whit Cain's gun cabinet first chance he got, a lawyer like Rita Fiore could come up with fifty reasons why his prints might have been on the .22.

"So you went there trying to bluff him and he called yours," Sunny said.

"Hell yeah."

"You knew you couldn't make it stick?"

"Not unless he confessed," he said. "I just needed to know for sure it was him."

"Now you do."

"Hell yeah," he said again.

"Is it enough?"

"Hell no."

He'd texted Sunny after he left Bryce Cain and asked if there was a chance he could see her after her dinner with Richie, that he needed to talk through some things with somebody other than Molly. She'd told him to come over.

She'd been resting her head on his shoulder. Now she pulled back and sat up, making no attempt to cover herself. She rarely did.

"You're not happy."

"Happy being here," he said.

"You know what I mean."

"I keep thinking there should be a way for me to nail the bastard," he said. "I keep thinking that even after everything Lily did, starting with what she did to that baby, she didn't have to die. Hell, I was even thinking on my way down here how close I came to getting Candace Pennington killed."

"But you didn't."

She reached over, touched his cheek with her hand, left it there.

"Let's change the subject," he said.

"Fine by me."

"Want to talk about us?"

Sunny smiled and slowly shook her head.

"How's Richie?"

"Not tonight, dear," she said. "I know it's a big bed. But two people in it is more than enough."

Now she kissed him where her hand had been.

"I wanted a drink tonight after I left Cain," he said. "Wolf was right back there at the door. I'm pissed off at Bryce Cain. Pissed off at myself." He exhaled. Loudly. "Same old same old. I just wanted to take the edge off."

"Why didn't you?"

"You responded to my text," he said.

"You need to let this go," Sunny said.

"Hard to do," he said.

"The last Boy Scout," Sunny said.

He turned to her, grinning, and told her a known criminal had called him the same thing not long ago.

"I never told you," he said. "But I actually was a Boy Scout once. For about a week."

"No way."

"Cains aren't the only ones with secrets," he said.

He reached over and pulled her closer to him.

"I can still recite the Scout's Oath," he said. "Want to hear it?"

"Not tonight, dear," she said.

"The key part is about being physically strong," he said.

She smiled a wicked smile.

"I can tell," she said.

# Acknowledgments

I could not write these books without the skill and talent—and patience—of my guide through the world of Robert B. Parker: Sara Minnich.